VIOLENCE OF THE MOUNTAIN MAN

D0090124

VIOLENCE OF THE MOUNTAIN MAN

William Johnstone
with J. A. Johnstone

PINNACLE BOOKS
Kensington Publishing Corp.
www.kensingtonbooks.com

PINNACLE BOOKS are published by

Kensington Publishing Corp.
850 Third Avenue
New York, NY 10022

PUBLISHER'S NOTE
Following the death of William W. Johnstone, the Johnstone family is working with a carefully selected writer to organize and complete Mr. Johnstone's outlines and many unfinished manuscripts to create additional novels in all of his series like The Last Gunfighter, Mountain Man, and Eagles, among others. This novel was inspired by Mr. Johnstone's superb storytelling.

All Kensington titles, imprints, and distributed lines are available at special quantity discounts for bulk purchases for sales promotions, premiums, fund-raising, educational, or institutional use. Special book excerpts or customized printings can also be created to fit specific needs. For details, write or phone the office of the Kensington special sales manager: Kensington Publishing Corp., 850 Third Avenue, New York, NY 10022, attn: Special Sales Department; phone: 1-800-221-2647.

ISBN-13: 978-0-7860-1839-0
ISBN-10: 0-7860-1839-9

First printing: December 2008

10 9 8 7 6 5 4 3 2 1

Printed in the United States of America

Chapter One

Sugarloaf Ranch

"Oh, that smells so good," Lucy Goodnature said as she watched Sally Jensen pull apple pies from the oven. "You'll have to tell me all your secrets."

"Lucy, one thing you must learn is that a woman never tells," Sally said.

"Oh, of course, I didn't mean all your secrets," Lucy said. "I just meant—"

Sally cut her off with a laugh. "I know what you meant," she said. "I was just teasing you."

Lucy laughed with her. "Well, I do want to learn how to make apple pie the way you do. I know Pearlie really likes your apple pies."

"Honey, here's one thing that isn't a secret," Sally said. "When it comes to eating, there is very little that Pearlie doesn't like."

From outside there was a loud whoop, followed by laughter. Lucy walked over to look through the window. "All of the cowboys seem to be having such a good time," she said. "It is very nice of Mr. Jensen to give them all a going-away party like this. And it was very nice of you to invite me. Thank you."

"Oh, you are welcome, Lucy. You have been a big help to me today. I know that Pearlie was glad to see you. And any friend of Pearlie's is always welcome at Sugarloaf."

Lucy was the nineteen-year-old daughter of Ian Goodnature, the owner of a ranch that was adjacent to Smoke Jensen's Sugarloaf Ranch. Tall and willowy, with long black hair and green eyes, she had attracted Pearlie's attention as no other woman ever had.

"I would like to think—" Lucy began. Then, after a pause in mid-sentence, she began again. "What I mean to say is, I would like to think that I am more than just a friend to Pearlie."

"I wouldn't be surprised if you weren't more than just a friend," Sally said. "But take it from someone who is older, if not wiser. You don't rush these things. Men always like to believe they are in charge, so you are going to have to let Pearlie take the lead."

"Yes, ma'am," Lucy said. "I know."

"Yes, ma'am?" Sally replied. She laughed. "Lucy, I said I was older, but I'm not ancient. Ma'am is something you say to old people."

"Yes, ma'am, I'm sorry," Lucy said. Then she covered her lips with her hand. "Oh, I said it again." Both women laughed.

On the large and well-kept lawn outside the house, Smoke Jensen walked over to a wood fire to check on the meat. He stood there for a moment watching as Juan Mendoza turned the spit slowly and Carlos Rodriguez applied barbeque sauce to the already glistening carcass of half a steer.

The employer of the cowboys, and the owner of the ranch, was Kirby "Smoke" Jensen. Smoke stood just over six feet tall and had shoulders as wide as an ax handle and biceps as thick as most men's thighs.

"How does the beef look, Señor Smoke?" Carlos asked, a broad smile spreading across his face.

"Amigos, I do believe that is the prettiest thing I have ever seen," Smoke replied.

"Oh, Señor, I think maybe you should not let Señora Sally hear you say such a thing," Juan said. "I think she would not want to hear that you think a side of beef could be prettier than she is."

Smoke laughed and pointed a finger at Juan. "You're right, Juan," he said. "And don't either of you dare tell her I said that, because if you do, I will be in hot water for sure."

The two men laughed appreciatively, then turned their attention back to the task at hand.

The aroma of the cooking meat filled the grounds between the group of small houses where Juan, Carlos, and the other permanent hands lived, and the house where Smoke and Sally Jensen, owners of Sugarloaf Ranch, lived. The American cowboys called the ranch house the "Big House." The Mexicans called it Casa Grande.

The cowboys, separate from the permanent hands, lived in the bunkhouse. The bunkhouse, which was between the Big House and the barn, was a long, low building that had ten bunks—five on each side of the building, as well as private rooms at each end of the bunkhouse. The private rooms provided quarters for Pearlie and Cal, the only two cowboys who were permanent employees.

The rest of the cowboys who rode for Sugarloaf were, as most cowboys, men who worked the ranches as temporary hands hired in the spring for the roundup and branding, then let go during the winter months. This was typical of all the ranches, and the cowboys not only accepted it, but many of them had chosen this particular line of work for the very reason that it was seasonal and temporary.

The time of employment for the extra hands was now coming to an end and, as they did every year, Smoke and his wife, Sally, were hosting a barbeque and party for the cowboys. Juan and Carlos had started cooking the beef the evening before, taking turns watching it through the night. Their long efforts had been rewarded and now the meat was nearly done. In the meantime, many of the Mexican women had prepared their own dishes to bring to the meal, and Sally had baked pies.

Some of the Mexicans were pretty good musicians and they had been providing music off and on during the day, but the cowboys were providing their own entertainment by way of bronco riding, steer wrestling, and target shooting.

One of the American cowboys, Lucas Keno, was pretty good with a pistol, and in head-to-head shooting with the others, he had bested them all. Keno was a singularly unattractive man, with an oversized, hawklike nose, thin lips, bad teeth, and a weak chin.

"Ha!" Keno said. "There ain't a cowboy on this ranch can beat me," he bragged. "Hell, there ain't a cowboy in the whole county can beat me, and none in the state either, I'm bettin'."

Cal laughed. "Keno, you might want to think about that some. No matter how good you are, there's always someone who is better."

"Yeah? Well, if there's somebody better, I'd like to know who it could be," Keno said. "I've done beat ever'body on Sugarloaf, and that's a fact."

"You haven't beat everybody," Cal said. "I've seen you shoot, and I've seen Pearlie shoot. And I think Pearlie is better."

"Do you now?" Keno asked. He laughed. "Is that right, Pearlie? Are you better'n me?"

"I don't know," Pearlie said.

"Tell you what. I just got paid out my thirty dollars. Why don't me and you bet that thirty dollars on which one of us is the best? I could use an extra thirty."

"I don't want to bet you," Pearlie said.

"Ha! I reckon you don't. What you mean is, you don't want to lose the money."

"No, I don't want to lose the money," Pearlie said.

"Don't know why you'd be so worried about losin' thirty dollars," Keno said. "Hell, bein' as you and Cal are Jensen's pets, you don't get fired like the rest of us. You'll get yourself another thirty come next month."

"We ain't bein' fired, Keno," one of the other cowboys said. "We know'd comin' in that this was a temporary job. All roundups are temporary jobs. Hell, that's what cowboyin' is all about."

"Yeah, so you say. But from the way I'm lookin' at it, it is the same as bein' fired," Keno said. Then, turning his attention back to Pearlie, he continued his pitch. "All right, you don't want to bet. At least shoot against me so I can prove I'm better."

Aiming at one of the empty cans that had been set up for a target, Keno pulled the trigger. He hit the can, knocking it into the air. Then he shot again, hitting the can a second time and knocking it farther back.

"Can you do that?" Keno asked Pearlie.

"Probably not," Pearlie answered.

"Ha! Then admit it, I'm better than you."

"We aren't going to find out," Pearlie said.

"Yeah, well, I don't blame you none," Keno said as he blew the smoke away from the barrel of his now empty pistol, then began punching the empty shell casings out to replace them with fresh cartridges. "I mean, let's face it. As long as you don't shoot against me, you'll have your puppy, Cal, convinced that you can beat me."

"It's not something we'll ever want to find out," Pearlie said.

"Oh? And why not?"

"Because if we do find out—one of us will be dead," Pearlie said flatly.

Before Keno could respond, the ringing of an iron triangle called everyone back up to the lawn of the big house. There, two long tables had been set up under the arching aspen trees and were now loaded with dishes, eating utensils, and several large bowls of such things as beans, rice, corn, steaming tortillas, and cornbread. Juan and Carlos stood proudly by the glazed beef, carving off generous portions to serve the men.

Pearlie filled his plate with beef.

"Tell you what, Pearlie, why don't you pass your plate around for the rest of to divide up, and you just eat the rest of the cow your own self?" one of the cowboys shouted. "Hell, we'd wind up gettin' more meat that way."

The rest of the cowboys laughed at the tease.

"Folks say you show a cook how much you enjoy their cookin' by how much of their food you eat. I just don't want Juan or Carlos thinkin' I don't appreciate them," Pearlie said, and again, there was more good-natured laughter from the men.

"Hey, Slim, what say you'n me head for California?" one cowboy asked another.

"What for do you want to go to California?" Slim replied.

"There's gold out there. I read about it in a book. You can just go out there and pick it up off the ground, gold nuggets as big as pecans."

"I never heard of such a thing," Slim said.

"Tell 'im, Miz Sally," the gold hunter said. "Tell 'im there's gold out there. I know about it 'cause I read about it in a book. It's called forty-niner."

Sally chuckled. "You're partially right, Mickey, " she said. "Gold was discovered there in 1849—that's where the term 'forty-niner' comes from. And there may still be some gold out there, but I doubt it is lying around on the ground like pecans."

"Yeah, well, I want to go anyway," Mickey said. "What about it, Slim? You want to go with me?"

"Sure, why not?" Slim replied. "There's an ocean out there, ain't there? I ain't never seen me no ocean. I think I'd like to see one. They say it's so big you can't see the other side."

"Really?" Mickey said. "Well, now, I think I'd like to see that my own self."

As all the cowboys and the permanent hands continued to enjoy their meal, Smoke stood up and tapped his spoon against the glass in an attempt to get everyone's attention.

When it appeared that he wasn't succeeding, Cal put his fingers to his lips and let out an ear-piercing whistle.

Around the tables, all conversation and laughter stopped as everyone looked toward Smoke.

Smoke laughed. "Thank you, Cal, for that whistle."

The others laughed.

"I want to thank all of you, cowboys and ranch hands, for helping to make Sugarloaf one of the most successful ranches in the entire state."

"State? In the entire West!" Cal shouted, and the others mouthed their own agreement with the statement.

"Now that the seasonal employment is over, many of you will be going on to other things, and I wish you all the best and hope that you can all come back to ride for us again next spring. And now, I think Sally has something to say."

"I hope so," one of the cowboys shouted good-naturedly. "She's a lot easier on the eyes than you are." Again, the others laughed.

Sally stood up then, still smiling at the cowboy's comment.

"As I'm sure you know, I run a school here on the ranch for the children of our permanent hands. Maria Rodriguez is one of my students. She is only nine years old, but already she is exceptionally talented as a flamenco dancer, and I thought you might enjoy watching her. Pearlie?"

Pearlie and Cal had brought another table up, and now Pearlie helped the young girl onto it. Maria was wearing a low-crowned black hat, and her dark hair hung in curls down her back. Her costume consisted of a white ruffled shirt, a black beaded vest, and a long flared red skirt. She was holding castanets, and she held her hands up, jutted out her hip, then looked over at the guitarist and nodded.

The guitarist started playing, a weaving, single-string melody that worked up and down the scale, all the while providing a strong rhythmic beat from the lower register. To the accompaniment of the guitar, Maria danced, whirling and dipping so that her wide skirt spun out and her hair tossed from side to side. Her booted feet beat a loud staccato on the table and the castanets clicked in counterpoint. Everyone watched her, transfixed by the talent and beauty of the young girl. Then, with a crescendo, the music ended and Maria curtsied.

Maria was cheered and applauded by all, but none so loud as the cowboys, who added loud whistles to their applause. Maria looked over toward Sally, then smiled in appreciation at Sally's reaction to her performance.

Finally, with the dinner ended and the ladies of the ranch cleaning up, the cowboys who were leaving mounted their horses, then gathered near the porch, where Smoke stood to bid them all good-bye.

"Boys," he said. "I want you to know this. If the going gets too hard for you come winter, you are more than welcome to come back here. I won't have any work for you to do, but if all you need is food for your bellies, a place to keep warm, and a pillow to lay your head, you've got it at Sugarloaf."

"Thanks, Boss," one of the cowboys said. "I'll see you next spring."

With a shout, the cowboy spurred his horse and galloped away, followed by all the other temporary hands. Smoke and Sally waved to them from the porch, and those ranch hands who were permanent employees had come out of their cabins to wave good-bye as well.

"We had a good bunch of hands this year," Sally said.

"Except for one," Smoke said. "I've already told him privately not to come back next year."

"You have to be talking about Lucas Keno," Sally said.

Smoke nodded. "Yes, I'm talking about Lucas Keno. He was all complaint and little work. I should have fired him weeks ago."

Pearlie and Cal were standing over in front of the bunkhouse and like the others, they had waved and shouted their good-byes to the cowboys as they rode out.

"How many of them you think will be back come spring?" Cal asked.

"Most of 'em, I reckon," Pearlie said. "You're too young to know any better 'cause this is about the only place you've ever worked. But I've worked at other ranches and I tell you true, there is no better place on God's green earth for a cowboy to work than to work for Smoke and Sally here on Sugarloaf Ranch."

"I know this is the only place I've ever worked," Cal said. "But I had already figured that out myself."

"Come on, Cal, what do you say we give Carlos and Juan a hand getting things cleaned up?" Pearlie suggested.

"All right," Cal said, and the two of them started across the yard toward the older men.

"Oh, Pearlie, wait a minute," Sally called from the porch of the Big House.

Stopping, Pearlie looked back toward Sally. "Yes, ma'am?"

"When Mr. Goodnature dropped Lucy off, I promised we would get her back home. Would you mind doing it? You can use the surrey."

"Why, I'd be glad to," Pearlie said, smiling broadly. "Miss Lucy, you just wait right here. I'll hitch up the team and be back for you before you can say Jack Robinson."

"Thank you, Pearlie," Lucy said. "That's very kind of you."

"Want me to come along with you, Pearlie?" Cal asked.

"I—uh," Pearlie began.

"Cal, if you don't mind, why don't you stay here and help me with something?" Sally suggested.

"Oh, sure, I don't mind," Cal said, walking over toward the porch.

True to his promise, Pearlie was back in very little time. Hopping down from the surrey, he helped Lucy in, then drove off, with the two of them engaged in conversation.

"What do you have for me to do?" Cal asked as they watched the surrey pass under the entry arch.

"What?" Sally asked.

"You said you wanted me to help you with something," Cal said. "What is it?"

"Oh. Uh, nothing, I guess."

"But you said—" Cal began, then chuckled. "Oh, I know now," he said. "You just said that because you wanted to give Pearlie a chance to be alone with Miss Lucy, didn't you?"

"Something like that, yes," Sally replied.

"Well, I hope it works," Cal said. "Pearlie sure is crazy about that girl, but I don't think she even knows he is alive."

Sally smiled. "She knows."

"You mean she's sweet on him?"

"Let us just say that nature is gradually beginning to work its course," Sally said.

Cal laughed. "I like that. Nature working its course. Well, if you really don't have anything for me, I think I'll give Carlos and Juan a hand," Cal said, starting toward the lawn where Carlos, Juan, and several others were beginning to clean up from the barbeque.

"I'm sure they will appreciate it," Sally said.

"What was all that about?" Smoke asked after Cal left.

"You haven't noticed Pearlie and Lucy?" Sally asked.

"Notice them? What do you mean, notice them?"

Sally laughed. "Smoke Jensen, to be as smart as you are in so many things, I'm sometimes surprised to discover how incredibly dumb you are in other things."

"Oh?" Smoke said. Then, it dawned on him. "Oh!" he said. "You mean Pearlie and Lucy are, uh—like that?"

Sally reached up to kiss him on the cheek. "Maybe you aren't all that dumb after all," she said.

Chapter Two

The drive from Sugarloaf over to Crosshatch, which was the name of the ranch Ian Goodnature owned, was about five miles, and with a spirited team pulling the surrey, Pearlie covered the distance in about twenty minutes. He and Lucy talked during the drive, but it was of inconsequential things, because Pearlie was too self-conscious to bring up any subject more substantive than the scenery or the weather.

He turned off the main road and up the long drive to Lucy's house, feeling a sense of frustration and disappointment with himself because he had been unable to let her know how he felt about her, or to feel her out as to how she felt about him. He pulled the team to a halt in front of the steps, then, wrapping the reins around a davit on the dashboard, hopped down from the surrey and hurried around to help Lucy down.

"I—uh—am glad you were able to come over today," he said.

"I wouldn't have missed it for anything in the world," Lucy replied. "It was great fun."

"Wasn't Maria good?"

"Yes, she was wonderful. And she is such a lovely little girl," Lucy replied.

"Yes. And she is a very sweet little girl, too. Everyone on the ranch just loves her."

There was a beat of silence, finally broken by Lucy.

"Well, I suppose I had better get on inside."

"Yes, I suppose so."

"Thanks for driving me home."

"It was my pleasure."

Lucy started toward the porch.

"Miss Lucy?"

Turning back toward Pearlie, Lucy had a big smile on her face. "Pearlie, don't you think you and I are good enough friends now, for you to call me Lucy? Without the Miss?"

"Uh—yes, I think so. I just didn't want to be too forward."

Lucy chuckled. "Pearlie, believe me, no one could ever accuse you of being too forward," she said.

"There's a dance Saturday night. Actually, there's a dance in town every Saturday night."

"Yes, I know."

"Will you be going?"

"Why, would you like me to go?"

"Yes. I mean, that is, if you are going anyway. I mean, if you want to go."

"I will be there," Lucy said, a little disappointed that he didn't ask to escort her to the dance.

"Good, good," Pearlie said. He touched the brim of his hat. "I'll see you there then."

Fontana, Colorado

Lucas Keno was at the Brown Dirt Cowboy Saloon in Fontana. It was still too early in the day for the evening trade, so there were few in the saloon. An empty beer mug and a half-full ashtray conveniently placed by the piano provided the only evidence that anyone ever played the instrument. Keno ordered a beer, then found a table and looked around.

There were two people were sitting at the table nearest the piano—a middle-aged cowboy and the only bar girl who was working at this hour. The fact that both of them had only one glass before them, and that the glass was still half-full, indicated that the bar girl either found the cowboy's company pleasant, or had accepted the slowness of the afternoon.

There were brass spittoons conveniently spaced around the room, but despite their presence, the floor was riddled with expectorated tobacco quids and chewed cigar butts.

The other cowboys who had worked for Jensen during the roundup just passed had gone on to other jobs, and even though he had not been particularly popular with the others, a few of them had even invited Keno to come with them.

"Thanks anyway, but I got me some other plans in mind," Keno replied.

"What plans you got?" one of the cowboys asked.

"Just plans," Keno answered.

Keno was vague about his plans because it wouldn't do for anyone else to know what they were. But before leaving Sugarloaf, Keno had moved fifty head of unbranded Sugarloaf cattle into a hidden box canyon and penned them up inside. His plans were to sell the cattle and get enough money to head down to Arizona or New Mexico or even Texas. It didn't really make that much difference to him where he went, just as long as he left Colorado.

Keno was here to meet a man who was going to help him carry out those plans, and as he looked up, he saw the man he was to meet coming in through the batwing doors. Toby Jeeter was considerably older than Keno, and his hair and beard were laced with gray. He nodded at Keno, then stopped at the bar to buy a beer before he joined Keno at the table.

"I found a buyer," Jeeter said.

"Who is it?"

"His name is C.D. Montgomery. He's a cattle dealer from over in Wheeler."

"Did you tell him when and where to meet me?"

"He'll be here to talk to you this afternoon," Jeeter replied.

"Good."

"When do I get my money?"

"As soon as I get my money, you'll get your thirty dollars," Keno promised.

"You didn't say nothin' 'bout me havin' to wait," Jeeter said. "You told me to find a buyer and you would pay me."

"How do you expect me to pay you before I sell the cows?" Keno asked.

Jeeter scratched at his beard, then pulled out a flea. He examined it for a moment, then crushed it between his fingernails. "All right, I'll wait. But I want fifty."

"What do you mean? Thirty dollars is a month's wages and you didn't do anything for the money. "

"I set up a meeting for you with a cattle buyer. That's what you asked for."

"All right, fifty dollars," Keno said. "But it better pay off."

"It will," Jeeter said. "Montgomery buys cattle all the time."

True to his word, Jeeter brought Montgomery to the saloon that afternoon. Montgomery was an older man, but his well-kept silver hair, clean-shaven face, and tailored clothes made him a very distinguished-looking figure.

"Keno, this here is Mr. Montgomery," Jeeter said. "This here is Keno," he added.

"Mr. Montgomery," Keno said. "Have a seat."

Taking out his handkerchief, Montgomery brushed off the chair before he sat down.

"Would you like a beer?" Keno asked.

"Thank you, no," Montgomery replied.

"I, uh, reckon that Jeeter told you what this was all about, didn't he?"

"He said you had some cattle for sale."

"Yeah, I do. Fifty head. I know it ain't all that much, but it's all I got at the moment."

"All right, deliver them to me at the railhead in—" Montgomery began, but Keno interrupted him.

"You're goin' to have to come get 'em your own self," Keno said.

"I'm going to have to come get them? See here, that is most unusual," Montgomery said. "Most of the time when I buy cattle, they are delivered to me."

"Yeah, well, this ain't most of the time," Keno said. "And you ain't never got no cattle this good for this cheap."

"I don't have any idea how cheap they are," Montgomery said. "You haven't mentioned a price."

"What do you normally pay for cattle?"

"About twenty-five dollars a head," Montgomery answered.

Keno smiled broadly. The broken and discolored teeth the smile displayed caused Montgomery to glance away in quick but repressed revulsion.

"I'll sell 'em to you for five dollars a head."

"Five dollars a head?" Montgomery said, reacting to the price.

"Does that sound good to you?" Keno asked.

"Yes, it sounds very good," Montgomery replied. "But I don't understand. Why so cheap?" Montgomery frowned. "Are these stolen cattle, Mr. Keno?"

"There ain't a brand on a one of them," Keno said.

"You didn't answer my question, Mr. Keno. Are these stolen cattle?"

"Five dollars a head," Keno said. "Do you want them or not?"

"Where are they now?"

"They are safe."

"Five dollars a head," Montgomery repeated. "You aren't going to change your mind later on now, are you?"

"No, I ain't goin' to change my mind," Keno said.

Montgomery was quiet for a long moment as he thought about the situation. Finally, he nodded.

"Yes, I'll take them," he said. "When and where do I come for them?"

"Do you know where Sugarloaf Ranch is?"

"Yes, of course I know. I don't think there is anyone in Eagle County who doesn't know where Sugarloaf is."

"All right, you come out there just after noon tomorrow," Keno said.

"Where exactly should I come?" Montgomery asked. "Sugarloaf is a big ranch. I suppose I could stop by the Big House and ask for directions."

"No! No, don't do that," Keno replied quickly and earnestly. "Look, you know where Old Woman Creek goes into the canyon? It's at the far west end of the ranch."

"Yes, I know the place."

"There's a little thicket of trees there. You come to the trees, I'll meet you there. Bring the money with you. Two hundred fifty dollars."

"You'll have the cattle?"

"Yeah, I'll have them," Keno said.

"Then I will have the money."

"Say, Mr. Montgomery, is there any way you could maybe pay fifty dollars now?" Keno asked. "Sort of on good faith, so to speak?"

"Can you produce ten cows now on good faith?" Montgomery replied.

"No, how would I do that?"

Montgomery stood up and pushed the chair back up under the table. "Very well, then I'll see you tomorrow afternoon," he said. "Good day to you, Mr. Keno." He looked toward Jeeter and nodded. "And to you, Mr. Jeeter," he added.

Jeeter chuckled as Montgomery walked out of the saloon. "Did you really think he would give you fifty dollars now?" he asked. "What the hell were you thinking about?"

"I was thinking that if he would give me some of the money in advance, I would be able to pay you thirty dollars right now and save myself twenty more dollars later on," Keno said.

"Hell, I could'a told you a man like C.D. Montgomery wouldn't go along with nothin' like that," Jeeter said. "He is a very rich man. Rich men don't do dumb things, and believe me, asking him for fifty dollars before he had ever seen so much as one cow . . . Yes, sir, Mr. Keno, that was one dumb thing." Jeeter laughed out loud.

The next afternoon

When Lucas Keno saw the cattle buyer approaching, he rode out of the copse of trees and down the little hill to meet him.

"Mr. Montgomery, it's good to see you again," Keno said. "Do you have the money?"

"I have the money, two hundred fifty dollars. That's what you asked for," Montgomery said. "Where are the cattle?"

"They're right back here in the—" Keno began, but when he turned around he saw Smoke Jensen along with Pearlie and Cal riding up behind him, having just emerged from the same copse of trees where he had been waiting for Montgomery.

"Jensen!" Keno said.

"Keno," Smoke replied.

"Uh—Mr. Jensen, this here fella is C.D. Montgomery," Keno said quickly. "If you want to know where some of your cows have been goin', well, he's been buyin' 'em from the thieves that's been takin' 'em. I just smoked him out for you."

"Did you now?" Smoke asked.

"Yes, sir, you can check him out for yourself. He's got the money right there in his hand. Two hunnert 'n fifty dollars. That's what I told him I wanted for the cows—just to see if he would take the bait, you see."

"Here is your money back, Smoke," Montgomery said, handing the money over to the ranch owner. "I appreciate the loan."

"Thanks, C.D. I appreciate you coming to me about this," Smoke said.

"Your money?" Keno asked, looking at the exchange. "What do you mean your money? What's goin' on here?"

"C.D. is a friend of mine," Smoke said. "When

you went to him with the offer to sell him fifty cows for five dollars a head, then told him to meet you on Sugarloaf, he came straight to me."

Keno glared at Montgomery, his eyes flashing intense anger and hatred.

"Why, you sorry son of a bitch!" Keno said. He went for his gun, but before he could draw it, Pearlie moved his horse quickly toward him, and the action knocked Keno from his saddle.

Keno fell heavily alongside his horse; then started again to reach for the pistol he had just dropped. A shot sounded out and Keno's pistol was knocked across the ground, the wood on the grip shattered by the impact of the bullet.

"Don't push it any further," Smoke cautioned. Smoke was holding a pistol. A small wisp of smoke curled up from the barrel.

"All right, so what are you going to do now?" Keno asked, getting up and brushing his hands together. "Are you plannin' on takin' me into town and throwin' me in jail?"

"No," Smoke said. "You didn't do anything. You were plannin' it, but you didn't do it. Be on your way, Keno. And don't bother to ever come back to Sugarloaf."

"You don't have to worry none about that," Keno said. "If I don't never see this place again, it'll be too soon."

Remounting his horse, Keno glared at Montgomery, Smoke, Pearlie, and Cal.

"Here, I believe this is yours," Cal said, handing

Keno's pistol back to him. "I hope you don't mind, I took out all the bullets."

Continuing his hateful glare, Keno stuck the empty pistol down into his holster, then turned his horse and rode away.

The four men watched Keno for a moment to make certain he was leaving. Then Smoke turned toward Montgomery. "C.D., how about having lunch with us? I'm sure Sally can come up with something worth eating."

Cal laughed.

"What's so funny?" Smoke asked.

"Your sayin' you're sure Miss Sally can come up with somethin' worth eatin'. That's what's funny," Cal said. "Why, Miss Sally is that good a cook, she could stew a boot and it would be good."

"A boot?" Montgomery said.

Smoke laughed. "Don't worry, C.D. It'll be more than a boot, I promise you."

"It sounds good to me," Montgomery said. "I'd love to join you."

"Come on, Cal," Pearlie said. "What say me and you get these cows back where they belong?"

"I'm right behind you," Cal answered.

"More mashed potatoes, Mr. Montgomery?" Sally asked, holding up a bowl of the white, steaming viand.

"Yes, please, and a little gravy, too, if you don't mind."

"I don't mind at all," Sally said, "Sugarloaf is so

far out that having a guest for a meal is actually quite a treat for us."

"Trust me, Mrs. Jensen, with the way you cook, it's a lot more of a treat for the guests," Montgomery said, holding out his plate for seconds.

"Mr. Montgomery, do you know a man named Byron Davencourt?" Sally asked as she spooned the potatoes on to his plate.

Montgomery looked up in surprise. "Why, yes. As a matter of fact I do know Byron. Quite well, in fact. Why do you ask?"

"I read in the newspaper that he has signed a contract with the U.S. Army to supply beef," Sally said.

"Well, I'll be. So, the deal came through for him, did it?" Montgomery said. "I knew that Byron was working on it. Good for him, I'm glad he was able to pull it off."

"The reason I'm asking is, that's going to take a lot of beef, isn't it? I mean for him to fulfill the contract?"

"I'll say it's going to take a lot," Montgomery answered. "As a matter of fact, if there is any problem at all with the deal Byron has, it's going to be in managing to buy enough cows to fill the contract."

"Do you think Mr. Davencourt would be willing to pay a premium price for the beef? Say, more than you can pay right now?"

Montgomery looked up at Sally, then chuckled. "Well, now," he said. "And here, all this time, I thought we were just having a friendly conversation. You are looking at the business side of it, aren't you?"

"C.D., anyone who knows us knows that Sally is the

one who has the business head," Smoke offered. He cut a piece of meat and shoved it into his mouth.

"I can see that," Montgomery replied. He smiled at Sally. "Yes, ma'am, Mrs. Jensen, I expect ole Byron will have to pay a little extra in order to get all the cows he needs."

"The paper said he'll be shipping out of Frisco," Sally said. "So, I expect that means that anyone who plans to do business with him would probably have to take their cows there." Walking over to the pie saver, Sally removed an apple pie.

"I expect so," Montgomery agreed. "Oh, my!" he said, his eyes growing large with anticipation and appreciation when he saw what Sally brought to the table. "Apple pie? I do believe I have died and gone to heaven."

"I know that you have bought cattle from us in the past. I hope you would not be put out if we sold to Mr. Davencourt," Sally said as she cut a particularly generous piece of pie and put it on a plate for Montgomery.

"Oh, heavens, no, Mrs. Jensen," Montgomery said. "As I told you, Byron is a friend of mine. I want to see him succeed. Besides, I know we will do more business together."

"Would you like a piece of cheese on top of the pie?" Sally asked.

"Oh," Montgomery said, his eyes rolling up in bliss. "You are an angel."

That night, as Smoke lay in bed with his hands laced behind his head, he was looking at Sally. Sally was sitting at the dresser, brushing her hair, the action lighted by a single candle. Just outside the window, rustling aspen leaves caught the moon and sent slivers of silver through the night. Some of the moonlight spilled in through the window, and it glowed silver in the folds of Sally's silken nightgown.

"I'll ride down to Frisco sometime next week and see this man Davencourt," Smoke said. "If he is needing beef the way Montgomery says he is, then he'll probably take at least fifteen hundred head."

"Maybe we shouldn't have let all the cowboys go just yet," Sally said as she continued to brush her hair.

"We had to let them go now," Smoke replied. "Most of them already have other jobs lined up that they need to get to. If they didn't get there in time, they'd lose out. Why do you think we shouldn't have let them go?"

"If we do sell some cattle to Byron Davencourt—"

"It's not if, it's when," Smoke said. "We will sell him fifteen hundred head. I've no doubt about that."

"All right, let's say we do sell him fifteen hundred head. So, the next question is, how are we going to get them over to Frisco?" Sally asked.

"Up to fifteen hundred head is no problem," Smoke said. "Pearlie, Cal, and I can take them over."

"Are you sure? Sally asked. "Maybe you ought to take Juan and Carlos with you."

"No need to take Juan and Carlos away from their families. I'm sure Pearlie, Cal, and I can do it," Smoke replied. "Now, I have a question."

Sally turned toward him and as she did so, the

silk nightgown clung to her figure, beautifully displaying every curve.

"What is your question?"

"Do you really want to talk business now? Or would you rather—" He left the question unfinished.

"Would I rather what?" Sally asked. But her flirtatious smile told Smoke that she knew exactly what he was talking about.

Returning her smile, Smoke folded the bedsheet back in invitation. "Would you rather—not talk?" he asked.

Sally leaned over the dresser, blew out the candle, then crossed the room to crawl into bed with her husband.

"Does this answer your question?" she asked.

Chapter Three

Reece Van Arndt, prison inmate number 2551, stood in the chamber just outside the warden's office. Half an hour earlier, Van Arndt had taken off his black-and-white-striped prison uniform and was now wearing an ill-fitting, dark blue suit. The suit looked even darker when contrasted with Van Arndt's alabaster complexion, for Van Arndt was an albino.

"Prisoner Van Arndt," the guard on duty said.

"I ain't a prisoner no more," Van Arndt said. "I get out today."

"Van Arndt, you are a prisoner until you step outside to the other side of the penitentiary gate," the guard said. "And we don't have to let you do that until midnight tonight, so I'd watch my step iffen I was you."

Van Arndt glared at the guard, but didn't say anything.

"Go on into the office. Warden Parker will see you now," the guard said.

Van Arndt nodded, then stepped up to the door that led into the warden's office. He put his hand on the doorknob.

"Knock, damn you!" the guard said sternly.

Van Arndt knocked.

"Come in."

Van Arndt walked into the warden's office, then stopped at the line on the floor beyond which no inmate was ever to pass. Parker was sitting behind his desk, and he leaned forward as Van Arndt came in.

"Well, Van Arndt, you are leaving us today. I didn't think you would make it. I thought you would do something dumb enough to get your sentence extended—or else, I thought someone might kill you. And to be honest, I was sort of hopin' for the latter."

"Sorry to disappoint you, Warden," Van Arndt said.

"Yes, well, I don't plan to be disappointed for long. If you aren't killed within the next six months, you'll be back," the warden said. "And the next time you come back, I have no doubt but that you will be staying with us for the rest of your miserable life."

"You give that kind of enouragin' talk to ever' prisoner that leaves this place?" Van Arndt asked.

"Not all of them," the warden replied. "Just the no accounts like you."

Van Arndt shook his head. "Well, I hate to disappoint you, but you have seen the last of Reece Van Arndt. I ain't never comin' back to this hellhole."

"So you say, Van Arndt, so you say," the warden said. He sighed, then shoved an envelope across the desk. "This is yours," he said. "According to Colorado state law, I am required to give you a train ticket to wherever you want to go in the state. You said you wanted to go to Fairplay, so you got a ticket to there. I must say, though, pickin' a place by the name of Fairplay for someone like you seems a little strange. You'll find five dollars in there as well, which is also required by state law."

"Five dollars?" he said. "I've busted rocks and sweated in this hellhole for three years, and all I get from it is five dollars?"

"Five dollars," the warden repeated. "Don't spend it all in one place," he added, laughing derisively.

Van Arndt picked up the envelope.

"Smitty!" the warden called.

The guard stuck his head into the warden's office. "Yes, sir?"

"Get this maggot-looking bastard out of my sight," the warden said.

"Let's go, you," the guard said.

Van Arndt shifted positions in the hard seat of the day coach, then looked through the window at the wide-open spaces outside. No more than one hundred yards away he saw a couple of coyotes running parallel with the track, actually outpacing the train. Finally it grew dark outside and, passing through the car, the conductor began lighting kerosene lanterns, including the one just over Van Arndt. Van Arndt reached up and turned it off.

"Thank you, sir, that was very kind of you," the man in the seat across from Van Arndt said.

"What?"

"You saw that I was trying to sleep, so you put out the lantern so as not to keep me awake."

"Yeah," Van Arndt said. He had actually put it out just to keep people from looking toward him and his chalk-white skin.

The man stretched, then sat up and yawned. "But I can't sleep none anyway." He chuckled. "Don't know why I can't sleep. I stayed up pret' nigh all night last night celebratin' my good fortune."

"Your good fortune?"

"Well, it might not be a fortune to most folks, but four hundred fifty dollars is a fortune to me."

Van Arndt had just been tolerating the man; now he began listening with interest.

"Oh, I would say that four hundred fifty dollars is a lot of money to just about anyone," Van Arndt said. "What did you do? Get lucky at cards?"

"Oh, no, sir, my wife, Suzie, there is no way she would put up with my playin' cards. There was a time when I gambled, but no more." He stuck his hand out. "Gibbs is the name, Donnie G. Gibbs."

"Eddie Mason," Van Arndt said, taking Gibbs's hand and lying about his own name. "So, how did you come by so much money?"

"Well, sir, I'll tell you. Me and Suzie, we got us this real small little place just outside Como, you see. And for the last three years, Suzie and me have survived just mostly by raisin' our own vegetables, sellin' eggs, and the such. But all along what we been doin' is, we've also been raisin' a few head of cows until we built us up to around thirty head or so. Then last week what I done is, I cut me out fifteen head of cows and drove them down to Frisco where I sold 'em to a fella there for thirty dollars a head." Donnie stuck his hand into his pocket and pulled out a roll of money. "Here it is," he said. He chuckled. "Just in case you ain't never seen that much money at one time."

Van Arndt smiled. "That is a good-looking wad of money, I have to admit."

"If you think that's a lot of money, you should see what they have on deposit in the bank in Frisco. Why, I'll bet they have over one hundred thousand dollars there."

"A hundred thousand dollars? That's a lot of money for a small-town bank, ain't it? Why is it that they have so much money, do you reckon?"

"They got all that money because there's a cattleman there, a fella by the name of Byron Davencourt, and he is buying up all the beef he can," Gibbs said. "He only bought fifteen head from me, but I reckon he'll be buyin' three thousand head or so before he's all finished and done."

"A hundred thousand dollars in the bank of Frisco," Van Arndt said. "That would sure be some sight to see."

"Ha, I reckon it would," Gibbs said. "Not that nobody is goin' to ever get a chance to look at it, though. I expect they'll keep it locked up good and safe."

Gibbs looked more closely at Van Arndt. "Say,

Mr. Mason, I don't mean no insult or nothin', but why is it you're so pale? Are you sick?"

"I'm what you call an albino," Van Arndt said. "My skin doesn't produce any color. There are a lot of colored people who are albinos, and they are as white as any white man."

"You don't say? Are you a colored man or a white man?" Gibbs asked.

"I'm a white man," Van Arndt answered.

"Well, I'll be. I ain't never seen anything like that," Gibbs said. "Like I say, I don't mean to be insultin' or nothin'. I hope you ain't takin' offense."

"No offense taken," Van Arndt said.

The conductor came through the car again. "Folks, the next stop is Grant. We'll be there about twenty minutes, just long enough for you to get yourselves some supper. Grant, next stop," he said again as he moved through the car and out onto the vestibule, heading for the next car.

"Would you care to have supper with me?" Van Arndt said.

"Why, I would be pleased to," Gibbs said. "Hardest thing about travelin' alone is havin' to eat alone. But when you are lucky to find someone that's good company, such as I've just done, why, sittin' down to a meal with such a person can be a pure pleasure."

After a supper of ham and fried potatoes, Van Arndt and Gibbs walked out of the depot café and stood for a moment on the darkened patterned-brick platform. The train that had brought them to Grant was sitting on the track, puffing as it vented steam from the pressure the fireman was maintaining.

"Do you think there is any depot café anywhere in the country that serves anything other than ham and fried potatoes?" Gibbs asked with a little laugh.

"That seems to be the standard fare all right," Van Arndt answered. The truth was, Van Arndt was just agreeing with Gibbs, because he had not ridden on enough trains to be able to comment.

"I have to admit that it wasn't bad eatin', though it could have been that I was just hungry," Gibbs said.

"Yeah, I suppose, but—" Van Arndt paused in mid-sentence. "Damn, look at that!" he said excitedly, pointing toward the front of the engine.

"Look at what?"

"I think I saw, no, I know I saw a little child crawling across the track in front of the engine."

"What? Are you sure?"

"I'm positive. It was a little girl. She must have gotten away from her mother."

"Good heavens, she's got no business crawling around on the track!" Gibbs said. "What if she is under the train when it starts? There's no way the engineer could possibly see her. Good Lord, she could be run over and killed."

"Yeah, that's what I think, too. Come on," Van Arndt said, starting toward the front of the train. "Let's see if we can find her."

"Yes, by all means, let's do!" Gibbs agreed.

The two men hurried toward the front of the train, then around to the other side.

"Where is she?" Gibbs asked. "I don't see her!"

"I don't see her either. Maybe she's under the train."

"Oh, heavens, I certainly hope not," Gibbs said.

"We'd better look. I'll look under the tender, you look under the express car," Van Arndt suggested.

Van Arndt leaned over to look under the tender while Gibbs headed for the next car behind. Once Gibbs passed Van Arndt, Van Arndt stood up, pulled his knife, then moved quickly until he was standing right behind Gibbs.

Sensing Van Arndt's presence, Gibbs turned around. "What is it? Did you see her under the—unhh!"

Van Arndt, holding the blade sideways and palm up in his hand, plunged the knife into Gibb's left side, aiming for the heart. Gibbs grunted in pain as the blade slipped easily in between his fourth and fifth ribs. His eyes grew large, and he looked at Van Arndt with an expression of confusion on his face and in his eyes.

"Mason! What—what are you—?"

That was as far as Gibbs got before his eyes closed and he fell off the knife. Quickly, Van Arndt took Gibbs's money before pushing him under the car. Then he walked back around to the depot platform, and was standing there when the other passengers came out of the café and boarded the train.

Van Arndt didn't reboard. Instead, he remained on the platform until the train started to leave; then he hurried into the depot. He saw a man behind the counter. The man was wearing a billed cap with a shield that read: STATIONMASTER.

"Are you the stationmaster?" Van Arndt asked.

"That's what it says on my hat," the man said, pointing to the shield. "The name is Travelsted. What can I do for you?"

"Mr. Travelsted, you'd better come quick!" Van Arndt said. "I think the train just ran over someone as it was leaving the station."

"What?" the stationmaster gasped. "What are you talking about? What do you mean you think the train ran over someone?"

"It was a fella named Gibbs," Van Arndt said. "I'm pretty sure he must've got run over."

"You are just pretty sure? Good Lord, man, that's not something that you can just casually speculate about. What makes you think this man—Gibbs, did you call him?"

"Yes, Donnie Gibbs."

"What makes you think the train ran over Gibbs? Did you see it happen?"

"No, I didn't exactly see it. But I'm pretty sure it happened."

"Are you and Gibbs friends?"

"Not in particular," Van Arndt said. "The thing is, we met on the train, and we come in here to take our supper together. Then, after supper, we was standin' out here on the depot platform waitin' to get back on the train. That's when Gibbs said he seen a baby crawling on the track. I have to tell you, Mr. Travelsted, I looked, but I didn't see nothin'. I told him I didn't see nothin', but he was bound and determined to go rescue the baby, so round the train he went. I waited for him, but he didn't come back.

Then, when the train pulled away, I thought maybe he'd be standin' on the other side, but he wasn't."

"Are you sure he didn't come back? Don't you think it could be that he got on the train without you seein' him?"

"I suppose that could be so," Van Arndt said. "But I have to tell you, I was watchin' pretty close and I sure didn't see him come back. I hate to say it, Mr. Travelsted, but I got me this awful feelin' that somehow poor ole' Gibbs fell on the track and got hisself runned over."

Travelsted sighed. "Well, I reckon we'd better check," the stationmaster said. "Sanchez?"

An elderly Mexican was moving luggage around and he looked up. *"Sí?"*

"Get Chavez and you two come with me."

"Chavez, Señor Travelsted quiere que nosotros vayamos con él," Sanchez called out in Spanish.

Van Arndt went out with Travelsted and the two Mexican employees.

"Where'd you see him last?" Travelsted asked.

"Let me see," Van Arndt said, scratching his chin. "I believe the engine was sittin' right about there," he said, pointing to a place on the track. "And ole Gibbs, after he seen the little girl, or else thought he seen the little girl, went around in front of the engine. So I reckon right about there is where I seen him last."

"The track is too dark to see from here. Let me get a lantern and we'll take a closer look," Travelsted said.

"A lantern I brought, Señor Travelsted," Sanchez said.

"Walk up there ahead of us, Sanchez, and hold the lantern down low so we can get a good look at the track," Travelsted ordered, stepping down from the platform and walking up the ties between the twin rails.

Sanchez went a few feet up the track, then summoned Chavez over and gave him the lantern. Chavez went on ahead for a few feet. Then he stopped dead in his track.

"Madre de Dios, Sanchez, es un hombre muerto," Chevez said with a gasp. *"El tren mutiló su cadaver!"*

"What did he say?" Travelsted asked.

"He has found a man's body, but it has been mutilated by the train," Sanchez translated.

Van Arndt, Travelsted, and Sanchez moved up to stand by Chavez, who was holding the lantern in a way to illuminate what was left of the body. The body had been completely split into two halves, from head to crotch, with half lying on one side of the track and half on the other. Blood and intestines were everywhere, as well as brain matter from the severed head.

Whereas Chevez and Sanchez stared at the remains in morbid fascination, Travelsted turned away, then began to throw up.

"My God," Travelsted said. "This is awful." He looked at Van Arndt. "What did you say your friend's name was?"

"He said his name was Gibbs. Donnie Gibbs. But he wasn't my friend exactly. We was just on the train together is all," Van Arndt said. "Like I told you, all we done is, we just ate supper. Then, after supper we come back outside, and was standin' here talkin' when he said he seen a little girl crawlin' across the track. That's when he went up to the front of the train lookin' for it."

"Should we look for the baby?" Sanchez asked.

"You can if you want to," Travelsted said. "But I don't think there was a baby. If so, the mother would have come to me to ask about it."

"*Sí*, I think so too," Sanchez said.

"I'll send a telegram back to all the stations along the line and try to find out if anyone knows anything about this man Gibbs. In the meantime, Sanchez, you and Chavez pick him up. We can't leave him on the tracks like this."

"Pick him up? Señor, we cannot pick him up," Sanchez replied. "He is in many pieces. We will have to scrape him up."

"All right, then scrape him up," Travelsted said.

Chapter Four

Frisco, Colorado

The ill-fitting blue suit that had literally screamed prison issue was gone, replaced by a pair of denim trousers and a white shirt. The clothes, like the black hat and the brown boots he was wearing, were new. Van Arndt had used Gibbs's money to buy himself new duds to include a new pistol and holster. He had bought a new horse and saddle as well, but rather than ride the fifty miles to Frisco, he had taken the train, buying passage for his horse in the attached stock car.

Stepping down from the train, Van Arndt saw a town that was alive with commerce. The streets were filled with the traffic of wagons, buckboards, and horses. Men and women moved up and down the boardwalks, and went in and out of the many stores that fronted Center Street. Across the street from the depot, a new building was going up and men hammered, sawed, and shouted at each other. Next to the depot was a large holding pen, and though it was almost empty at the moment, the ground was redolent with the droppings of thousands of cattle deposited over the last several months. This was both visual and olfactory evidence of the cattle commerce carried on at the Frisco railhead.

Retrieving his horse from the attached stock car, Van Arndt led the animal down the street to a livery, where he made arrangements for it to be boarded. Then he walked back up the street to the Railroad Hotel, which was just across from the depot, and there, he took a room. After that, he went to the bank to have a look around at the way the bank was laid out. If this little bank really did have one hundred thousand dollars, as Gibbs had stated, than Van Arndt intended to relieve it of that burden.

He chuckled to himself as he realized how he had just thought of it as "relieving the bank of its burden."

The bank was unremarkable in that it resembled all the other banks in all the other towns Van Arndt had seen. Just inside the door was a table, on which there were bank deposit slips and counter drafts. A little farther back were the tellers' cages.

"May I help you, sir?" one of the tellers asked, seeing Van Arndt standing by the table. "Do you wish to make a deposit?"

"I might," Van Arndt replied. He stepped up to the cage and handed the teller three twenty-dollar bills. "But first, I would like to have these bills changed into tens, if you don't mind."

"Why, I don't mind at all, sir," the teller said, taking the money and making the change.

"I have a lot of money in the bank in Denver,"

Van Arndt said. "I plan to buy some cattle while I'm here, and so I would like to move my money to this bank. But I'm a little worried."

"Worried? May I ask what you are worried about, sir?" the teller asked. "Perhaps I can ease your fears."

"Well, I'm sure you can understand why I'm worried," Van Arndt said, continuing the charade. "It's just that the bank in Denver is rather substantial, and I am absolutely certain that my money is safe as long as it is there. Please don't get me wrong, sir," Van Arndt said obsequiously. "I truly mean no insult, but you must admit that this is a rather small bank, and I just imagine you don't have a lot of money on deposit."

"Well now, that's just where you are wrong, sir," the bank teller said. "It just so happens that we have well over one hundred thousand dollars on deposit right now. And at least eighty thousand dollars of that money is deposited in one account."

"Is that a fact?"

"Yes, sir, it is a fact," the teller insisted.

"That must be quite a wealthy man, to have so much money in one account."

"I think he represents an industry that is wealthy," the teller said. "But he is not in the least worried about the safety or efficiency of our bank. So, I'm sure you can see that, regardless of the size of your account, we will quite able to handle it."

All the time the teller had been talking, he had been counting out money. "There you go, sir," he said, shoving a small pile of money through the teller's cage. "Sixty dollars in ten-dollar bank notes."

Van Arndt picked up the six ten-dollar bills, folded them over, and stuck them in his pocket.

"Well, I thank you very much," he said. "You have been very helpful. I'll be returning to Denver soon and, when I do, I'll draw the money out and bring it back here for deposit."

"We'll look forward to doing business with you, Mister—" The teller dragged the word out, waiting for Van Arndt to supply the name.

"Yes, thank you, I'll see you when I get back," Van Arndt said, making no effort to supply a name.

In his hotel room that night, Van Arndt developed the plan he would use in order to relieve the bank of its money. During his time in prison he had met three men that he believed would be helpful to him. One thing that made them particularly valuable to him was the fact that he knew them, but they didn't know each other. And, for the time being, they wouldn't know him, for he had no plans to sign the letters.

It was going to cost him sixty dollars to put the plan into operation, but sixty dollars was little enough to spend for the return he expected from his investment.

Van Arndt wrote the three letters. Then, as he put the letters into the addressed envelopes, he also included two ten-dollar bills in each one. Because he knew the men, he was certain that the money would get their attention. Tomorrow he would take the letters down to the post office and put them in the mail.

A line shack in Gunnison County

Zeb Tucker had been the first to arrive, reaching the line shack by following the directions in the letter. The letter had contained two ten dollar bills along with a promise for much more money if he would follow the directions.

> *Following the directions above, you should arrive at the shack no earlier than one o'clock and no later than two o'clock on Thursday, the seventh, instant. You will be the first to arrive. You will find that the shack has been stocked with enough food and coffee to provide supper that night and breakfast the next morning for three people. You are to be one of the three I have chosen.*
>
> *Stick a white feather in your hatband. The other two men are also being instructed to mark their hat with a white feather. This will be the signal of recognition among you. Be wary of anyone who is not wearing this signal of recognition.*
>
> *Each of you will be given a few random words. When you put the random words together, it will form a sentence of instruction that will prepare you to take the next step. Your words are:*

TUCKER READ INSTRUCTIONS FOUND

Tucker had no idea where the instructions he was supposed to read were found, but he assumed it would be made clear to him when the two others arrived. He located the coffee, and had just made a pot when he heard a horse approaching from outside. Making certain he had a white feather in his hat, he pulled his pistol, then stepped into a shadowed corner of the room so he could watch the door.

The man who stepped in through the door was also wearing a white feather in his hat.

"Anybody in here?" the man called out.

"Yeah, I'm over here," Tucker said. "You have a letter with you?"

"Yeah."

Tucker put his pistol away. "The name's Tucker," he said.

"I'm Clay."

"That your first or last name?"

"Clay," he repeated without being any more specific. "According to my letter, there will be three of us."

"Yeah, that's what my letter said as well," Tucker said. "Do you have any idea who sent the letter?"

Clay shook his head. "I don't have a clue," he said. "But there was twenty dollars in it, with the promise of more."

As the two men were talking, they heard the third man approaching, and they stepped out front so they could watch him as he rode up. He was wearing a white feather in his hat.

"Do you know who this fella is?" Clay asked.

"No. I've never seen him before in my life."

"Interesting. Whoever the fella is that sent us

these letters, seems like he just don't want us to know each other," Clay said.

Because the two men standing in front of the line shack were both wearing white feathers in their hat, the rider continued his approach without apprehension. "Hello, boys," he said as he swung down from his horse. "The name is Rawlins. Either one of you boys know what this is all about?"

"No, but now that all three of us are together, I reckon we'll be findin' out soon enough," Tucker said.

When Rawlins went inside, the three men compared their letters and found that each of them had only one part of a cryptic message. Putting it together gave them the first step.

TUCKER READ INSTRUCTIONS FOUND ON THE TOP BUNK UNDER THE RED BLANKET

Tucker opened the envelope they found under the red blanket, read it quickly, then looked up at the others. "I'll be damned," he said.

"What is it?" Rawlins asked.

"Why don't I just read it to you?" Tucker said and, clearing his throat, began to read aloud.

> *If you have found this letter, that means all three of you are together. What I propose is difficult and dangerous, but the reward is great. If all goes as it should, we will be dividing one hundred thousand dollars.*

"One hundred thousand dollars?" Rawlins said. "Is that what you said?"

"That's what it says here," Tucker said, holding out the letter.

"Holy shit! I ain't never seen that much money at one time in my life. I didn't even know there was that much money in the world."

"Go on, finish reading the letter," Clay said.

At this point, make certain that you are agreed to carry out my instructions. Tucker, if even one man says he does not want to do this, do not read any further.

Tucker looked up. "Are you both in?" he asked.

"Hell, yes, I'm in!" Rawlins said.

"Me, too," Clay said. "Read the rest of the letter."

At the present time there is on deposit at the bank in Frisco, Colorado, over one hundred thousand dollars. I have checked the bank out myself. There are no armed guards and only two tellers. The tellers are meek-mannered men and unarmed. Use your guns and you will get no resistance. After you get the money, return to this cabin. I will be here to meet you and, at that time, we will divide the money four ways.

"Wait a minute. I don't know about this," Clay said. "I mean, if you think about it, we're the ones takin' the risk, but whoever this fella is who wrote the letter is goin' to get his share? That don't seem right."

"Yeah, but don't forget, it's one hundred thousand dollars," Tucker said. "And even split four ways, one hundred thousand dollars is, uh . . ." Tucker paused for a moment, trying to divide one hundred thousand by four.

"Twenty-five thousand dollars," Clay said.

"Yeah, twenty-five thousand," Tucker agreed.

"Son of a bitch, that is a lot of money," Clay said.

"So, what do you say? Do we do it?" Tucker asked.

"Yeah, hell, yes, I say we do it," Rawlins said.

"What do you think, Tucker?" Clay asked. "Do you feel all right with this?"

"Well, for one thing, you've already said that you would," Tucker replied. "And for another thing, whoever wrote this is the one who found the bank. And he is also the one who found us. It appears to me that he seems to have it all planned out. So, you tell me, Clay. Are you willin' to just walk away from your share of one hundred thousand dollars just because you think it's not fair?"

"No, I guess not," Clay answered. "If you two are goin' along with it, well, I reckon I will, too."

"There's one thing I don't understand," Rawlins said. "How does this fella, whoever he is, know that we aren't going to just take the money and ride away without givin' him his share?"

"Well, think about it. Do you know who he is? Or what he looks like?" Tucker asked.

"No, I don't," Rawlins said.

"Do you know who it is, Clay?"

"No," Clay answered, shaking his head.

"Uh-huh, and neither do I. But the thing is, he does know who we are. And not only that, I'd bet a dollar to a dime that he knows exactly what each one of us looks like."

"So what does that have to do with it?" Rawlins asked.

"Well, suppose we took the money and didn't give him his share. He could come right up to one of us—shoot us if he wanted to—and we wouldn't even know to be worried because we wouldn't know who he was," Tucker explained.

"Yeah," Rawlins said. "I see what you mean. I guess you have got a point at that. Anyway, like I said, I'm all for it. Clay, it's up to you."

"No, it ain't up to him," Tucker said. "At this point, I figure on doin' it with or without him."

"I'm in," Clay said.

Chapter Five

Sugarloaf Ranch

Not one for riding in a buckboard, Smoke let Sally drive the rig while he rode next to it. As he rode down the trail toward town, Smoke glanced down at Sally, recalling the way the moon had made her silk nightgown glimmer like molten silver the other night. When it suited her to do so, Sally wore men's pants, and she was doing so this morning, but it did not detract one bit from her femininity. This morning she was carrying a silver-plated .32 revolver. She wasn't a fast-draw artist, but she was smooth with the revolver, and she always hit where she aimed.

Smoke was actually leaving for Frisco this morning in order to meet with Byron Davencourt so he could make arrangements for selling his cattle. It would have been a lot quicker to go by train, and he did intend to return by train, but he intended to go on horseback all the way from Big Rock to Frisco in order to scout the best route for driving the cattle. Sally chose this morning to come into town as well, not only to prolong her good-bye to Smoke, but also so she could do some shopping. They rode together into Big Rock, laughing and talking as they did so. Despite the length of time they had been married, they still enjoyed each other's company, and this morning was no exception.

When they reached Big Rock and rode down Main Street, they saw Sheriff Monte Carson standing on the boardwalk in front of his office, drinking a cup of coffee.

As Smoke and Sally rode past the sheriff's office, the sheriff raised his cup in a salute. "Good mornin', Smoke, Sally. Where are you two headed?" Carson called.

"Meet me at Longmont's and I'll tell you all about it," Smoke called back.

Carson nodded and then he pitched his coffee onto the dirt. Smoke and Monte Carson had become very good friends over the past few years. Carson had once been a well-known gunfighter, though he had never ridden the owlhoot trail.

Smoke was responsible for the fact that Carson was the sheriff of Big Rock. It had all come about when an ambitious and totally unscrupulous rancher named Tilden Franklin made plans to take over the county. He hired Carson to be the sheriff of Fontana, a town just down the road from Smoke's Sugarloaf spread. When Carson learned that the man's plans were to have a sheriff who would wink at his lawlessness, he put his foot down and informed Franklin that Fontana was going to be run in a law-abiding manner from then on.

Franklin, with the intention of showing Carson who was the real boss of Fontana, sent a bunch of his riders into town to teach the upstart sheriff a lesson. The men seriously wounded him and killed Carson's two deputies, taking over the town. In retaliation, Smoke founded the town of Big Rock, and he, Sheriff Carson, and a band of aging gunfighters returned to Fontana to clean house and make things right.

When the fracas was over, Smoke offered the job of sheriff of Big Rock to Monte Carson. Carson accepted the offer, and wound up marrying a grass widow and settling into the sheriff's job as if he had been born to it. Neither Smoke nor the citizens of Big Rock ever had cause to regret the fact that Carson had taken the job.

Now, aging somewhat, heavyset, and growing a bit of a paunch thanks both to his wife's excellent cooking and his aversion to any real physical labor, Carson still had the qualities that made a good sheriff. He was quick and deadly accurate with a handgun, and he was honest. If you obeyed the law and didn't cause any trouble in his town, you would have no trouble with him. Cross the law, and a significant number of young gunnies learned that age and weight had not lessoned the sheriff's effectiveness.

"Smoke, you go on down to Longmont's. I'll join you in a little while," Sally said. "I need to stop in to Lucy's Dress Emporium for a few minutes."

"You are buying another dress, with as many

dresses as you have in the armoire?" Smoke asked. Before Sally could answer, Smoke held up his hand as if waving her off. "Don't get me wrong, I think you are beautiful in any dress you choose to wear." He chuckled. "Heck, you are beautiful even when you aren't wearing anything at all," he added.

Sally smiled. "If you are trying to make me blush right here in front of everybody, it isn't going to work."

Smoke laughed again. "Sally, I gave up trying to make you blush a long time ago. It's just that you don't choose to wear dresses all that often. I mean, look at what you are wearing right now. I'm just wondering why you would even want another dress, is all."

"For your information, *Mister* Jensen, it just so happens that the dress I am buying this morning will not be for me," Sally said. "It just so happens that Maria's birthday is coming up this week, and this dress is for her."

"Oh, yes, Maria's birthday," Smoke replied. "I had forgotten about that. Yes, if this is for Maria, be my guest."

"Thank you, *Mister* Jensen, for your permission. Not that I needed it," she added, though her smile and the twinkle in her eyes softened her words.

After Sally stopped in front Lucy's Dress Emporium, Smoke rode on down to Longmont's, dismounted, then went inside. As was his custom upon entering any saloon, he stepped immediately to the side and pressed his back up against the wall. He stood there a moment, letting his eyes adjust to the lower light inside while he looked for possible trouble among the patrons. Even though he knew he was almost as safe in his friend's restaurant as he was in his own house, he'd been hunted and tracked for more than half his life, and the habit of caution was so ingrained in him that when he was cautious, he didn't even notice it.

The owner of the saloon and restaurant, Louis Longmont, was sitting at his usual table in a corner. He smiled as he watched his friend go through his regular ritual. Louis was a lean, hawk-faced man, with strong, slender hands, long fingers, and carefully manicured nails. He had jet-black hair and a black pencil-thin mustache. He was dressed in a black suit, with white shirt and a crimson ascot. He wore low-heeled boots, and a pistol that hung in tied-down leather on his right side. The pistol was nickel-plated, with ivory handles, but it wasn't just for show, for Louis was snake-quick and a feared, deadly gunhand when pushed.

Although Louis was engaged in a profession that did not have a very good reputation, he was not an evil man. He had never hired his gun out for money. And while he could make a deck of cards do almost anything, he had never cheated at poker. He didn't have to cheat. He was possessed of a phenomenal memory, could tell you the odds of filling any type of poker hand, and was an expert at the technique of card counting.

Louis was just past thirty. When he was a small boy, Louis left Louisiana and came West with his parents. His parents had died in a shantytown fire, leaving the boy to cope as best he could.

Louis had coped quite well, plying his innate intelligence and willingness to take a chance into a fortune. He owned a large ranch up in Wyoming Territory, several businesses in San Francisco, and a hefty chunk of a railroad.

Though it was a mystery to many why Louis continued to stay with his saloon and restaurant in a small town, Louis explained it very simply.

"If I left the business, I would miss it," he said. Smoke understood exactly what he was talking about.

Still standing just inside the door, Smoke glanced over and saw his friend smiling at him. He returned the grin, then moved across the floor to take a seat at Louis's table.

Louis was shuffling a deck of cards and dealing poker hands. He turned up three hands, studied them for a moment, then pointed to the hand that was still facedown.

"If I were a betting man—and incidentally I am—I would bet on this as the winning hand," he said.

"What makes you think so? This one has a pair of aces," Smoke said, pointing to one of the hands.

"I think this will have three of a kind," Louis said. "Small cards to be sure, but three will beat a pair of aces." He turned up the cards to expose three sixes, a jack, and a queen.

"I'm glad I didn't bet," Smoke said.

"Did Miss Sally remain behind at Sugarloaf?" Louis asked as he picked up all the cards and folded them back into the deck.

"No, Sally came with me. She will here shortly."

Louis's smile broadened. "Ah, good, good. I am

always glad to see you, my friend, but the lovely Mademoiselle Sally?" Louis raised his hand to his lips and, putting his thumb and forefinger together, made a kissing motion. "It is well known that Mademoiselle Sally's beauty brings joy to a dreary world."

"Do I have to keep reminding you, Louis, that Sally is not a mademoiselle? We are married."

"Yes, *mon ami*, I know you are married," Louis said, "but *l'espoir est éternel*. Hope is eternal," he translated.

Smoke laughed, and was still laughing when Sheriff Carson came into the saloon, breathing a little heavily from having walked down from his office.

"Have I missed a joke?" he asked.

"Alas, my *gendarme* friend," Louis said. "The joke is on me."

"How about a round of beers on me?" Smoke said. "I'm heading down to Frisco and could use one for the trail."

"Why Frisco?" Louis asked as he signaled the bartender.

"Yes, Mr. Longmont?" the bartender called to him.

"Bring us three beers, will you, Andrew?"

"Yes, sir, right away."

With the beers ordered, Louis turned his attention back to Smoke. "You were about to tell us why you were going to Frisco."

"I'm going there to meet a cattle buyer named Davencourt. Turns out he has a contract to supply beef to the army, and I figure he is going to be in the market."

"But can't you sell your beef here? To C.D. Montgomery, or one of the other buyers?"

"I could," Smoke said. "But Davencourt is paying more, providing I deliver the cattle to the railhead in Frisco."

"I see," Longmont said. "Do you think he will pay enough to make it worth your while to take your cattle to Frisco?"

"I think he will. At least, that's what I intend to find out with this trip."

"That sounds smart to me," Carson said. "No wonder Sugarloaf is the most successful ranch around. You are always on top of things."

"Ha, don't give me credit for this," Smoke said. "This was all Sally's idea."

"Yes, I know. She is not only beautiful, she is also very smart," Louis said. He sighed. "Ah, what a woman."

"Oh, say, Smoke, do you remember a fella by the name of Van Arndt?" Carson asked. "Reece Van Arndt?"

"Yes, I remember him," Smoke said. "As I recall, he tried to hold up a train a few years ago."

"As you recall," Carson said with a chuckle. "Tried is right. He tried, but he didn't succeed because of you, my friend. His gang was killed and he wound up going to prison."

"Good place for him," Smoke said.

"I would agree with you," Carson said. "Unfortunately, he is no longer there. I got a wire a few days ago from Warden Parker at the prison."

"Don't tell me Van Arndt has escaped."

Carson shook his head. "He didn't escape, he was

let out. He served his time and is now a free man. The warden thought you might like to know that."

"Why would he think that?" Smoke asked. "Has Van Arndt made any specific threats?"

"I don't know and Warden Parker didn't say," Carson replied. "All I know is that his telegram just said that I should advise you that Van Arndt has served his time and has been released. If you want to know the truth, I expect Parker is just being extra cautious is all."

"I don't fault him for his caution and I appreciate you bringing me the information," Smoke said. "I've had a passel of people after me in my life—so if somebody new is added to the bunch that call themselves my enemy, it's always good to know his name."

"Smoke Jensen, let's just see how good you really are with a gun! I'm callin' you out, you son of a bitch!"

The loud shout and angry challenge got the attention of everyone in the saloon, and all talking stopped in mid conversation as the other patrons looked up to see what was going on.

Looking toward the sound of the voice, Smoke saw Lucas Keno standing just inside the door. There was an expression of rage and hatred on the cowboy's face, and he was holding a pistol leveled at Smoke.

"What are you doing, Keno?" Smoke asked.

"Cal and Pearlie have both told me that you are the best with a pistol they ever saw. So, I was just wonderin' how good you really are. Because, you see, I'm pretty good myself. And what I thought is, we'd just see which one of us is the best in a fair fight."

"It's hardly a fair fight when you are already holding a gun in your hand," Longmont said.

Keno smiled, an evil, mirthless smile.

"Well, now, you see, the way I look it, that's what is going to make it a fair fight," he said. "I figure if you really are as good as ole' Cal and Pearlie say you are, then I might just need me an advantage."

"That's quite an advantage, Keno," Sheriff Carson said. "In fact, it is so much an advantage that if, by some wild chance, you would happen to kill Smoke or anyone else in here, it would be considered murder in the first degree. We hang people for that in this state."

"Yeah, I reckon it is a big advantage, ain't it?" Keno replied, his smile growing larger. "I tell you what I'll do for you, Jensen. I'll give you a chance to stand up and face me. And I won't shoot until I see you start to pull your gun."

Smoke smiled, and his smile was broad and genuine.

"What are you smiling at, you son of a bitch? Don't you understand what's goin' on here?"

Now Sheriff Carson and Longmont were smiling as well.

"Have you all gone crazy?" Keno asked, his voice rising in pitch as his frustration and anger intensified. Smoke was showing no fear, and that wasn't the way it was supposed to be. "I'm the one that's holdin' the gun here. Or ain't you people noticed that?"

"Oh we've noticed all right," Smoke said. "Drop the gun, Keno. Drop the gun and you might live."

"What are you talking about?" Keno asked, still confused by the strange reaction. "Why would I do a foolish thing like that?" Keno asked.

"Because if you don't drop your gun right now, I will be forced to put a .32-caliber ball in your head," a woman's calm and well-modulated voice said.

Sally's words were augmented by the deadly double click of the cylinder being engaged as the hammer was being pulled back by her thumb.

"Hi, Sally," Smoke said easily. "Do you want a beer?"

"Don't mind if I do," Sally replied. "Louis, tell Andrew to draw one for me while I shoot Mr. Keno in the back of his head for not dropping his pistol when I told him to."

"No! No!" Keno said. "I'm dropping it, I'm dropping it. Don't shoot!" He opened his hand and the pistol fell to the floor with a loud thump.

"Damn," Sheriff Carson said. "I walked all the way down here. Now I have to put Keno in jail before I can even have a beer."

"Darlin', pick up Keno's gun and bring it to me," Smoke said.

Stepping around Keno, Sally reached down to pick up his pistol; then she took it over to the table. The wooden pistol grip was still shattered from the impact of the bullet when Smoke had shot it a few days earlier. Smoke held it out toward Keno.

"Damn, you haven't gotten that fixed yet?" he asked. "I thought you were supposed to be so all-fired good with a gun. Nobody who is good with a gun would let one stay in such a bad condition as this."

Smoke removed the cylinder and slipped it into his pocket. Then, using his pocketknife, he extracted the firing pin. After that, he walked over and dropped the gun into a half-full spittoon.

"No need to put him in jail, Sheriff, he didn't actually do anything," Smoke said, handing the empty cylinder to Carson. "Suppose you hold on to this for a couple of days."

"All right," Carson said, taking the cylinder from Smoke.

"You don't have to be doin' me no damn favors," Keno said.

"Oh, don't get me wrong, Keno, I'm not doing you any favors," Smoke said. "I'm just telling you straight out to get out of my sight and stay out of my sight. Because next time I see you, I'll kill you."

Smoke delivered the words in an even, calm, and cool voice. That had the effect of making the threat much more frightening and believable than if he had spoken the words in anger.

Keno stood in the door for a moment longer, as if trying to digest the words.

"What?" Keno said. "Sheriff, did you hear that? This man just threatened to kill me."

"Yes, I heard the man," Sheriff Carson said. He made a dismissive motion with his hand. "Get out of here, now, before I kill you myself."

"I ain't goin' nowhere without my pistol."

Carson pointed to the spittoon where Smoke had deposited Keno's pistol.

"There it is," Sheriff Carson said. "Fish it out, and it's yours."

Keno walked over to the spittoon, looked down into it, hesitated for a moment, then, making a face of disgust and revulsion, stuck his hand down into the little brass pot. A few seconds later, he pulled his pistol without the cylinder out, and with it, and his hand, dripping a brown, slimy oozing liquid, walked quickly out of the saloon.

Keno was chased from the saloon by the laughter of nearly a dozen customers.

Chapter Six

Frisco, Colorado

It was late afternoon when Tucker, Rawlins, and Clay rode into Frisco. They had purposely chosen this time because they figured that the nearer to closing time it was when they held up the bank, the fewer chances there would be for any of the citizens of the town to be present. Also, by the end of the day the tellers would be tired and less responsive, which should make the outlaws' job easier. The three men were wearing long, white dusters, and hats that were pulled low. Dismounting about half a block away from the bank, they stood there for a moment, looking up and down the street.

"Anyone see anything that looks unusual?" Tucker asked.

"Looks normal to me," Rawlins said.

"See any law?"

"No. No law," Clay said.

"Check your guns."

The three men pulled their weapons and spun the cylinders, then put the weapons back in their holsters.

"All right, Rawlins, you wait here with the horses," Tucker said. "When you see us come out of the bank, you bring the horses up to us fast. Do you understand me? Because I swear, if you ain't in front of the bank by the time we reach the street, I'll shoot you myself."

"I'll be there," Rawlins said.

"You'd better be." Tucker looked over at Clay and nodded. "Are you ready?"

"I'm ready," Clay said.

"Then, let's go."

Tucker and Clay moved down to the front of the bank, looked up and down the street, then at each other.

Tucker nodded. Then the two men pulled their bandannas up to cover their faces and stepped into the bank.

In addition to the two tellers, there were two customers in the bank, a woman who was in front of one of the teller windows, and a man who was standing at the table, filling out a deposit slip.

"Everybody put your hands in the air!" Tucker shouted.

"Oh, my God! It's a bank robbery!" one of the tellers said.

"You," Tucker said. "Put all the money in this bag."

Tucker handed the teller a cloth bag and he started scooping money up from the cash drawer.

"From the safe," Tucker said.

"The safe? There's no money in the safe," the teller said.

Tucker pointed his pistol at the other teller. "Mr. Bank Teller, I know that there is one hundred thousand dollars in the safe, and I am going to kill this man right now unless you empty the safe like I told you to."

"For God's sake, George, do it!" the second teller shouted, his voice edged with panic.

The teller took the bag, then walked to the back of the bank where there sat a large safe that was black with gold trim. Opening the safe, George began filling the sack with bound stacks of bills. It took but a moment to empty the safe. Then he brought the bag back and handed it to Tucker.

"Very good," Tucker said. Tucker looked over at Clay. "Let's go."

As the two men started out of the bank, the one male customer who was in the bank drew a gun from somewhere. Neither Tucker nor Clay had noticed it when they came into the bank, because the customer was not wearing a holster.

"Drop that money!" the bank customer shouted.

Tucker fired at the customer. Then he and Clay dashed outside, both of them turning to fire back toward the bank as they left.

"Rawlins! Where the hell is Rawlins?" Clay shouted. "That son of a bitch is supposed to be here!"

"Here he comes," Tucker said, pointing to Rawlins, who was approaching them at a rapid trot, leading two more horses.

"Did you get the money?" Rawlins shouted.

"Yeah," Tucker answered, holding up the cloth bag as he and Clay swung into the saddles.

"One hundred thousand dollars!" Rawlins shouted happily. "Son of a bitch! One hundred thousand dollars!"

"Shoot!" Tucker shouted.

"At what?" Rawlins asked.

"At the town! Shoot up the town! Get everyone off the street!"

The three men, shooting as they galloped away from the bank, were rewarded by the sight of all the townspeople scattering to get out of their way. "Get off the street if you don't want to get shot!" one of the bank robbers cried out, and he punctuated his shout by firing a couple of shots down the street. The shots had the effect he wanted, because everyone scattered.

A third man suddenly appeared from the alley that ran between the bank and the neighboring apothecary. He was riding one horse and leading two others. Leaning down, he handed the reins to the two bank robbers and, quickly, they climbed into the saddles. Mounted now, they started shooting up the town in order to keep people off the street.

Smoke Jensen had just ridden into town when several gunshots erupted from down at the far end of the street. Looking in the direction of the shooting, he saw two men, wearing long white dusters, backing out of a building. A sign, protruding over the boardwalk from the front of the building, identified it as the Bank of Frisco. Both men were holding their right arms stretched out in front of them, and Smoke could see the muzzle flashes and smoke as the two were shooting back into the bank.

"Bank robbery!" someone called. "They're holdin' up the bank!"

The announcement wasn't really needed. Everyone on the street, from the grocer who was arranging potatoes for display in a bin in the front of his store to a man who was whitewashing a fence, to a woman who was walking down the boardwalk with a little boy, knew that the bank was being robbed.

Most of the townspeople had cleared out of the way, but looking across the street, Smoke saw that the little boy, whether reacting from curiosity or fright, had broken away from the woman's grip to run out into the street.

"Johnny!" the woman shouted, her voice rising in terror. "Johnny, come back here!"

Slapping his legs against the side of his horse, Smoke galloped toward the little boy. Leaning over, he scooped the boy up, then galloped toward the woman and set the boy down on the boardwalk beside her.

"Ma'am, you and the boy get inside, quick!" he shouted.

With an appreciative nod, the woman wrapped both her arms around the little boy and ran to get inside the nearest shop, even as a bullet from one of the robbers' guns smashed through the window beside her, sending out a tiny shower of splintered glass.

Smoke's immediate goal had been to get the boy and his mother to safety, but in so doing he had put himself right in the middle of the action. He heard a snapping sound right by his ear. He didn't have to wonder what it was, because he had heard that sound many times over the last two decades of his life. Smoke was being shot at, and one bullet had come within inches of his head.

Turning toward the bank robbers, Smoke saw all three of them bearing down on him, their dusters flying in the wind behind them. All three were firing specifically at him, and he could hear the bullets buzzing angrily by his head. The smart thing for him to do would be to gallop up one of the alleys and out of danger. He knew that they wouldn't chase him because the only thing on their minds at the moment was escape and the only reason they were shooting at him was to frighten him into getting off the street and out of the way.

But their reckless endangerment of the young boy, in addition to their shooting at Smoke, made him just angry enough not to do the smart thing. Instead, he sat his saddle for what to onlookers appeared to be an agonizingly long moment. Then, as calmly as someone retrieving an umbrella, Smoke pulled his Winchester from the saddle holster just in front of his right leg. Methodically, Smoke jacked a shell into the chamber, raised his rifle to his shoulder—almost leisurely, some thought—and aimed at the bank robber who was riding in the middle.

"Damn! Look at that crazy son of a bitch! Why

don't he move?" someone yelled as he pointed toward Smoke.

"He's goin' to get hisself kilt, is what he is goin' to do," another suggested.

Smoke fired. A flash of flame and smoke issued from the front of his rifle, and the recoil of the rifle rocked him back slightly. His shot was deadly accurate for, in the center of the robber's chest, a puff of dust and a mist of blood flew up from the impact of the bullet. The robber fell from his saddle, but even before he hit the ground, Smoke had already snapped the lever down and back up and fired a second time. A second robber fell as well, but this one didn't fall as cleanly as the first, because his foot got hung up in the stirrup and he was dragged through the dirt for several feet before his foot came loose. From Smoke's position on the side of the road, he watched as the two horses, now riderless and terrified by the shooting, galloped by.

Smoke's action had not only alerted, but inspired some of the other townspeople, because the third robber was brought down by a fusillade of bullets, not one of which had been fired by Smoke. The third robber had been carrying the cloth bag, and it fell with him. As it did so, several of the bound bundles of bills spilled out into the street.

Almost before the echoes of the gunshots had died down, people began coming out into the streets, many of them armed. Cautiously, they approached the three men who were sprawled out in the street.

"This one's dead!" someone shouted.

"Yeah, this one, too!"

Someone came moving up the street to check the man who was lying no more than ten yards away from Smoke.

"Deader'n a doornail, this here one is!" the person shouted back.

A few of the townspeople started picking up the bundles of bills that had fallen into the street, and putting them back into the bag.

Slipping his rifle back into its sheath, Smoke dismounted and stood by, talking soothingly to his horse as someone started toward him. The one who was approaching was wearing a sheriff's star pinned to his vest.

"Mister, I reckon the town owes you a debt of thanks," the sheriff said. "Not many people would have taken hand in this, especially bein' if they were a stranger in town."

Smoke smiled. "Believe me, Sheriff, I had no intention of taking part," he said. "I just rode into town and all of a sudden sort of found myself right in the middle of a bank robbery."

"You may not have had any intention of participatin', but I expect Mrs. Foley is mighty glad you're here."

"Mrs. Foley?"

The sheriff pointed, and looking in the direction of the point, Smoke saw the woman and the little boy who had, but a few moments earlier, been in the line of fire. With the shooting stopped, they had both come back out of the shop in which they had taken shelter.

"Are you and the young boy all right, ma'am?" Smoke called over to them.

"Yes, sir, thanks to you," the woman replied. "God bless you for saving my child."

"He's a brave little boy," Smoke said. He could have also said a very foolish little boy for running into the street at such a time, but he didn't.

"The name is Bryant. Gary Bryant. I'm the sheriff here," the man with the badge said, extending his hand.

"I'm Smoke Jensen," Smoke replied, taking the sheriff's hand. Smoke saw the reaction in the sheriff's face, and knew that the sheriff had heard of him.

"Well, Mr. Jensen, you have quite a reputation," the sheriff said, "I don't know what brings you to Frisco, but I have to say that the town couldn't be any luckier than to have someone with your reputation here at this exact time."

"I hope you mean reputation in a positive way," Smoke said. Although it had been many years earlier and all the dodgers had been pulled, there was a time when there were hundreds, if not thousands, of wanted posters out for Smoke.

Those posters, some of which still turned up from time to time, had often put Smoke in difficult situations. With the law, he could generally talk his way out simply by having them send a wire to check up on him.

It was a different story with the bounty hunters, though. Most "regulators" didn't care whether the reward posters were valid or not, and many had no plans to take him in alive. It was their modus operandi to bring their subjects back in belly-down across their horses. Smoke had found it necessary to shoot himself out of those situations on more than one occasion.

Sheriff Bryant laughed. "I know any dodgers on you have long since been pulled," he said, almost as if reading Smoke's mind. "Sheriff Carson, back in Big Rock, is a friend of mine. And unless he was lying to me, not only are you not a wanted man, you are one of his full-time deputies as well as a part-time justice of the peace."

"Unpaid deputy, unpaid justice of the peace," Smoke said quickly. "And both positions are more or less honorary, you might say, though, to be truthful, I am fully empowered to perform, and have performed, the duties of both offices."

"Well, anytime you would like to be an honorary, and fully empowered, deputy for Frisco, you just let me know," Sheriff Bryant said. "And I mean that in all sincerity."

"I appreciate that," Smoke responded.

"What brings you to our town, Mr. Jensen?"

"I'm here on business, Sheriff," Smoke answered. "I'm looking for a man named Byron Davencourt. Do you have any idea where I can find him?"

"Ah, so your business is with the cattle buyer from Chicago, is it?" Sheriff Bryant asked.

"Yes. I want to arrange to sell him some cattle, so I thought I would look him up before I had my dinner."

"I'll tell you what you do, Mr. Jensen. Why don't you just mosey on down to Mama Lou's Café for dinner? It's right down the street here, a real nice place. Order anything you want and tell Mama Lou that I said the town is going to pay for it. And while you are having your dinner, I'll look up Mr. Davencourt and bring him to you." The sheriff chuckled. "I said the city will pay for your meal, and we will. But truth to tell, seein' as most of the money you saved today was his—that is, belonging to the company he's with, why, I reckon Mr. Davencourt will be so glad to see you that he would be more than willin' to pay for the meal his own self."

"Thanks," Smoke said. "Give me a minute or two before you bring him to the restaurant, will you? Just long enough to get my horse taken care of."

"Tell McGee over at the livery that the town will pay for boarding your horse as well," Sheriff Bryant said as, with a little wave, he started out to find the man Smoke had come to see.

Chapter Seven

Mama Lou's was typical of many of the cafés Smoke had seen over the years. It was located in a building that was thirty feet by forty feet. There was a counter painted green that ran three quarters of the way down the left side of the room. Out on the wide plank floor sat a dozen or more round tables, while along the back wall were two very long tables that could seat at least ten people each.

Behind the green counter there was a blackboard upon which a sign, written in chalk, advertised the day's fare.

Special Today
**ham, butterbeans, mashed potatoes – 25 cents
cherry pie – 5 cents**

A rather large woman, wearing an apron over her rose-colored dress, was wiping the counter with a damp cloth.

"Just take a seat anywhere, honey," she said. "Someone will be with you in a moment."

"Thanks," Smoke said, picking his way through the tables until, by habit, he took one that would put his back against the wall.

Although a few customers nodded and smiled, no one spoke to him. As he sat down, he saw one of the patrons get up from his table and move over to the counter and say something to the large woman. Both the customer and Mama Lou looked in his direction. Then the woman nodded, put down the towel, and came over to talk to him.

"I'm Mama Lou," she said, though the introduction was unnecessary. "I want to thank you for what you done for the town a while ago'."

"No thanks are needed," Smoke said. "I just suddenly found myself in the middle, and had to do what I did in order to stay alive."

"No you didn't have to, mister," the restaurant patron who had spoken to Mama Lou said. "I seen the whole thing. All you would have had to do is skedaddle up the alley alongside Bloomfield's apothecary and you would have been out of danger. But instead, you scooped up the little Foley boy, got him and his mama out of the way, then you come back and faced down them robbers just as cool as a cucumber. You was a hero in my book. Hell, you was a hero in the eyes of anyone who seen you."

"Hear, hear!" one of the other customers shouted out loud, and everyone in the café began applauding.

"I guess I just wasn't thinking straight," Smoke said,

trying to deflect the accolades, which were beginning to make him uncomfortable.

"Mister, from what I seen, not thinkin' straight ain't likely to ever be a problem with you."

Mama Lou laughed. "Well, whatever the reason was that you stood up to them, the point is you did stand up to them. That means the town owes you thanks, and to express that thanks, I'm pleased to tell you that your dinner is on the house."

"Well, I appreciate that, Miss Mama Lou," Smoke said. He didn't mention that Sheriff Bryant had already offered to pay for it.

"Would you like a cup of coffee while you wait?"

"Yes, thank you, a cup of coffee would be very nice."

"Do you want any of the fixin's with it?" Mama Lou asked. "Sugar? Cream?"

"No, I'll take it black, please."

"Black it is, cowboy," Mama Lou replied as she stepped up to the large, blue coffeepot.

Smoke took his seat at a table, then noticed that everyone else in the restaurant was still looking at him. When he looked back at them with a pleasant smile of acknowledgment, he thought the reaction he got was interesting. Some nodded back at him, but a few looked away, as if intimidated by the fact that they had even been noticed by someone like Smoke Jensen.

In a few moments, Mama Lou brought the coffee herself.

"Here is your coffee, Mr. Jensen, and if you want

more, just let me know. There is a lot more where that came from," she said.

"Thank you."

Mama Lou was just walking back from the table when Smoke saw Sheriff Bryant and a very round, very bald man step in through the front door. Unlike Bryant's denims and plaid shirt, indeed unlike the clothes of anyone else in the café, the bald man was wearing a three-piece suit, brown in color, with a green bowtie.

Bryant pointed to Smoke's table and, with a nod to the sheriff, the round, bald man came toward him as the sheriff walked over to the counter to say something to Mama Lou. Smoke didn't hear what the sheriff said, but he did hear Mama Lou's response.

"I already took care of that," Mama Lou's voice said, carrying throughout the room.

"No need for you to do that, Mama Lou," the sheriff replied, raising his voice to the level of Mama Lou's. "I told you, the town's goin' to take care of it."

"And I told you that I already took care of that," Mama Lou replied. "You let the town do something else for him. His meal is on the house."

"Yes, ma'am, whatever you say," Sheriff Bryant said, acquiescing to Mama Lou's forceful personality.

"You'd be Smoke Jensen, would you?" the bald man asked as he approached the table.

"I am."

The bald man extended his hand and smiled.

"I'm Byron Davencourt. I understand from the sheriff that you have some cattle to sell?"

Smoke took his hand.

"Yes, sir, Mr. Davencourt, I surely do have some cattle for sale," Smoke replied. He pointed to one of the chairs. "Would you join me for dinner?"

"Thank you, I have had my dinner," Davencourt said. "But I'll sit with you, if you don't mind."

"I don't mind a bit. Please, have a chair," Smoke offered.

"Thanks," Davencourt said, settling his girth into a chair in such a way as to make it obvious that he was glad for the opportunity to sit down. "First, let me thank you for thwarting the bank robbery. The money you saved belonged to my partners and me and I don't mind telling you, it would have been disastrous if we had lost it."

Before Smoke could respond, Mama Lou brought his dinner out and put it on the table.

"Oh, here, let me pay for that, it's the least I can do," Davencourt said, reaching for his billfold in his inside jacket pocket.

"It's all been taken care of," Mama Lou said.

"You don't say."

"The sheriff said he wanted to pay for it, but I told him his money was no good here. Mr. Jensen's dinner is on the house."

"My, you seem to be a very popular man, Mr. Jensen. And rightly so," Davencourt said.

Smoke laughed. "If I could just bank all these offers to buy my meal, I could eat free for a couple of days."

Mama Lou laughed as well as she walked away from the table.

"Where are your cattle, Mr. Jensen?" "Are they nearby?"

"They are at my ranch."

"I see. And how long would it take you to get the beeves from your ranch to the railhead here in Frisco?"

"I can have them here within a week," Smoke answered. "My ranch, Sugarloaf, is very near Big Rock."

"Big Rock? Interesting that you would come here, Mr. Jensen. I know that there is a railhead at Big Rock, and there is a cattle-processing company that will buy your cattle there."

"Yes, there is," Smoke said. "But I'm gambling on getting a better price from you by bringing the beef here. And, seeing as you've just signed a contract to provide the army with beef to give to the Indians, I'm sure you are in the market."

The cattleman nodded. "You are right about that. To be honest, I may have bitten off more than I can chew with that army contract. But I'll say this for you. If you understand that, then you are a good businessman, because that means you have done your homework."

"I don't want to fly under false colors here. I must confess that it was my wife who did the homework," Smoke said. "Sally read about it in the paper and suggested I come down here to see you."

"Did she now?" Davencourt replied. "Well, having a smart wife is almost as good as being smart yourself," he said. "How many head of cattle do you run on your ranch?"

"On my ranch? I have around thirty thousand on the hoof," Smoke replied.

"*Whew,*" Davencourt whistled. He cocked his head and looked at Smoke with a measure of awe and respect. "Mr. Jensen, I must say, that is a very substantial operation. In fact, I don't believe I have ever dealt with anyone who had such a large herd. How many were you planning on bringing to Frisco? Not the whole herd, I hope?"

"I thought I would bring about fifteen hundred head," Smoke said. "I've only two cowboys to help me with the drive over here, and fifteen hundred head is about the maximum I can handle."

Davencourt nodded. "Good, good. Fifteen hundred I can handle," he said. "And what if I said thirty dollars a head? How would that sound to you?"

Smoke did a rapid calculation, then smiled. That was five dollars a head better than anything he could get at Big Rock. "That sounds good to me," he said. "In fact, it sounds very good."

"Thank you, I thought you might like that," Davencourt said. He smiled. "Also, Mr. Jensen, I do have to be honest with you. I know that the top price being offered by the Red Cliff processing company, which is who would handle cattle coming through Big Rock, is only twenty-five dollars a head. I offered you my top price, which is thirty dollars, to see if you would try and hold me up for more. If you had done that, I would have walked away from the deal. But you didn't, which means you are an honest man. And I like doing business with honest men."

"Yes, I like dealing with honest men as well,"

Smoke said, and even though he was smiling, the look in his eyes gave fair warning to Davencourt that he expected total honesty and fairness in the transaction.

Davencourt stuck his hand out. "Fifteen hundred head, thirty dollars a head. Have your cows here one week from today, Mr. Jensen, and I'll present you with a bank certified draft for forty five thousand dollars."

"I'll be here," Smoke said as he shook Davencourt's hand.

"Are you ready for your cherry pie, Mr. Jensen?" Mama Lou asked, returning to the table.

"Yes, thank you, a piece of pie would be nice."

"Oh, cherry pie, you say?" Davencourt said. "Well, I have eaten my dinner, but there is always room for a piece of pie." He rubbed his rather considerable stomach. "If you don't mind, Miss Mama Lou, would you bring me a piece as well? And, maybe you could put some whipped cream on top of the pie. Oh, and bring me a cup of coffee with sugar and lots of cream."

"I'd be happy to," Mama Lou said.

Davencourt smiled across the table toward Smoke. "Some folks like to conduct business over a drink," he said. "But I say, give me a good piece of freshly baked pie anytime and I'm just real easy to do business with."

Smoke chuckled. "I hope you never have to do business with my wife," he said.

"Oh? And why is that?" Davencourt asked as Mama Lou put the pie before him.

"Because she is the smartest business person I've ever known, and she is the best cook I've ever known. I think that would be a dangerous combination for you."

Davencourt laughed out loud. "I think you are right, my friend," he said as he forked a big piece of pie toward his mouth. "I think you are right."

Chapter Eight

The three wooden coffins were standing upright against the front of Norman Prufrock's undertaking establishment. Inside the boxes, their faces ashen with death, stood the bodies of Tucker, Rawlins, and Clay. But nobody knew who the bank robbers were, because the sign that was posted above the bodies read: DO YOU KNOW ANY OF THESE MEN?

Tucker, Rawlins, and Clay were wearing the same clothes they had been wearing during the aborted bank robbery, though Mrs. Prufrock had washed them and had done a pretty good job of getting the blood out. She had made no effort to patch the bullet holes, though, and the shirts of Tucker and Clay, both of whom had been shot by Smoke Jensen, had a single hole over the heart. Rawlins, who had been shot down by the rest of the town, had several holes in his shirt and pants, as well as still visible bullet wounds in his neck, his left cheek, and over his right eye.

Nearly the entire town had come to view the

bodies during the day, including children of the town who were now scattered about, acting out the grizzly event, taking turns being the bank robbers and vying for the right to be Smoke Jensen. Even now, after nightfall, and with the bodies glowing in the reflected light of the street lamps, several of the townspeople were still hanging around in front of the undertaker's, staring at the bodies, their morbid curiosity not yet satiated.

"Bang, bang!" a child shouted.

Another ran to the front of one of the coffins, then stood very still with his head tilted to one side like the body behind him.

"Look at me!" he shouted. "I'm dead! I'm dead!"

"You kids, get out of here!" Prufrock shouted, running out of his building to chase them away.

Although there was no legal division to the town of Frisco, there was a de facto division into an American and a Mexican section. On the Mexican side of the town, in a cantina called Pedro's, an American sat alone at a table in the back. Conversations and laughter swirled around him, but he paid little attention. Instead, he just drank tequila, often refilling his glass from a bottle that he held clenched in his left hand.

"Señor, do you want food?" Pedro asked, stepping up to his table.

"When I want food, I'll tell you."

"Sí, Señor," Pedro replied, stung by the harsh reply.

Reece Van Arndt was replaying the events of the

day. The bank robbery had been his idea. He was the one who had recruited the men and he was the one who had made the plans. He didn't personally take part in the robbery because being an albino meant he would be too easily identified. Even if he tied a handkerchief around the lower part of his face, he could still be identified.

Van Arndt held his hands out and looked at them, wondering, perhaps for the millionth time in his life, why he had been so cursed.

His plan would have gone off without a hitch had it not been for the fact that it occurred at the same moment Smoke Jensen happened to be riding into town. Van Arndt knew all about Smoke Jensen, and had even had a run-in with him once.

Five years earlier

Van Arndt and his gang had stopped the train by the simple expedient of building a fire in the middle of the track. Of course, there was always the chance that the engineer wouldn't stop. He might get suspicious and plow on through the fire, so, to back up the fire, they had built up a pile of rocks and logs sufficient to derail the train.

Van Arndt, who was sitting on his horse in the dark of a tree line about thirty yards away from the track, wondered if the engineer would stop. It would be much easier if he did stop, because then the robbery would be a simple thing. Van Arndt would take whatever was on the express car; then he would send a couple of men through the passenger cars to relieve the travelers of any money they might be carrying with them.

Most of the time they wouldn't get that much from the passengers, but from time to time they would find one who was well heeled. These would generally be businessmen who traveled with a great deal of money. Such people would be moving from one place to another, perhaps to buy a ranch or a business, or even a house. They tried so hard to look like all the other passengers, blending in so as not to call attention to themselves, but Van Arndt was particularly adroit at recognizing them. In fact, he enjoyed the game of finding them almost as much as the money he took.

"She's backin' down, Van Arndt," one of his men said, and the shower of sparks coming from the drive wheels as they slid along the track validated his observation.

"Hell, I think I would almost rather see it run into the pile of rocks," one of the other men said. He laughed fiendishly. "That would have made one hell of a wreck now, wouldn't it?"

The train came to a complete stop about ten yards shy of the burning pile, then sat there, venting steam and popping and snapping as bearings and journals cooled. Van Arndt could see the engineer, backlit from within the cab, lean through the window to look ahead.

"What is it, Frank?" Van Arndt heard the engineer ask the fireman. "Can you see anything on your side?"

Van Arndt didn't know if the fireman answered or not. He might have, but he was too far away to hear.

"Get up there," Van Arndt said to the three men with him. "Get up there and blow the express door."

The three men with Van Arndt rode up to the train.

"Here, what is this?" the engineer asked, seeing the three men ride up so quickly. "What are you men doing here?"

One of the three answered by shooting toward the cabin window, driving the engineer back. One of the others put a stick of dynamite, its fuse sputtering, into the jamb of the express door; then the three rode away quickly to avoid the blast.

It took about five seconds for the fuse to burn down. Then the dynamite exploded. There was a loud noise, accompanied by a ball of fire and a billowing cloud of smoke as the door was blown off the hinges.

A passenger from one of the dimly let cars stepped out onto the vestibule then, and looked out to see what was going on. Seeing the armed men heading back toward the express car, the passenger darted back inside.

"It's a holdup!" the passenger shouted excitedly. "They just blew the door off the mail car, and I seen some men on horses, holdin' guns."

Van Arndt was so distracted by watching his men work that he didn't notice someone step out from the rear of the train, then climb the ladder to the top of the car. There, lying down, the passenger used the center ridge of the car, not only for concealment, but also as a rest for his rifle.

Van Arndt heard a shot fired from inside the baggage car. That was followed almost immediately by more shots from outside the car, the gun blasts lighting up the darkness with their muzzle flashes.

"No, no, don't shoot no more!" a muffled voice called from inside the car. "You done kilt the guard!"

"Throw out the money pouch, or we'll kill you too!" one of the robbers shouted.

Van Arndt saw the money pouch being tossed from the train. Then, just as the money pouch hit the robber's hands, Van Arndt heard the sound of a rifle shot. A bullet plowed into the robber's chest, raising a little spray of blood, which flashed pink against the ambient light of the train and the fire. The robber was knocked from his horse, and he lay flat on his back with both arms spread out to either side. The money pouch lay on the ground beside him.

"Muley!" Van Arndt shouted from the darkness. "Get the money pouch and let's get out of here!"

One of the other riders leaned over to pick up the money pouch, and a second round was fired. This bullet caught Muley in his elbow, leaving the arm dangling loosely from a few ragged tendons. With a scream of pain, Muley rode off, leaving the money sack where it lay.

"Van Arndt, I seen the muzzle flash! He's on the . . ."

That was as far as the third robber got before another shot brought him down.

Van Arndt hesitated for a long moment, trying to decide whether to make a try for the money pouch or to turn and run. He hesitated too long, because he suddenly felt his horse go down under him, tossing him to the ground. By the time he stood up, half a dozen armed men were running toward him from the train.

"Put your hands up, mister, now!" one of the men shouted.

Van Arndt had no choice but to respond. He was taken prisoner and put into the baggage car, and after the track was cleared, taken to the nearest town, where he was turned over to the sheriff.

It wasn't until his trial that Van Arndt learned who the man was who climbed onto the top of the train to stop the robbery. It was Smoke Jensen, and Van Arndt's run-in with him wound up costing him five years in prison.

The events of today represented the second time Jensen had spoiled one of Van Arndt's robbery attempts. Also, by a strange coincidence, the second time it had gotten his partners killed. It was too bad Van Arndt didn't know Smoke Jensen was coming to town today. If he had known that, he would have made plans to ambush the son of a bitch and kill him.

"Señor, would you like to have a good time with Rosita?" a bar *puta* asked, interrupting Van Arndt's musing.

Van Arndt was wearing wide-brimmed hat and staring into his glass. Because of that, the brim of his hat covered his face so that Rosita had not yet gotten a good look at him. When Van Arndt looked up, Rosita gasped in surprise and shock at the white face and pink eyes.

"Madre de Dios, eres usted un fantasma?"

Van Arndt laughed at the effect he had on her.

"Why, yes, honey," Van Arndt replied. "I am a ghost."

Rosita hesitated.

"You aren't going to change your mind on me, are you now?" Van Arndt asked. "I would be really angry with you if you changed your mind. If you change your mind, I will haunt you in your sleep."

"No, Señor," Rosita stammered. She crossed herself. "I beg of you, do not haunt my sleep."

Rosita was trapped now, damned if she did and damned if she didn't. She had no choice but to smile and try to keep her fear from showing.

"I will go with you, Señor," she said.

Over at the Railroad Hotel, Smoke Jensen went to bed with the satisfaction of knowing that his trip had been successful. One week from now, he would deliver fifteen hundred head of cattle to the loading pens here in Frisco, Colorado.

Lying in bed, he listened to the sounds drifting up from outside: the low rumble of men's voices, the soft, seductive replies of the women, interspersed with occasional guffaws of laughter. Through the open window he could hear piano music from the saloon, and from the Mexican part of town, the sound of a trumpet. Hollow hoofbeats echoed from a horse being ridden slowly up the street, and from far off came the mournful wail of a coyote. Gradually, the sounds subsided and, one by one, the lights across the town were extinguished until at last it lay as a cluster of dark buildings, visible only because of the silver wash of the three-quarter moon. Despite the fact that Smoke had been engaged in a life-and-death struggle earlier in the day, his conscience was clear and he drifted off into a peaceful, non-dreaming sleep.

Over on the Mexican side of the town, Van Arndt stood in a splash of moonlight, looking down at the woman on the bed. Rosita's eyes were open but unseeing. Blood spread out from her slit throat, staining the pillow. Van Arndt, who was still holding a bloody knife in his hand, reached under the pillow and took out his roll of money.

"Bitch," he whispered in the dark. "You picked the wrong man to steal from."

Van Arndt wiped the blade of his knife off on the bedsheet, leaving smears of blood that, because they were illuminated only by the splash of moonlight that spilled in through the open window, looked black rather than red.

When Van Arndt returned to the hotel ten minutes later, the lobby was dark except for a dimly glowing lantern that sat on the front desk. The lobby was in deep shadow and though he could see the sofas and chairs, he had to look twice before he saw that someone was sleeping on one of the sofas.

At first, Van Arndt thought the sleeping figure might be the night clerk. Then he saw that it was just someone who had come in off the street. Glancing back toward the front desk, he saw that the night clerk was sitting in a chair, but the chair was tipped back against the wall and the occupant's eyes were closed. Van Arndt could hear a soft, fluttering snore coming from the night clerk's lips.

Van Arndt started toward the stairs, then stopped and walked back over to the desk. Making certain the clerk was still asleep, Van Arndt turned the registration book around and ran his pasty white finger down the list of names. If Smoke Jensen was still in town, it was likely that he would be staying here at this very hotel, since this was the only place where lodging could be secured.

> *Byron Davencourt*
> *Ed Meeker*
> *Kirby Jensen*
> *John Caldwell*
> *Abner Smith*

Who the hell is Kirby Jensen? Is that Smoke Jensen? He drummed his fingers lightly on the registration book for a moment, then saw an envelope lying on a table behind the desk. The name on the envelope was "Smoke Jensen."

Van Arndt smiled. That answered his question.

Checking the guest named Kirby Jensen again,

Van Arndt saw that he was upstairs in Room Six. By a fortuitous coincidence, Van Arndt was right next door, in Room Four.

Behind the counter was a board filled with hooks. Each hook had a key or, in case the room wasn't occupied, two keys. Moving as quietly as he could, Van Arndt leaned over the counter and lifted the key from the hook for Room Number Six.

If you aren't the right one, I'm sorry, Van Arndt thought. But I don't intend to take any chances. I'm going to kill you whether you are Smoke Jensen or not.

With the key in hand, Van Arndt went up the stairs to the second floor. The hallway ran down between facing doors. Even-number rooms were situated on the left, while odd-number rooms ran down the right side. The hallway was illuminated by half a dozen wall-mounted kerosene lanterns, all of which hissed as they burned. From two of them, little coils of black smoke worked up through the chimney. The doors to each of the rooms were painted brown, the rooms identified by the brass numbers that were attached to the middle of the upper frame.

The hall was partially carpeted by a long, narrow rug that ran down the middle of it, leaving approximately six inches of uncarpeted and unfinished wood to either side. The runner was wine-colored and decorated with woven baskets of flowers and fruit. A roach was crawling along the unpainted wooden floor beside the rug and as Van Arndt approached, it scurried through the gap under the door of Room Number Five.

As he moved up the hallway, approaching Room Six, the one that he believed to be occupied by Smoke Jensen, Van Arndt reached up to extinguish each of the lanterns, causing the shadows to grow longer. By the time he reached Room Number Six, the hallway was dark except for the ambient light of the moon that spilled in through the open window at the end of the hall. The window allowed for a slight breeze to cool the hallway, but the breeze did not come without a price, for it also brought in the pungent aroma of a street that was literally filled with horse apples.

Stopping in front of the door to Room Six, Van Arndt quietly slipped the key into the keyhole, then turned it slowly to minimize the sound of the tumblers.

Smoke was sound asleep, dreaming of Sally and Sugarloaf, when something penetrated his dreams—something that was amiss.

He opened his eyes and lay in the darkness for just a moment, wondering what it was that had awakened him. Then he felt a slight change in air pressure, and he looked toward the door. Because the room was dark in front, and the hallway dark behind, he could see nothing—but he sensed that the door had just opened.

Smoke rolled off his bed and onto the floor beside his bed just as the first shot was fired. Smoke heard the bullet hit the bed he had just vacated. The flame pattern of the muzzle flash lit up the room, and Smoke could see someone illuminated by the very gun he was shooting.

The would-be assailant shot three more times, then Smoke heard him turn and run up the hallway.

Quickly, Smoke was on his feet with his gun in hand. Stepping out into the hallway, he strained to see into the black maw, but he could see nothing. By now other doors were opening as people—many of them holding flickering candles or brighter lanterns, and all in their nightclothes—were sticking their heads out to see what was going on.

"What is it? What is all the shooting about?" someone asked.

"Did anyone get hurt?"

"What's going on?"

"Get back! Get out of the way!" Smoke shouted.

For a moment everyone jerked back, but as they did so, they took their candles and lanterns with them so that, once more, the hallway was dark. Smoke stared into the darkness, but could see nothing.

Gradually, the other guests of the hotel opened their doors and stuck their heads out again. Again, they brought light with them.

Smoke stood there for a moment, looking at all the people who were in the hallway, but nothing about any of them stood out enough for him to know who shot at him. One of the people who had come out into the hall to have a look around was Byron Davencourt, the cattle buyer.

"Are you all right, Mr. Jensen?" Davencourt called anxiously up the hallway to him.

Smoke realized then that he was the only one holding a gun. He lowered it.

"I'm fine."

"What was the shooting about? Do you know?"

"Yeah, I know," Smoke answered. "Someone was trying to kill me."

"Good heavens!" some woman said.

"Who?" a man asked.

"I don't know who it was," Smoke said. "I don't even know why."

The hotel clerk came on the scene then, having clambered quickly up the stairs when he heard the gunshots.

"What's going on here?" he asked.

"Someone tried to kill this man," one of the other hotel residents said.

"What happened to the hall lanterns? Why are they out?"

"You're worried about hall lanterns when someone tried to murder one of your guests?"

"I have to relight them," the clerk said. "Does anyone have a match?"

"Mr. Jensen, you take care of yourself," Davencourt said. "If you get killed, who will I give that forty-five thousand dollars to?" He laughed.

"Forty-five thousand dollars?" some one repeated in surprise. "You're giving him forty-five thousand dollars?"

"Oh, yeah," Davencourt replied. "But not until he delivers fifteen hundred head of cattle."

* * *

Van Arndt had been able to get away before Smoke saw him because his own room was next door to Smoke's room, and he had managed to get inside before Smoke reached the hallway. Now, he stayed in his own room with the door shut and listened to the conversation from the hallway.

"Forty-five thousand dollars?" he whispered, repeating the number he heard mentioned.

Van Arndt looked at his pistol, then slipped it back into his holster. "Damn," he whispered. "I'm glad I didn't kill you, Jensen." Van Arndt smiled broadly. "It turns out you're worth more alive than you are dead."

Even before all the commotion died down in the hallway, Van Arndt had taken off his boots, shirt, and trousers and crawled into bed. Now he lay there with his arms laced behind his head, staring up at the moon shadows on the ceiling.

"You're going to have all that money," he said. "The question is, how am I going to take it from you?"

Chapter Nine

All who saw Sugarloaf Ranch agreed that its location in the Eagle River Basin provided one of the most beautiful landscapes imaginable: creeks, springs, wetlands, lakes, prairies, and mountains. It was here that Smoke Jensen had established his one-hundred-thousand-acre ranch, a huge spread traversed by fourteen miles of the Frying Pan River, plus a handful of smaller streams. Its vast expanse of prairie, pools of water, and meandering creek bottoms easily supported his herd of some thirty thousand cows, plus a rich wildlife population, including one of the highest densities of pronghorn in North America. Its sweeping vistas captivated all who visited Sugarloaf, and from many locations on the ranch there was an unobstructed view of a 120-mile panorama of the Rockies, including the Sawach and the Mosquito ranges, through which the Denver and Rio Grand Railroad traversed by way of Tennessee Pass.

Sugarloaf, like all ranches in the area, had two

levels of employees. There were the cowboys who drifted from place to place, finding work during roundup and branding time, then leaving as soon as they were paid off, so they could drift on as they preferred. There were also those permanent employees who were required for the day-to-day operation of the ranch year-round. To such men fell the task of riding and repairing fence lines, feeding the herds when snow covered the ground, keeping the outbuildings in good repair. These were, quite often, settled men, with wives and children to support. There were ten such full-time employees at Sugarloaf, nearly all of whom were Mexican.

Smoke's wife, Sally, was his full-time partner in managing the ranch, and on those occasions when Smoke had to be gone, Sally was perfectly capable of running the ranch by herself. Those who had known Smoke for a long time fully appreciated the impact marrying Sally had had on his life.

Growing up in New Hampshire, Sally was from a family of great wealth. She could have stayed in New Hampshire and married "well," meaning she could have married a blue blood from one of New Hampshire's old, established, and wealthy families. She would have hosted teas and garden parties, and grown old to become a New England matriarch.

But while such a future promised a life of ease and tranquility, that wasn't what Sally had in mind. She envisioned a much more active—some might suggest uncertain—future. Thus, she announced to one and all that she intended to leave New Hampshire.

"You can't be serious, Sally!" her family and

friends had said in utter shock when she informed them that she intended to see the American West. "Why, that place is positively wild with beasts and savages."

"And not all the savages are Indian, if you get my meaning," Melinda Hobson said. Melinda Hobson was of "the" Hobsons, one of New Hampshire's founding families.

But Sally had a yen to see the American West, as well as a thirst for adventure, and that brought her to Bury, Idaho Territory, where she wound up teaching school.

It was in Bury that she met a young gunman named Buck West. There was something about the young man that caught her attention right away. It wasn't just the fact that he was ruggedly handsome, nor was it the fact that, despite his cool demeanor, he went out of his way to be respectful to her. That respect, Sally saw, applied to all women—including soiled doves, even though he was not a habitué of their services.

But it was the intensity of the young man that appealed to Sally—a brooding essence that ran deep into his soul.

Then, she learned that his name wasn't even Buck West, it was Smoke Jensen. And the hurt he felt was the result of a personal tragedy of enormous magnitude. Smoke's young wife, Nicole, had been raped, tortured, murdered, and scalped by men whose evil knew no bounds. They had also murdered Arthur, his infant son.

Those same men owned ranches and mines

around the town of Bury. In fact, one might say they owned Bury itself, including nearly every resident of the town. If ever there was a Sodom and Gomorrah in America, Sally thought, it was Bury, Idaho Territory.

And, like the Biblical cities of sin, Bury was destroyed, not by God, but by Smoke Jensen, who, after allowing the women and children to leave, killed the murderers and the gunmen and then put torch to the town. When Smoke, with Sally now by his side, set out en route to the "High Lonesome," there was nothing remaining of Bury but the smoldering rubble of a destroyed town and the dead killers he had left behind him.

The rage that had burned at his soul was gone and he had put Nicole and Arthur to rest in a private compartment of his heart. With the fire in his gut gone, Smoke was free to love once more, and to be loved, and Sally was there for him. Smoke asked Sally to marry him, and she accepted, knowing from the depth of her soul that it was the right thing for her to do.

Even before Sally met and married Smoke, her public teaching career had come to an end, due to her refusal to kowtow to the evil directors of the town of Bury, but she still had the call. Because of that call, and the fact Sugarloaf was far enough from town so as to make it difficult for the children of the ranch to attend public school, Sally started a private and fully accredited school on the ranch. There, she taught the children of the employees.

"Señora Sally, look what I have made for you."

Smiling broadly, Maria, the same little girl who had danced the flamenco so brilliantly at the time of the barbeque, held out a small piece of cloth upon which was embroidered a red flower perched upon a green stem and encircled by green leaves.

"Why, Maria, that is absolutely lovely," Sally Jensen said.

"It is a handkerchief," Maria said proudly.

"I can see it is a handkerchief," Sally said. "And I've never seen one more beautiful."

The little nine-year-old girl beamed under the praise.

"It is not as beautiful as the dress you bought for me," Maria said. "But I wanted to give you something in return."

"What are you talking about? It is every bit as beautiful as the dress," Sally replied. "Haven't you ever heard the expression 'Beauty is in the eyes of the beholder'?"

Maria shook her head. "No, Señora."

Sally chuckled. "Well, call that your lesson for today. It means that something is as beautiful as you believe it to be, and I believe this handkerchief to be one of the most beautiful things I have ever seen."

"I am glad you feel that way. It makes me happy to know that you like it," Maria said.

"Have you been studying your lessons?" Sally asked.

"Si, Señora," Maria's mother, Consuela, replied.

"Maria has studied very hard. Her father and I are very proud of her."

"As indeed you should be proud of her," Sally said. "Maria is a very smart little girl. Why, some day she could grow up to be president of the United States."

"But she is Mexican, Señora," Consuela said. "She cannot be president of America."

"No, Mama, I am American. I was born in this country," Maria said. "But I can't be president because I am a girl and a girl cannot be president. Girls cannot even vote."

Sally laughed. "Well, you tripped me up on that one," she said. "I had no idea you had studied your civics lessons so well."

"But I think maybe someday girls will be able to vote," Maria said. "I think girls should be able to vote, don't you?"

"Yes, I do think so," Sally replied. "And I think you are right. I believe the day will come when women will be able to vote."

"So, maybe someday I can be president after all. And you can be my vice president," Maria said. She wrapped her arms around Sally's legs.

"Señora Jensen," Consuela said. The word Jensen came out as Hensen. "I think maybe Maria would come live with you if her father and I would let her."

Sally knew that she was not supposed to have favorites, but she was particularly fond of Maria, who was, she believed, the smartest and most talented of all the children in her school.

Marrying Smoke might have ended Sally's public teaching career, but it did not end her acquisition of new experiences and adventures. Indeed, she had already packed more experiences into her young life than most other women would have in three lifetimes.

Being Mrs. Smoke Jensen carried certain responsibilities, not only as the wife of a successful rancher, but also as someone who could cope with the many and varied activities of a man like Smoke. Learning from Smoke, Sally was an excellent shot, a skilled rider, and a good tracker.

Sally was also an excellent cook whose specialty was "bear sign," a doughnut-type confection that was a particular favorite of Pearlie's. In fact, Sally's pastries had earned such a reputation that cowboys who worked seasonally for Sugarloaf had carried stories of them to other ranches. As a result, travelers sometimes rode out of their way, just on the chance that Sally had recently turned out a batch.

"What? What are you talkin' about?"

The loud voice caused Sally and the others to look over toward the bunkhouse, where she saw Pearlie and Cal just exiting.

"You know what I'm talkin' about. I'm just sayin' don't you be embarrassin' me now. That's all," Pearlie was saying.

A few years earlier, Pearlie had been a gunman, hired by a man who wanted to run Smoke off so he could ride roughshod over those who were left. But Pearlie didn't take to killing and looting from innocent people, so he quit his job, stopping by not only to tell Smoke that he was leaving, but also to warn him of the trouble that lay ahead. That was when Smoke offered to hire him. Since that time, he had worked for Smoke and Sally.

Pearlie stood just a shade less than six feet tall, was lean as a willow branch, and had a face tanned the color of an old saddle and a head of wild, unruly black hair. His eyes were mischievous and he was quick to smile and joke, but underneath his slap-stick demeanor was a man that was as hard as iron, snake-quick with a gun, and as loyal as they come to his friends.

Not too long after Pearlie had joined the ranch, a starving and destitute Cal, who was barely in his teens at the time, made the mistake of trying to hold up Sally. Sally, who was nearly as good with a gun as Smoke, easily got the drop on Cal. But instead of turning him over to the sheriff, she brought him home and made him one of the family, along with Pearlie. Now Calvin Woods was not only loyal for life to Smoke and Sally, he had become Pearlie's best friend and protégé.

"Well, I don't know what you are talkin' about when you say don't embarrass you. How could I em-barrass you?" Cal asked.

"By standin' around at the dance like some dimwit when all the pretty girls are just waitin' for you to ask them to dance," Pearlie replied.

"What? How's that goin' to embarrass you?"

"'Cause I'm responsible for you," Pearlie replied. "Folks will think I'm not doin' my job, that I haven't taught you anything. It's bad for my reputation to see you just standin' on the side with a hangdog look on your face."

"I'm just always afraid that none of the girls are goin' to want to dance with me," Cal said.

"Well, who can blame 'em?" Pearlie replied. "Standin' around with a sour expression on your face all the time—why, it makes you so ugly that one look at you would make a train take five miles of dirt road."

Pearlie laughed as Cal took off his hat and began hitting him.

"I don't think Cal is ugly," Maria said. "Do you think he is ugly, Señora Sally?"

"No, not at all," Sally said.

By now, Pearlie and Cal had reached the front stoop of the main house where Maria and her mother had been talking to Sally.

"Are you still my girlfriend, Maria?" Cal asked the little nine-year-old.

"Sí," Maria answered.

"And you're still going to wait until I'm old enough to get married so you can marry me?"

Maria laughed. "Señor Cal, you are old enough to be married. I am the one who is not old enough."

"Oh, yeah, that's right, isn't it?" Cal said. "I always seem to get that mixed up."

"Wait a minute, what do you mean you are going to marry Cal?" Pearlie asked. "I thought you were going to marry me when you grew up."

"Oh, no, Señor, I cannot marry you," Maria said seriously. "Señorita Lucy is going to marry you."

"Ha!" Cal said. "She sure has your number!"

At that moment, Sally looked up, then smiled broadly as she saw a familiar figure riding through the arched gate.

"It's Smoke!" she said, starting toward him.

Smoke urged his horse into a trot, then reaching her, dismounted. Embracing his wife, Smoke kissed her.

"Smoke, you want us to all turn our back so you and Sally can have a little privacy?" Pearlie called.

"Nah, you can watch if you want to," Smoke replied. "Maybe you'll learn something." The others laughed.

"Well, just so's you don't get embarrassed or anything," Cal said.

"What are you two boys all gussied up for?" Smoke asked. Then, seeing Maria, he chuckled. "I knew it. Get a young pretty girl on the ranch, and none of my cowboys will work," Smoke said. "Are these men bothering you, Maria? Because if they are, I'll just fire both of them."

"No, Señor!" Maria said quickly, not understanding that Smoke was teasing her. "Don't fire them."

"You're right, I can't fire both of them, who would do the work? I tell you what, I'll just fire one of them. You pick the one you want me to keep around."

"Señor!" Maria gasped.

"Smoke, don't tease her like that," Sally said sharply.

Smoke laughed. "All right, you win," he said. "I can't fire them anyway. All my other cowboys are gone and I'll need the two of them to help me drive some cattle into the railhead at Frisco."

"You got the deal?" Sally asked.

"Yes," Smoke said. "It worked out just as you said it would, Sally. He's taking fifteen hundred head, and for five dollars more per head than we could get in Big Rock. That means we will be able to give everyone a bonus and still have enough left over to pay off the mortgage on the land we bought last year."

"Oh, Smoke, that's wonderful!" Sally said.

"It's going to be a long drive, especially with just these two worthless cowboys to help me," Smoke said, taking in Pearlie and Cal with a wave of his hand. His otherwise unkind words were contradicted by his broad smile. "But it's worth it."

"When are we leaving?" Pearlie asked.

"Tomorrow."

"Tomorrow?"

"At first light."

"First light?" Pearlie repeated. "Come on, Smoke, me and Cal's goin' into town for the dance tonight. The night'll just be gettin' started at first light."

Sally laughed. "You're going into Big Rock, aren't you?"

"Yes, ma'am," Cal replied.

"What do you mean the night will just be getting started at first light. You know as well as I do that they roll up the sidewalks at ten o'clock in Big Rock."

"Well, yes, ma'am, I reckon they do," Pearlie said. "But just in case they don't, why, me and Cal's got to be ready."

"It's Cal and I," Sally corrected.

"Sally, when are you going to learn that trying to teach these two worthless cowboys anything is a waste of your time?" Smoke said. Then, to Pearlie and Cal, he added, "Stay in town as long as you want."

Pearlie smiled broadly. "That's more like it."

"As long as you are back here, bright-eyed and bushy-tailed, by first light in the morning."

"Bushy-tailed?" Maria said, her eyes wide in wonder. "Señor Cal, Señor Pearlie, do you really have bushy tails?"

"I don't have a bushy tail," Pearlie said. "But Cal does. He has a tail just like a squirrel."

Maria's eyes opened wider and she put her hand over her mouth.

"He's teasing you, child," Sally said.

"Oh. I am glad," Maria said. "I do not think I would like Señor Cal to have a tail like a squirrel."

"Come on, Cal," Pearlie said. "You want to stand around here and gab, or go into town and have some fun?" Pearlie started toward the barn to saddle his horse.

"I'm coming," Cal said, trailing after him.

"Good Lord, look at them," Smoke said as they walked away. "They'll be dead in their saddles tomorrow. Like as not, I'll wind up leading their horses and herding the cattle all by myself."

"Don't give them a hard time, Smoke. Don't you remember what it was like to be young?" Sally asked.

"Do I remember? What kind of question is that? I am still young," Smoke replied. "But if you have trouble remembering, just ask me and I'll tell you what it's like."

"Oh, you!" Sally said, laughing as she hit Smoke on the shoulder. Smoke retreated into the house, and Sally started to go after him, but realized that Maria was still standing at the foot of the steps. She turned back to the little girl.

"Maria, thank you again for the beautiful handkerchief," she said.

"You are welcome," Maria said, beaming at the praise.

"Consuela, tell Carlos to take extra good care of Smoke's horse tonight. It brought us good news."

"*Sí, Señora.*"

Sally watched young Maria and her mother walk away, then turned to go into the house after Smoke. She had in mind a very special welcome home.

Chapter Ten

Big Rock

Every Saturday night, the Morning Star Hotel in Big Rock held a dance. It wasn't part of a big city-wide event such as the annual Cattlemen's Appreciation Day or the Fourth of July. Those events often brought in professional bands from Denver or San Francisco, or even from as far away as St. Louis. On such special occasions, entire families would show up, not only from town but from all over the county. Of course, then the dance would be only one part of a much larger celebration.

The music for the Saturday night dances was provided by local talent, the quality of the music varying according to the skill of the musicians. Very few families, or, for that matter, very few married couples, came to the Saturday night dances. These were primarily a means whereby young, unmarried men and women could socialize. From time to time, couples would meet here, get married, then drop out of the Saturday night scene.

Pearlie and Cal tied their horses off at the hitching post, then went inside. The ballroom of the hotel was brightly lit with hanging chandeliers and wall sconce lanterns, and approximately two dozen young men and women were milling about, waiting for the music to begin. Pearlie and Cal saw a couple of friends from Twin Peaks Ranch, and went over to talk to them.

"Cal, wherever did you get that hat?" one of the cowboys asked.

Cal took off his hat and looked at it. "What's wrong with the hat?" he asked.

The young cowboy laughed. "What's wrong with it? Look at it."

"I am looking at it," Cal said. "I don't see anything."

"That's it!" the cowboy said.

"What's it?" Cal said. "For the life of me, Moe, I don't see anything."

Moe laughed. "Like I said, that's it."

"Moe, if you don't tell me what the hell you are talkin' about, and tell me quick, I'm goin' to go right upside your head," Cal said.

"Look at my hat," Moe said, putting his alongside Cal's. "Do you see any difference?"

Cal's hat was black, Moe's was brown. Cal shook his head. "Yours is brown," he said.

"Pearlie, ain't you learned this young pup nothin'?" Moe asked. "Look at the hatband, Cal. What do you see?"

"You got one of leather and turquoise," Cal said.

"Uh-huh. And what do you have?"

"I don't have a hatband."

"That's my point," Moe said. "You want to show off to the girls, you need to get yourself sharpened up a bit. Maybe a red kerchief, or a silver belt buckle, or a hatband like this."

"How much does somethin' like that cost?"

"What do you care? You work for Smoke Jensen, don't you?"

"Yes, but what does that have to do with it?"

"Well, hell, he's one of the richest men in the state. Surely, he pays you enough to be able to buy a hatband," Moe said.

"I think you should get a silver hatband," a young woman said, overhearing the conversation.

Looking toward the sound of the voice, Cal saw Lucy Goodnature. "Do you really think so?" he asked.

"Absolutely," Lucy said. "What do you think, Pearlie? Don't you think our young friend should have a silver hatband?"

It did not escape Pearlie's notice that Lucy had referred to Cal as "our" friend. It was an intimate way of alluding to a shared friendship, thus suggesting a relationship between them.

"Yes, I think he should have a silver hatband," Pearlie said.

"How come you never said anything like that before?" Cal asked.

"I guess I never thought of it."

"Ha. The only reason you are saying it now is because Miss Lucy said it, and you are so crazy about her that you'll do anything she says," Cal said.

"Cal!" Pearlie said sharply, giving his friend an angry glance.

Lucy smiled, obviously pleased by the way the conversation was going.

"Ladies and gents, choose your partners and form up your squares!" the dance caller shouted, ending an embarrassing moment for Pearlie.

"Come on," Lucy said, reaching for Pearlie. "Let's be in the first square."

In a moment, there were three squares formed and waiting. Pearlie and Lucy were in the square nearest the band. The music began, with the fiddles loud and clear, the guitars carrying the rhythm, the accordion providing the counterpoint, and the slide guitar singing over everything. The caller began to shout, and he stomped his feet and danced around on the platform in compliance with his own calls. He was the center of fascinated attention from those who weren't dancing as he bowed and whirled just as if he had a girl and was in one of the squares himself. The dancers moved and swirled to the caller's commands.

Pearlie danced two more sets with Lucy, but because she was a pretty, and popular girl, others came around afterward so that, for the next several dances, Pearlie either danced with someone else— or stood on the side and watched the activity.

One of the dances was nearing the end when Cal heard Lucy's voice. Her voice was agitated, and he looked toward her to see what she was upset about. He saw a tall, lanky cowboy reaching for her, and he saw Lucy draw back from him. It was Lucas Keno.

"Just 'cause you're the daughter of a ranch owner

don't mean you're too good for an ordinary cowboy," Keno said.

"You being a cowboy has nothing to do with it," Lucy said. "I don't want to dance with you because I don't like you."

"Yeah? Well, you've come to the dance, and that means you're supposed to be willin' to dance with anyone who asks you to dance. So I'm askin', and you're goin' to dance me whether you want to or not," Keno said, reaching for her.

"Lucy, I believe you had promised me this dance," said Pearlie, coming up to her.

The frown on Lucy's face was replaced by a relieved smile. "Yes," she said. "Yes, I had promised this dance to you. I was afraid you had forgotten."

"No way I would forget something like that," Pearlie said, extending his hand toward her.

"Like hell you are going to dance with her!" Keno said angrily. Once more he reached out to grab Lucy by the shoulder, this time pulling her forcefully away from Pearlie.

Pearlie didn't say a word. Instead, he stepped in and hit Keno hard. The cowboy went down.

By now, several others had noticed the commotion and had stopped in mid-conversation to watch. When they saw Pearlie knock Keno down, they applauded.

Pearlie offered Lucy his arm and they started to walk away from the cowboy. The others at the dance, thinking the episode was over, also turned their attention away from the cowboy as they prepared for the next dance.

"You son of a bitch!" Keno shouted, getting to his feet. "I've had about enough of you!"

"He's got a gun!" someone yelled.

One of the women screamed.

"So have I," Cal said, and everyone in the room could hear the deadly click of the hammer being pulled back on Cal's gun. "And my gun is cocked," he added.

Keno's thumb was on the hammer of his pistol, but he hadn't yet pulled it back.

"Keno, if your thumb so much as makes one little twitch, I'm going to blow your brains out," Cal said.

"This ain't your fight," Keno said.

"Oh, you mean the one between you and Pearlie when he knocked you on your ass? You're right, that one wasn't my fight. But this one is. This one is just between you and me."

Keno's face broke out in perspiration; then, slowly, he lowered his pistol.

"I—I don't want no trouble," he said.

"I'll tell you what. The best way to avoid any more trouble now would be for you to just put your pistol on the floor, then leave."

"I ain't puttin' my pistol on the floor," Keno insisted.

"Have it your way, Keno. I'll just kill you, then you *and* your pistol will wind up on the floor," Cal said easily.

"No!" Keno said. "No, wait, wait."

"Put it on the floor and walk away from it."

The cowboy did as instructed, and Cal walked over to retrieve the pistol. Cal took out all the bullets, then stepped to the front door and threw the pistol as far as he could out into the night."

"Damn, Keno, I hear Miss Sally took that gun away from you, too," one of the other cowboys said. "Seems to me like you need to tie a rope around that thing.

The others at the dance laughed.

"Show's over, folks," Pearlie said. "Bandleader, play us some music."

The band struck up a Virginia reel and, almost instantly it seemed, the incident was forgotten and merriment returned.

"You want to dance again?" Pearlie asked.

"We could do that. Or, we could take a walk. Don't you think it is awfully hot in here?"

"Oh, I don't know that it is that hot," Pearlie replied.

Lucy laughed. "Tell, me, Pearlie. Just how hard is it to get you to take a hint? Can't you tell when a girl is asking you to take her for a walk?"

"Oh!" Pearlie said. "Oh, I'm sorry, I guess I *am* being a little dense. Miss Lucy Goodnature, might I have the pleasure of your company for a stroll around town?" He offered her his arm.

"You may, indeed, sir," she answered with a smile, putting her hand through his arm.

Leaving the hotel, they stepped out onto the boardwalk, then walked, arm in arm, down Main Street all the way to the tracks at the far end of town.

Behind them, the lights around the dance floor glittered brightly. The rest of the town was dark, or nearly so. Here and there, a candle or lantern gleamed. Overhead, the moon was just over half full, and shining brightly enough to paint the surrounding countryside in shades of silver and black. The sky was filled with stars, some so bright that it looked as if you could almost pluck them from the sky. Then, between the very bright ones were thousands of stars of lesser magnitude, then lesser still, until the entire night sky seemed to glow dimly with a soft blue light from those stars that couldn't quite be seen. That made the night sky just a little lighter than the nearby mountains so that the range stood out in bold, black relief on the distant horizon.

"Have you ever seen anything so beautiful?" Lucy asked.

"No," Pearlie replied. "I haven't."

There was something in the tone of Pearlie's voice that caused Lucy to look back at him and when she did, she saw that he was staring at her.

"I mean the sky," she said self-consciously.

"I mean this," Pearlie answered. He put his hands on her shoulders, then leaned down toward her. She turned her face up, offering him her mouth, and they kissed.

Pearlie held the kiss for a long time, feeling, first Lucy's surrender to it, then her embrace of it as she wrapped her arms around his neck and pressed herself against him.

Suddenly, Pearlie pulled away from her and looked down at her. "Oh," he said. "Oh, Lucy, I'm sorry, I had no right to be so forward."

"Don't be silly, Pearlie," Lucy said. "That is exactly what I wanted." In the distance could be heard the whistle of an approaching train. "But maybe we should get back now."

"Yes, I think so," Pearlie agreed.

Halfway back to the dance floor, Lucas Keno suddenly stepped out of the darkness of the space between two buildings, holding an ax handle. He held it in his right hand and tapped it softly into the palm of his left hand.

"Get out of here, Lucy," Pearlie ordered.

"No, I'm not going to leave you with . . ."

"I said get out of here! Now!" Pearlie said more sternly.

Lucy hesitated just a second, then started running back toward the lights at the far end of the street.

Keno swung at Pearlie, and Pearlie danced back out of the way.

Keno swung again, this time managing to hit Pearlie a glancing blow on the shoulder. Pearlie felt the pain shoot down his arm, but he was sure it was a bruise and not a break.

Keno got overconfident then. With a triumphant yell, he raised the ax handle straight up over his head, intending to bring it smashing down onto Pearlie. But Pearlie stepped into him, not away from him, and Keno had no leverage. He tried to back up, but Pearlie grabbed the ax handle, jerked it from Keno's hand, then tossed it away.

"What the—?" Keno started to shout, but that was as far as he got before Pearlie took him down with a hard right to the chin.

Pearlie stood over Keno for a moment, then

turned to head back to the hotel. That's when he saw Cal and Lucy, standing no more than fifty feet away.

"I thought I told you to go back," Pearlie said.

"I—I couldn't just leave you," Lucy said. "Besides, Cal was with me."

"Yeah," Cal said. "If you had gotten into real trouble, I would have stepped in to help you out."

Pearlie chuckled. "Well, damn, Cal, he came after me with an ax handle. How much trouble would I have to be in before you thought I was in trouble?"

"I don't know," Cal answered. "It looked to me like you were handling it pretty well. Don't you think so, Miss Lucy?"

"I think it was the bravest thing I ever saw," Lucy said, the tone of her voice reflecting the genuineness of her statement.

After Pearlie, Cal, and Lucy left, Keno groaned, then got up onto his hands and knees. He stayed that way for a moment.

"Well, you are still alive, I see," a voice called from the darkness.

Keno looked toward the voice, but could see nothing. "Who is it?" he asked. "Who is there?"

A man stepped from the darkness. "It's me, Jeeter," he said.

"What are you doing down here?"

"Watching," Jeeter said.

Keno got to his feet, then rubbed his chin. "I was just aimin' to scare him," he said. "I should have gone after him for real."

"Yeah, you should have," Jeeter said.

"What do you mean, you're watching?"

"Well, maybe a little more than that," Jeeter said. "I followed you when you left the dance."

"Why?"

"Because I've got a proposition for you. I know how you can make some money and get even with Jensen."

"What do you mean, get even with Jensen? Pearlie is the one I want. And Cal."

"The way them all is joined at the hip, I reckon if you get even with one of them, you get even with all of them."

"You may have a point there. What do you have in mind?" Keno asked.

Let's get out of here," Jeeter said. "I'll tell you all about it on the way."

"On the way where?

Jeeter looked at Keno, then ran his hand through his hair. "Look, do you want in on this or not?"

"You say I can make some money and get back at Jensen?"

"Yes."

Keno nodded his head. "Yeah," he said. "Yeah, whatever it is, I want in on it."

"Good. Just don't ask so damn many questions. You'll find out everything you need to know soon enough."

"What time you reckon it is?" Cal asked as he and Pearlie rode under the arch that marked the beginning of the road up to the Big House.

"Oh, it's a little after ten o'clock, I reckon," Pearlie answered.

"Ha," Cal said. "We're some big partygoers we are, comin' back home by ten o'clock. And here we told Smoke we'd be gone till early mornin'.'"

"Ah, I don't reckon he thought we'd really be gone all that long," Pearlie said. "Besides, iffen we're goin' to be punchin' cows come first light, I'd as soon go ahead and get a little sleep anyway."

"I reckon you're right," Cal agreed.

The two boys rode on into the barn, dismounted, took the saddles off, then gave their horses some oats before turning them into the corral. It was a short walk from the barn to the bunkhouse.

"Hey, Pearlie," Cal asked as they started toward the bunkhouse. "Do you think Moe was right?"

"Right? Right about what?"

"The hatband," Cal said. "Do you think if I had a fancy hatband, the girls would pay more attention to me?"

Pearlie chuckled. "Hell, Cal, you don't need nothin' fancy. All you need to do is be a little more friendly at these dances. The girls look at you and get scared off."

"I don't ever know what to say to a girl," Cal said. "I'm shy. I don't know. Maybe Moe is right. Maybe if I had me somethin' like a fancy hatband, I could do better."

When dawn broke the next morning, Smoke, Pearlie, and Cal were in the saddle, cutting fifteen hundred head away from the main herd. They weren't alone at this point, for many of Smoke's Mexican hands were with them, dressed as vaqueros, wearing large sombreros and, in some cases, serapes as they dashed about, forming the cows into a manageable herd.

Sally was working with them as well, and she slapped her legs against the side of her horse urging it into a gallop as she dashed alongside the slowly moving herd until she reached the front, where a few cows were trying to break away from the right-hand side. Expertly, she pushed them back into position.

Cal was the flank rider on the left side, near the front, and Juan was on the same side, riding in the swing position, or near the rear. Pearlie was riding swing on the right, which would be his position once they were under way. For the moment, Carlos was riding flank on the right. Sally was in the point position, which would be Smoke's position.

Smiling, Smoke slapped his legs against the side of his horse, then gave a shout.

"All right, boys, we'll take it from here," he called out to the hands who would remain at the ranch.

"Who are you calling boy?" Sally asked, riding over to join him.

"Darlin', I might call you many things," Smoke said. "But boy ain't one of them."

"Ain't?" Sally replied with a wince. "Smoke Jensen, you know that everyone on this ranch looks up to you. How am I ever going to teach proper grammar if you don't set the example?"

"Sally, if they all look up to me, they have a sorry example, I'm afraid."

"False modesty does not become you. And they do look up to you, and you should be cognizant of that at all times."

"Cognizant?" Smoke said. He laughed again.

"Yes, cognizant," Sally repeated. "What do you find so funny."

"You," Smoke said.

"Oh?"

"Look at you," Smoke said. Taking his handkerchief from his pocket, he reached out to wipe a smudge of dirt from Sally's face. "I'll bet when you were a little girl growing up in New Hampshire, the daughter of a rich man, you thought you would be president of the garden club, hosting teas and the like. Never in your life would you have imagined yourself riding astride and pushing cattle."

"Well, that's where you are wrong, Smoke Jensen. I'm doing exactly what I used to imagine myself doing," Sally insisted.

Smoke chuckled again. "Now that I think about it, I'll just bet you are."

"Let me come with you," Sally said.

"No need. Pearlie, Cal, and I can handle it."

"But it would be easier with me along, and you know it would."

"Sally, someone has to stay and watch the place."

"Carlos can do that."

"What about school? Don't you have some kids depending on you to teach school?"

Sally sighed. "Yes," she said. "Yes, I do. But it's not fair," she pouted.

Smoke leaned over and kissed her.

"I won't be gone long," he promised. "And when I come back, why, we can go into Big Rock and you can go shopping."

"Big Rock my hind foot," Sally replied with a smile. "If I'm going shopping, I'm going to do it up right. We'll be going into Denver. Denver? Heck, we might even go all the way back to New York."

"Whoa, let's not get carried away with all this," Smoke said.

"Hurry back to me," Sally said. Then she let out a loud, piercing whistle. "Carlos, Juan!" she shouted. "Let's go!"

Turning her horse, she urged it into a quick gallop as she started back toward the house. Smoke watched, appreciating the easy way she sat the saddle and the way like she seemed to almost share the musculature of the horse so that the gallop was like a ballet involving horse and rider.

Smoke knew a lot of good horsemen, but he had never met anyone who was better than Sally.

Chapter Eleven

As they got under way to Frisco, the herd moved across the land, not in one large mass, but in a long plodding column, generally no more than three or four abreast. While it was on the move, flankers would ride on either side of the herd, keeping it moving, while one man rode drag. Drag was the least desirable position because the cowboy who rode behind the herd had to swallow all the dust. In many outfits, Cal, being the youngest and the least experienced, would have been selected to ride drag every day. But Smoke was fair about it, and he rotated the position, even taking drag himself when it was his turn.

Smoke had scouted all of the best places to camp for the night when he had ridden to Frisco the first time. As a result, there was no need to send anyone ahead, as one would during a normal drive. Smoke had carefully selected the nightly encampments to be about fifteen miles apart. That way he knew that they would cover the seventy-five miles in five nights, arriving at Frisco by mid-morning of the sixth day.

The hardest part of the drive was to get the cows moving each morning. By design, the campsites were picked where there was plenty of grass and water. In addition, there would be an occasional tree or an overhanging bluff to provide some respite from the sun, and that combination made the cows reluctant to leave. Each morning, they had every intention of staying right where they were.

In order to get the herd moving, Smoke, Pearlie, and Cal would have to shout, probe the animals with sticks, and ride at a gallop alongside, swinging ropes overhead. Eventually, their efforts would pay off, and the herd would begin to move. Then, once the herd was under way, it would change from fifteen hundred individual creatures into a single entity with a single purpose. The inertia Smoke, Pearlie, and Cal needed to overcome to get the herd moving in the first place now worked in their favor as the cows would plod along all day long at a steady clip, showing no inclination to stop.

There was a distinctive aroma to a herd this size. The smells came from sun on the hides, the dust in the air, and most pungently from the animals' droppings and urine.

While the odor was strong and, no doubt to most people, unpleasant, to Smoke, it was a scent as familiar and almost as agreeable as the fragrance of flour and cinnamon on Sally's apron.

It would be a long and labor-intensive journey for just three men to drive a herd this size, but as far as Smoke was concerned, there was no place in the world he would rather be than right here, right now.

Putrid Wells

At on time there had actually been a town called Putrid Wells, built during a silver strike in the nearby buttes. But the silver had played out quickly, so the townspeople had moved on. A score or more of abandoned buildings remained, some of wood and turning gray, others of adobe and disintegrating under the heat of the summer sun and the blows of winter. Of the buildings that lined both sides of a single street, only one was still occupied.

The one remaining business establishment was the Silver Strike Saloon. The Silver Strike, which was built of adobe brick, was the largest building in town. Nippy Jones, its owner, insisted to all who passed by that the silver was still there, still ready to be pulled from the mine. Only a few die-hard prospectors believed him. In fact, he didn't believe it himself. It was just his way of trying to breathe life back into the town. He managed to stay in business by providing drink and food to the few prospectors who did remain, hoping to find the mother lode, and to travelers who just happened through.

When Toby Jeeter and Lucas Keno rode up to the Silver Strike Saloon, there were at least eight other horses tied up out front.

"Damn," Keno said as he dismounted. "Who would think this place would be doing this much business?"

"This ain't normal," Jeeter said. "We're meetin' some folks in here."

Inside, there were two men standing at the bar, though as they were at opposite ends, they were obviously not together. There were six more men who were together, though, and they were sitting in the back of the room at a couple of tables that had been pulled together. One of the men sitting at the tables was the whitest person Keno had ever seen, and he stopped for a moment to stare in curiosity.

Jeeter noticed Keno staring. "I told you he was pale," Jeeter said under his breath.

"You said pale, you didn't say white."

"Yeah, well, don't say nothin' to him about it. He gets a bit peekid when folks carry on about it."

"I wasn't goin' to say nothin'. I was just lookin', that's all."

"Come on, I'll introduce you to him."

"Hello, Jeeter," the very white man said as Jeeter and Keno approached the table. "Is this the man you told us about?"

"Yeah," Jeeter said. "This here is Lucas Keno. He used to work for Smoke Jensen. Keno, this is Van Arndt. He's the boss."

"The boss of what?" Keno asked.

"You'll find out soon enough," Jeeter said. He introduced the others. "This here is Peters."

Peters was short and swarthy, with dark, beady eyes.

"Boswell," Jeeter continued, pointing to a man who had a purple scar running from his left eye down to the corner of his lip.

"Shardeen."

Shardeen suffered from hyperthyroidism, though it had never been diagnosed. The visual symptom, however, was quite clear in the bulging eyes that were his most prominent feature.

Kingsley and Miller, the last two men Jeeter introduced to Keno, were unremarkable in appearance, being of average size and coloring, and without any visible scars or abnormalities.

"I understand you worked for Smoke Jensen," Van Arndt said.

"I used to, yeah. I don't work for him anymore."

"You got any loyalties left for your old boss?"

"Loyalties?"

"Yeah. Any reason why you wouldn't want to steal anything from him?"

"Are you kidding?" Keno replied. "If I could, I would steal the nickels off the son of a bitch's eyes after he's dead. In fact, I wish I could do that very thing," Keno added, then chuckled at the humor of his remark.

Van Arndt chuckled as well. "Then I reckon you can ride with us," he said.

"What is all this about?"

Van Arndt looked at Jeeter. "You didn't tell him anything?"

Jeeter shook his head. "I figured you'd want to do that," he said.

Van Arndt nodded, then looked back at Keno. "We're goin' to take his herd," he said.

"Take his herd? Impossible. He has more than thirty thousand on the hoof scattered over a fifteen thousand acre ranch," Keno said.

"Not that herd," Van Arndt said. "Jensen and two of his cowboys are taking fifteen hundred cows to Frisco to sell to a cattle buyer there."

"Why is he taking them all the way to Frisco? Why not just take them into the railhead at Big Rock?"

"The buyer at Frisco is paying five dollars more per head," Van Arndt said. "That means he's paying forty five thousand dollars for those cows."

"Wheew," Keno whistled. "That's a lot of money."

"Yes, it is," Van Arndt replied. "And if you ask me, it's far too much money to be wasted on the likes of Smoke Jensen."

"So what is the plan?" Keno asked.

"It's a simple enough plan," Van Arndt replied. "There are only three of them taking the herd in. There are eight of us."

"Yeah—I don't know," Keno said, stroking his chin.

"What's there not to know? Eight against three seems like pretty good odds to me."

"What you don't understand is, them's not just any three men," Keno said. "Smoke Jensen may be the best man with a gun there is. And I don't reckon Pearlie and Cal are any too bad."

"I heard that you was pretty good with a gun," Van Arndt said. "Is that a lie?"

"No, that ain't no lie," he said. "I am good with a gun."

"Better than Jensen?"

"Yeah, I think I am," Jeeter said, recalling his "challenge" of Smoke a few weeks earlier. "And I know damn well I am better than Pearlie or Cal."

"Then there is no problem," Van Arndt said in a matter of fact tone of voice. "You can take out Pearlie and Cal, that will leave the rest of us to handle Jensen."

"When is all this supposed to happen?" Keno asked.

"The herd will come close by here tomorrow." Van Arndt answered. He looked over toward the bar. "Hey, barkeep," he called.

"Yes, sir. More liquor?" Nippy replied.

"How much will it cost for us to spend the night here in the saloon?"

"I got rooms upstairs, only cost you fifteen cents a room," Nippy replied.

"Nah, not upstairs. We don't need no rooms. We'll sleep here, on the floor," Van Arndt said.

"Well, sir, that won't cost you no more'n a nickel apiece," Nippy said. "Forty cents, I reckon."

"Here's four dimes. Come get 'em," Van Arndt said, holding out the money.

Nippy stepped around the bar, then walked over to get the money. "I won't be providin' no blankets or nothin'," he said. "Not at this price."

"We don't need no blankets," Van Arndt said.

As Nippy returned to the bar, Van Arndt continued explaining his plan to the others. "We'll spend the night here and hit 'em at mid-morning. They won't be lookin' for us, so we'll just ride in and kill Jensen and the two with him. Once they're dead, it won't be nothin' for us to then take the herd and drive 'em on in to Frisco our ownselves."

"You sure we can sell the herd?" Keno asked. "I mean, isn't the buyer expecting Jensen to deliver the herd?"

"From what I know, the buyer needs all the beef he can get for a contract he has with the army," Van

Arndt said. "I expect he'll buy from the first person who shows up." Van Arndt smiled, but the smile, instead of lessening his macabre appearance, stretched the white skin to the point that it made his head look almost like a living skull.

Up at the bar, one of the men who had watched and heard everything that transpired made a signal to the owner. "Nippy, you have any of that horehound candy left?"

"Yeah, Taylor, I have some left, but damn if you don't keep me run out of it most of the time. I swear, you are sure like a kid, what with always wantin' some of that horehound candy."

"What can I say, Nippy? I like horehound candy," Taylor said. "Fact is, when I strike silver, I plan to build me a factory making nothing but horehound candy, and I don't plan to sell none of it. I'll be eatin' it all my own self."

Nippy laughed, then dropped several pieces of the amber candy into a bag and handed it to the old prospector. "When you get that horehound candy factory built, you come tell me about it, Taylor. That is somethin' I would pure dee like to see."

"I'll do that." Taylor popped a piece of candy into his mouth. "I'll be back in a month or so," he said as he ambled slowly toward the door.

"You take care out there, old-timer," Nippy called to him.

"Hey, bartender," Van Arndt called.

"Yes, sir? More whiskey?"

"No. Who was that fella that just left?"

"His name is Taylor," Nippy said.

"Seems to me like he was a might too interested in what we was talkin' about," Van Arndt said.

Nippy laughed.

"Hell, you don't have to worry none about that old-timer. Truth is, I think he's been out in the sun too long. He's a bit addled in the head if you ask me. He's been prospecting for gold and silver for ten years or more."

"Has he ever found anything?" Boswell asked.

"Oh, I think he finds enough leavin's from the tailings of the old mine to stay alive, but he ain't never found nothin' to write home about," Nippy said. "Why do you ask? Are you interested in doing some mining? Because if you are, I've got some maps I'll sell you."

"Could be that I'm interested," Boswell began, but Van Arndt interrupted him.

"Nah, we ain't interested in nothin' like that," Van Arndt said, glaring at Boswell. "We got other things to think about."

"Yeah, well, I didn't mean now," Boswell said. "I was thinkin' about maybe later."

"Don't think," Van Arndt said. "I'll do the thinkin' for all of us."

It was nearly supper time when Cal spotted the rider coming toward the camp.

"Smoke, someone's coming," Cal said, pointing toward the north.

"Anybody we know?" Pearlie asked.

"I've never seen him," Cal said. "How about you, Smoke? Have you ever seen him?"

"No," Smoke replied. "But if he was looking for trouble, I don't expect he come in to the camp riding like this."

"No, I don't think so either," Pearlie agreed.

"Hello the camp," the rider hailed.

"Come on in," Smoke invited.

They studied the rider as he approached. He looked to be in his sixties at least. He was bony and angular, almost to the point of emaciation. He had a white, stubby beard, not one that was purposely grown, but the result of going several days without shaving.

"We're just about to have our supper," Smoke said. "You're welcome to join us."

"Well, now, I thank you kindly for that," the rider said as he dismounted. "I ain't never one to turn down a free meal." He pulled out his own mess kit and handed it to Cal, who reached for it. "The name is Taylor. Bogardus Taylor, though I don't normally tell folks my first name. I take it that one of you boys would be Smoke Jensen?"

"That would be me," Smoke said. Smoke squinted his eyes. "Do I know you?"

"No, sir, I don't reckon that you do know me," Taylor said. "But I know you. At least, I know about you. Sometime ago you was ridin' shotgun guard for my brother, Puddin'. Some men tried to hold up the stage. Puddin' said if it hadn't a'been for you, he would'a been kilt for sure."[1]

----

1. *Betrayal of the Mountain Man*

Smoke chuckled. "Puddin' Taylor, yes, I remember him. He got shot in the arm as I recall. How is he doing?"

"His arm still troubles him somewhat when it gets cold. But other than that, he is getting' along just fine, thanks to you," Taylor said. "Which is why I've come to tell you."

"You've come to tell me what?" Smoke asked, just as Cal passed the kit back filled with beans, bacon, and a biscuit.

"Uhmm, this is mighty tasty," Taylor said shoveling a spoonful into his mouth. "You know a feller by the name of Van Arndt? He's a real pale feller."

"Yes, I know him."

"Well, sir, he and some more fellers is a'plannin' to attack you tomorrow mornin'. What they are figurin' on doin' is killin' the three of you and then take your herd." He took a bite of the biscuit. "This biscuit is just real good. Who made it?"

"I did," Cal said.

"Sonny, you'd be a fine man to camp with. You ever get a hankerin' to look for silver or gold, come look me up. I'd be just real happy to take you on and learn you all about prospectin'. Most especial if you can cook like this all the time."

"How many of them are there?" Smoke asked.

"I beg your pardon?" Taylor asked, so involved with his eating now that it was almost as if the life-and-death discussion of ambush, robbery, and murder was no more than casual conversation.

"You said Van Arndt and some others are planning on killing us and taking the herd. How many of them are there?"

"Oh, there's about eight of 'em, I reckon. They're holed up back at the Silver Strike Saloon in Putrid Wells."

"Putrid Wells?" Cal said. He chuckled. "What kind of a name is that?"

"Hey, I know that place," Pearlie said. "It's a town just ahead of us by a couple of miles."

"It was a town," Smoke said. "It grew up around a silver mine, but when the mine played out, there was nothing to keep people there any longer. Especially given he fact that the water is bad. That is what gave the town its name. It's a ghost town now."

"Well, it ain't rightly what you would call a ghost town," Taylor pointed out. "A ghost town means there ain't nobody there at all, but there is a feller by the name of Nippy Jones that runs him a bar and café there in Putrid Wells. And they's folks that drop in on him from time to time, them bein' mostly travelers and the like." Taylor held his cup out. "You reckon maybe a feller could get hisself another cup o' that coffee?"

"Sure thing," Cal said, using his hat as a heat pad and taking the blue metal pot from the fire to pour another cup of coffee for the old prospector.

"I thankee there, sonny. I thankee right kindly," Taylor said.

"Mr. Taylor, I believe you said Van Arndt and the others are holed up in Putrid Wells?" Smoke asked.

"Yes, sir. I heard Van Arndt tell the others he plans on them spendin' the night right there in the saloon tonight. Then what he plans on doin' is, he plans on comin' after you boys and the herd around mid-morning tomorrow."

"Unless we go after them first," Smoke said.

"Go after them? What are you talking about, Smoke? Didn't you hear Mr. Taylor say there were eight of them?" Cal said. "That is what you said, isn't it, Mr. Taylor? That there are eight of them?"

"Eight, that's right. And one of 'em used to work for you. You know a feller named Keno?"

"Keno?" Pearlie replied. "Oh, yes, sir. We do indeed know a fella named Keno."

"He's one of 'em," Taylor said. "He claims to be somethin' special with a gun."

"He is good with a gun," Pearlie said.

"Is there some bad blood betwixt you boys and this feller Keno?"

"Why do you ask?"

"From listenin' to him talk, seems like he has a particular hard spot for the lot of you. I could be wrong, but that's the way it sounded to me."

"You aren't wrong, Mr. Taylor," Smoke said.

"So, how are we going to go after eight? There are only three of us." Cal asked.

"Four, if you count me," Taylor said.

Smoke reached out and put his hand on the old prospector's shoulder. "Thanks for the offer, Mr. Taylor," he said. "But you've done enough for us already. Anyway, there aren't three of us, there are fifteen hundred and three."

"Fifteen hundred? Ha!" Cal said. "I don't know

where you get fifteen hundred, unless you are countin' the cows."

"Don't you think they have a stake in this?" Smoke asked.

Cal laughed. "Well, I reckon they do," he said. "But I'm not sure how you plan to get them into the game."

"I'll show you," Smoke said without further explanation.

They had gotten their herd under way before dawn, and now, nearly two miles into the day's drive, the sun was barely above the eastern horizon. The early morning light picked up the blanket of dew on the meadow and flashed it back in a million sparkling points of color. From their position on the crest of a hill, Smoke, Pearlie, and Cal stared down toward the little ghost town of Putrid Wells.

"I hope they're still here," Cal said.

"They're here. See the horses down there?" Smoke said.

"Ha! They're probably plannin' on just how they are going to hit us," Cal said.

"I reckon we'll be upsettin' those plans somewhat considerable," Pearlie said.

"Are you boys ready?" Smoke asked.

Pearlie nodded. "We're ready." He giggled. "It's funny, because the thing you want to watch out for most on a long drive is a cattle stampede. And now here we are, planning on gettin' one a'goin'."

"The herd is well watered and well fed," Smoke said. "I don't expect they'll run too far."

The herd, having been moved up this morning, now stood motionless. The only movement within the herd came from those few animals who, not understanding why they had stopped so soon, and sensing that it was time to be under way again, were walking around as if expending nervous energy. Even they would make no effort to move until urged to do so, for with the water and graze that was available, the herd would be perfectly content to remain here indefinitely if not prodded.

Smoke, Cal, and Pearlie moved their mounts into position behind the herd. Cal and Pearlie had blankets in their hands and Smoke was holding his pistol. When all were in position they looked toward Smoke in expectation.

There was a long moment of waiting as Smoke held his hand up. Then he fired the gun into the air. "Now!" he called out, his shout concurrent with the firing of the pistol.

Almost immediately after his shout and gunshot, Cal and Pearlie began waving blankets, and the herd, startled by the sudden fury of noise and activity, broke into a rapid, lumbering gait, headed down the hill toward the little scattering of buildings below.

"*Yee hah! Yee hah!*" the three men shouted at the top of their voices, riding back and forth behind the herd. They had put away their blankets, and were now waving hats at the cattle to urge them into greater and greater speed.

* * *

Inside the Silver Strike, Van Arndt and the others were still sleeping off the effects of all the whiskey they had drunk the night before. Only Keno was up, a full bladder having awakened him. He stepped outside the front door of the saloon and, rather than walk across the street to the toilet, began relieving himself in the street right in front of the saloon door.

He thought of the sight he must make, standing here in front of a building, relieving himself on the main street of a town, and he found the thought funny.

"Ha," he said. "What I'd like to do is take a piss, just like this, in front of Longmont's back in Big Rock. Wouldn't that be a picture now?"

Keno said the words aloud, even though there was nobody there to talk to. Then, just as he was finishing, he heard thunder. Surprised by that, Keno looked into the sky. There wasn't a cloud to be seen.

Then, looking to the north, he saw something that first puzzled, and then startled him.

It was cattle! An entire herd of cattle was running hell-bent across the plains! He looked at them for a moment, unable to believe his eyes. Then he realized that they weren't just running, they were stampeding, and they were heading right for him.

"What the hell?" he asked quietly. Then, shock gave way to panic as he realized that he was in danger. "My God, my God, it's a stampede! *Stampede!*" he shouted at the top of his voice. He ran back into the saloon. "Stampede!" he shouted again.

"Keno, what the hell are you carrying on about?"

Jeeter asked, sleepily. Jeeter had pulled two of the tables together, and he was lying across them with his hat over his face. "You're dreamin'. Go back to sleep."

"The cattle are stampeding!" Keno said. "There are thousands of them and they are coming right for us."

"What do you mean they're coming right for us?" Shardeen asked irritably. Shardeen was lying on the floor near the bar. "What cattle?"

"Look outside, you'll see what I'm talking about!" Keno shouted.

By now, the sound of sixty thousand hooves drumming on the ground had grown loud enough for everyone to hear.

"What the hell is that? Thunder?" Kingsley asked. He got up from the table and walked over to look through the window. At that moment the herd was less than one hundred yards away. An outhouse on the outskirts of the settlement went down under the onslaught of the thundering herd.

"Holy shit!" Kingsley shouted.

Kingsley's shout alerted the rest of the men, though his warning wasn't really necessary, for by now the thundering sound of the stampede had become almost deafening, waking even the most hungover of all the sleepers.

"We've got to get out of here!" Kingsley shouted running toward the door.

"Kingsley, you fool! Get back in here!" Van Arndt yelled, but his yell went unheeded. The terrified man ran outside only to find himself trapped in the open with an ocean of brown crashing toward him. He tried to get back to the relative safety of the saloon, but it was too late. He was run over and crushed by the stampeding cows.

Those inside the saloon shuddered in terror as the ground shook around them. Now and again, the horns of one of the bolting cows would hook into the crusted adobe walls of the Silver Strike, gouging out large chunks of mud and dirt. With a crash, the window frame was pulled out, leaving a large, gaping hole in the wall. Through the hole, the terrified men could see a seemingly unending stream of wild-eyed cattle.

One corner of the wall came tumbling down, bringing the roof down with it. The men inside screamed, and fell to the floor with their arms over their heads. They gritted their teeth and cried in fear and felt the earth shake as the herd continued to rumble by. Finally the shaking stopped and the sound began to recede.

Then it was quiet.

"What . . . what the hell was that?" someone asked.

"I've never heard of cows stampeding through a town like that," another added.

"They weren't just stampedin' through the town," Keno said. "They was drove through the town."

"What? What do you mean they was drove through the town?" Van Arndt asked.

"I mean they was drove through the town," Keno repeated. "I seen Smoke Jensen, Pearlie, and Cal, all ridin' behind the herd, urgin' them on. Them cows was drove through here of a pure purpose. Those sons of bitches tried to kill us."

"How did they even know we was here?" Shardeen asked.

"I don't know how they knew, but they did. And they used them cows to try and kill us," Keno answered.

"Where's Kingsley? Does anybody see him?" Van Arndt asked.

"He's still out there," Boswell said, nodding toward the window. "The cows got him. He's deader than hell."

Van Arndt walked up to the door and looked outside. He could see the bloody pulp of what was left of Kingsley's body.

"What are we goin' to do with him?" Boswell asked.

"What do you mean, what are we goin' to do with him?"

"We can't just leave him there, can we?" Boswell said.

"Why not? The dumb shit brought it on himself. Anyone so damn dumb they would run out in front of a stampede don't deserve nobody to worry over them."

"Still, it don't seem right," Boswell said.

"You want to bury the son of a bitch, bury him," Van Arndt said. "I ain't stoppin' you."

"What do we do now, Van Arndt?" Peters asked.

"Did our horses survive?"

"Yeah, they all run off when they heard the herd stampedin' toward them," Keno said. "Fact is, they're all comin' back now."

"Good. What we do now is, we leave here."

"Are we still goin' to take the herd?" Keno asked.

"No. That's not possible now."

"So, are we givin' up?"

"Depends on what you mean by givin' up? We ain't goin' to try and take the herd," Van Arndt said. He smiled. "I've got a better idea."

"What's that?" Shardeen asked.

"Think about it. If we had taken the herd, we'd still have to drive it to Frisco. Why not let Jensen and his boys do all the hard work for us. We'll wait until he delivers the herd—then we'll take the money."

The others smiled.

"Yeah," Jeeter said. "Yeah, I like that a lot better anyway. Let Jensen and his boys do all the work."

Chapter Twelve

Frisco was a busy place when Smoke, Pearlie, and Cal brought the herd into town. Two trains were standing in the depot. One was a passenger train taking on passengers for its run to the East. Even though the engineer was at rest, the fireman wasn't. He could be seen through the cab window, shoveling coal into the firebox, working hard to keep the steam pressure up.

In contrast to the fireman's toil, the engineer was leaning out the window of the highly polished green and brass locomotive. Serene in the power and prestige of his position, the engineer was smoking a curved-stem pipe as he watched the activity on the depot platform.

A score of passengers were boarding or leaving the train as the conductor stood beside the string of varnished cars, keeping a close check on the time. Over on the sidetrack sat a second train, this one a freight, with its relief valve puffing as it opened and closed to maintain the delicate balance of steam pressure while it waited. The passenger train had priority over the "high iron," as the main track was called, and not until it departed would the freight train be allowed to move back onto the main line in order to continue its travel west.

Two stagecoaches and half a dozen carriages were also sitting at the depot, while out in the street behind the depot a horse-drawn streetcar rumbled by. Although pushing cattle through the town was not unheard of, it was a rare enough condition to cause everyone to look on. Of course, they had little other option, since fifteen hundred cattle filled Poindexter Street from side to side, and stretched out from Miners Creek to the feeder on the other side of Ten Mile Creek where the gate was already open and two of Davencourt's employees were counting the cows by putting a knot in a piece of string for every twenty-five head that passed by.

Davencourt came down to the holding pens and stood there for a while, watching as the cattle were moved into the pens.

"Mr. Jensen," he said. "If you have someone who can keep an eye on things for you here until all the cows are in the pen, why don't you come on over to the saloon with me and let me buy you a drink? Afterward, we'll walk down to the bank and I'll draw out the draft for you."

"Sounds like a good idea to me," Smoke said. "Pearlie," he called. "I'm going with Mr. Davencourt. When you're finished here, take care of our horses and get us a couple of rooms over at the hotel."

"Sure thing, Smoke," Pearlie said.

Smoke turned the reins of his horse over to Pearlie, then walked with Davencourt down to the Twin Branch Saloon.

The place smelled of whiskey, beer, and tobacco. There was a long bar on the left, with towels hanging on hooks about every five feet along the front. A large mirror was behind the bar, but the images Smoke could see were distorted by imperfections in the glass.

Over against the back wall, near the foot of the stairs, a cigar-scarred, beer-stained, upright piano was being played by a bald-headed musician.

"Barkeep," Davencourt called as soon as they stepped into the saloon. "I've just closed a business deal with this gentleman and I am in a magnanimous mood. Libations for all herein present."

The bartender and everyone in the saloon looked at Davencourt with puzzled expressions on their faces. Seeing that they had not understood him, Davencourt repeated his offer.

"Set everyone up, barkeep. The drinks are on me."

The others in the bar cheered.

With the cattle count secured and the horses taken to the livery, Pearlie and Cal started toward the hotel to get the rooms. They were walking past the mercantile store when Cal suddenly stopped and looked in through the window.

"What is it? What are you lookin' at?" Pearlie asked.

"Nothin'," Cal said. "You go on, I'll be along directly."

"You goin' into the store?"

"Maybe."

"I'll go in with you."

"No need for you to do that," Cal said. "Don't forget, Smoke wants you to get our hotel rooms for the night."

"Why you bein' so damn mysterious?" Pearlie asked.

"I ain't bein' nothin' of the sort," Cal replied. "You just go on and get them rooms like Smoke asked you to."

Pearlie chuckled. "All right, all right," he said. "Keep your damn secret, see if I care."

Pearlie started on down the street toward the hotel. By looking across the street, he could see Cal's reflection in the window of a leather-goods store. He saw that Cal was still standing in front of the store, watching him, as if making certain that he was going to the hotel. Then, when he saw Cal actually go into the store, he doubled back and looked in through the window. He saw Cal go over to a table and look at the display, but, from the window he couldn't see what it was Cal was viewing.

"Yes, sir, can I help you, sir?" a young woman asked as she stepped over to the table.

"Yeah, I'd like," Cal began, then, seeing that it was a very pretty young woman, stopped in mid-sentence and took off his hat. "I—uh—apologize for bein' so dirty, miss," he said. "But my pards 'n me just brung in fifteen hundred head of cows, an' I ain't had no chance to take me a bath yet."

"Oh, I saw you," the young woman said.

"Beg your pardon?"

"I saw all the cows coming down the street this morning. And you were one of the cowboys who brought the herd in?"

"Yes, ma'am, I reckon I was."

"Oh, how exciting!"

"Yes, ma'am, I reckon it was somewhat," Cal said. "Only, it's a dirty job, which is why I'm apologizin' to you for comin' in to your store like this."

"That's all right," the young woman replied.

"No, ma'am, it ain't all right a'tall," Cal said. "I mean, if you was a—" He paused. "I mean if you *were* a man, well, it would be different. But you are a girl and it's all the same to you, I figure on goin' over to the hotel and havin' me a bath. Then I'll come back when I'm more decent and buy the thing I come in here for."

"If you insist," the young woman said.

"Yes, ma'am, I reckon I do insist," Cal said.

The young woman smiled broadly. "Then I shall look forward to serving you," she said.

Pearlie saw Cal turn back toward the front of the store, and he had to run quickly to get down the street far enough so as to be in the hotel by the time Cal got outside. He hurried up the desk, then, seeing no one behind it, struck his hand on the bell to cause it to ring.

A clerk hurried out of the back room to answer the summons.

"Yes, sir?" The smile left the clerk's face when he

saw how dirty Pearlie was. He stared at the young man for a pregnant moment.

"You'll have to go somewhere else," the clerk finally said. "The hotel proprietor does not allow me to give alms to the poor. You can understand, I'm sure. Why, if I gave money to everyone who came around asking for it, the hotel would soon be filled with beggars and tramps."

Puzzled by the clerk's comment, Pearlie look around to see if anyone had followed him into the hotel.

"Mister, who you talkin' to?" Pearlie asked. "I don't see nobody in here askin' you for money."

"Well, I was talking to—" the clerk began, then stopped. "Are you telling me you aren't here to beg for money?"

"What? Hell, no!" Pearlie exploded. "Look at me, mister! Do I look like the kind of man who would be begging for money?"

In fact, the clerk thought, this man looked exactly like someone who would be asking for money.

"I beg your pardon, sir, my mistake," the clerk said. "What can I do for you?"

"I need a couple of rooms for tonight."

"A couple of rooms? May I inquire as to why you would possibly need more than one room?"

"Well, if you have to know, one room will be for Smoke Jensen, and the other room will be for me and Cal," Pearlie said. He smiled. "And Smoke has give me the authority to go ahead and sign for the rooms myself."

The expression on the night clerk's face changed. "Did you say Smoke Jensen?"

"I did indeed," Pearlie said. "Me and Smoke and Cal brung in to town slightly more'n fifteen hundred head of beeves in order to sell them to a fella by the name of Mr. Davencourt. Unless you are blind, you saw us bringin' them in a while ago. We took up the whole street, we did."

"Yes indeed, I did see the herd being brought in," the clerk said. "Mr. Davencourt you say. Well, Mr. Davencourt has been a hotel guest for nearly a month now. And Mr. Jensen stayed in our hotel the last time he was in town. I shall be very pleased to put him up again."

"And a tub and some hot water," a voice said from the lobby.

"I beg your pardon?" the clerk replied.

"We want us a tub and some soap and some hot water," Cal said. "I aim to get myself all spiffed up."

"Sir, I am serving this gentleman now," the clerk said.

Pearlie chuckled. "That's all right," he said. "This here is Cal. He's my pard."

"A tub of hot water, very good sir, I shall see to it," the hotel clerk said.

By the time Van Arndt and the others rode into Frisco, the cattle Smoke, Pearlie, and Cal had driven from Sugarloaf filled the feeder lot to near capacity. Van Arndt and the men with him rode down to the fence that held the milling cattle, then stopped to look over into the pen.

"That's quite a large herd, isn't it?" a man sitting on the top rail of the fence asked. He was one of the stock handlers. "Why, it'll take three trains to ship 'em all back to Kansas City."

"It's a lot of cows, all right," Van Arndt said.

"Yes, sir, fifteen hundred head. I know this because I counted them myself," the stock handler said. "They was brought in this morning by just three men. Can you believe that? Just three men drove this entire herd."

"Yeah, I can believe it," Keno said. "This is Smoke Jensen's herd, ain't it?"

"It is indeed Mr. Jensen's herd. Why do you ask? Do you ride for him?"

"There is no way in hell I would ride for that son of a bitch."

The smile left the man's face.

"You know Smoke Jensen, do you?" the man asked.

"Yeah, I know the son of a bitch. I don't like him, but I know him."

"Well, mister, I don't know what's put the burr under your saddle, but here in Frisco, we're sort of partial to the man."

"Are you now?" Keno said.

"Yes, sir. You may not know it, but there was a bank robbery here a week or so ago, and Smoke Jensen stopped it near about single-handed."

"Yeah? Well, I guess that makes him a hero then," Keno said.

The stockman chuckled. "Funny, though, because as it turns out now, a lot of the money he saved that day was his own."

"What do you mean?"

"Well, sir, he was paid forty-five thousand dollars for these cows. Can you imagine that? One man havin' forty-five thousand dollars."

"That's a lot of cash for a fella to be carryin'," Van Arndt said.

The stockman chuckled. "Yes, sir, I suppose it would be," he said. "Only thing is, he ain't bein' paid in cash."

"He ain't bein' paid in cash?" Boswell asked.

"No, sir, not a dollar of it."

"Well, just how the hell is he bein' paid?" Boswell asked.

"By bank draft, of course," the stockman said. "That's how it is always done when there's a whole lot of money. You see, that way the money is safe."

"What do you mean, the money is safe?"

"Well, say a fella is carring forty-five thousand dollars in cash," the stockman explained. "Someone could rob him and have all that money to spend," The stockman held up his finger. "But now say he's carryin' a bank draft. A bank draft is made out to one man and he's the only one that can take it to a bank and cash it. So even if a robber was to steal the bank draft, it wouldn't do him no good. It would just be a worthless piece of paper as far he is concerned. And the one who got robbed could just go back to the bank and get another one."

"I'll be damn," Boswell said.

"Yeah," Jeeter added, his words colored by his frustration. "I'll be damn."

Chapter Thirteen

When Cal went back into the mercantile store he was bathed, shaved, and wearing clean clothes. He smiled when the same young woman who greeted him earlier returned to welcome him again.

"Yes, sir," the young woman said pleasantly. "May I help—" She stopped in mid-sentence. "You are the young man who was in here earlier today, aren't you?"

"Yes, ma'am."

"I don't understand. Why did you leave with such haste?"

"I was embarrassed," Cal said.

"Embarrassed? Whatever for?"

"'Cause I was so filthy," Cal said. "Why, if Sally had seen me go into a store lookin' like I was lookin', she would'a turned me out for sure."

"I see," the young woman said. "This Sally, is she your wife?"

Cal laughed. "No, ma'am, she ain't my wife."

"Your girlfriend then?"

Cal laughed again. "No, ma'am, she ain't that neither. She's the wife of my boss. In fact, you could near 'bout say she is my boss, seein' as she does near 'bout as much bossin' around the ranch as Smoke does. If truth be told, miss, I have to confess that I ain't got me no girlfriend."

"Why, I can hardly believe that," the young woman said with a flirtatious smile. "Are you telling me that a handsome and adventurous young man like you doesn't have a girlfriend? Why, I would think the girls would just be all over you."

"Yes, ma'am, that's what I would think, too," Cal said. "But here is the thing that maybe you can help me with. I went to me a dance back in Big Rock, that's where I live. Well, not exactly Big Rock, truth is I live out on Sugarloaf, which is the name of Smoke Jensen's ranch. I cowboy for Smoke."

"Smoke Jensen? Oh, how exciting!" the shopgirl said, interrupting Cal's train of thought. "Why, everyone in town is talking about how brave he was to face down those bank robbers the way he did."

Cal smiled. "Yes, ma'am, well, that's just the kind of thing Smoke does all the time."

"And you cowboy for him?"

"Yes, ma'am, only, it's a little more than cowboyin'."

"What do you mean?"

"I mean, Smoke isn't just my boss, he is also my friend. He is Pearlie's friend also. Pearlie is the only other cowboy who works for him full time."

The young girl shook her head. "That's all the more reason I find it difficult to believe that the young women of Big Rock haven't all set their cap for you."

"Yes, ma'am, well, that brings me back to what I was tellin' you. I went to me this dance back in Big Rock, and met a feller there who told me that I need to wear somethin' that would cause the girls to look at me. He said it should be somethin' like a belt buckle, or a fancy red kerchief, or maybe a fancy hatband. What do you think about that?"

"Why, I think that would be a wonderful idea," the young woman said. "Yes, sir, all you need is something that would add just a little dash to get the attention of the girls."

"Which one of them ideas do you think would be best?" Cal asked. "The belt buckle, the fancy red kerchief, or the fancy hatband?"

"Well, any one of them would do," the young woman replied. "But I think the hatband would be best, and it just so happens that we've got a particularly beautiful one in stock that I think would be just perfect for you."

"Can I see it?" Cal asked.

"Of course you can," the young woman replied. "I have it right here."

Reaching down to the table, the young woman moved a few things around, she produced a silver hatband.

"Let me see your hat," she said.

Cal handed his hat to her and, with a slight adjustment, she slipped the hatband into position, then put the hat on Cal's head. Crossing her left arm across her waist, she cupped her right elbow.

She placed her right hand alongside her cheek, then tipped her head to one side as she studied Cal.

"Turn just a little to your left," she asked.

Cal did as instructed.

"Now, turn back to the right."

Again, Cal turned.

"Oh, my, how handsome you are in that," she said. "You simply must buy that hatband. Why, with it, you can't help but turn the head of every young woman in the county."

"How much is it?" Cal asked.

"It's only thirty dollars."

Cal blanched.

"Thirty dollars?" he asked. "Are you saying this silver hatband is going to cost me thirty dollars?"

"Yes," the young woman replied.

"I don't know. That seems awfully expensive."

"Oh, but you must believe me. It is well worth thirty dollars," the young woman said. "Why, when you wear that, it brings out your eyes just so. I swear if I don't think you are about the most handsome boy I've ever seen."

"Really?"

"Really. But be careful with it. You don't want to break too many hearts now. That wouldn't be very nice of you. And I don't think you really want to do that now, do you?"

"No, ma'am, I don't reckon I would like to break any girl's heart," Cal said. "That wouldn't be very gentlemanly of me." He took the hat off and examined the band. "It sure is a pretty thing."

"I think it is the most beautiful thing we have in the store," the young woman said enthusiastically.

"I reckon it is. It's just that it costs so much money," Cal said.

"Is that what's bothering you? How much money it costs?" the girl asked "What if I told you that you don't have to worry about that at all."

"I don't?"

"Not at all."

"Why do you say that I won't have to worry?"

"It's very simple really," the young woman explained. "Because the truth is, if you buy this band, you will still have your money."

"What do you mean I'll still have my money? I don't understand how that can be."

"Well, think about it," the young lady said. "If you are ever in financial difficulty and need money, you can always sell this to someone and recover every cent you paid for it. In fact, this is so reasonably priced that you might even get more than you paid for it. And that makes it just like money in the bank, only better. Your money just sits in a bank. With this, you'll be able to use the money, even as you are saving it."

"Yeah," Cal said. He repositioned the silver hatband. A big smile spread across his face. "Yeah, you're right. It ain't as if I'm spendin' the money a'tall, is it? It's kind of like I'm savin' it, but I'm usin' at the same time, just like you said."

"Exactly."

"All right, miss, I'll take it." Cal put the hat back on.

"Oh, wait," the young woman said, reaching up

to the hat. "Wear it like this. You are the kind of person who should wear his hat at a rakish angle."

"Rakish angle?"

"Yes," the young woman said. "You are definitely a rakish angle kind of person." She picked up a mirror and held it in front of him. "Here, take a look so you can see for yourself."

Cal looked at himself from a head-on view, then turned to the left, then to the right as he studied his image.

"Yes," he said. "I see what you mean."

Smiling, Pearlie sneaked back out of the mercantile store, unnoticed by Cal. He had started across the street toward the saloon when he saw some men riding out of town. He wouldn't have given them a second thought, except that he thought he recognized two of them. He couldn't be certain, because he was unable to see their faces, as they were riding away. But from their build, and they way they were sitting their horses, he believed that it was Keno and Jeeter. Pearlie stood there for a long moment, looking at the men as rode away, hoping that one or more of them would turn his face so he could see him. No one did.

"What you lookin' at?" Cal asked.

Turning, Pearlie saw his young friend standing beside him.

"Those riders," Pearlie said.

"What riders?"

"Those men, I thought I—" Pearlie paused. Looking toward the end of the street, Pearlie saw the riders were no longer in view, having already gone around the corner. "Never mind," he said. "It seems pretty unlikely they would actually be here. Not after the stampede."

"Are you all right?" Cal asked.

"Yes, of course I'm all right. Why do you ask?"

"You was just actin' funny, is all," Cal said.

"It was probably nothing."

"Ahemm," Cal said, clearing his throat. Reaching up, he thumped the brim of his hat.

Pearlie saw the silver band around his hat, and he knew that Cal was waiting for him to reply, but he showed no sign that he had seen it.

"Ahemm," Cal said again.

"You got a frog in your throat?"

"No, I ain't got no frog in my throat. Why do you ask?"

"You seem to be clearing your throat a lot."

"Ahem," Cal said again, thumping his hat.

"Come on, let's get us a beer," Pearlie said. "I'm pretty sure that will clear up your throat."

"A beer sounds good, but there ain't nothin' wrong with my throat."

"Really? Well, you can't prove it by me."

As Van Arndt started riding back toward the edge of town, Keno called out to him.

"Hey! Where are you goin'?"

Van Arndt neither answered, nor looked back. Instead, he kept riding toward the edge of town.

The others looked at each other for a moment, then started after him.

Keno caught up to Van Arndt.

"Are you just going to ride away and leave all this money?"

"You heard the fella," Van Arndt said. "There is no money. There is nothing but a worthless piece of paper. It wouldn't do us no good if we did take it. We couldn't spend it."

"Yeah? What if I told you I know a way we could get the money?"

Van Arndt looked over at Keno. "How?"

"It's simple," Keno said. "We find something that Jensen will pay forty-five thousand dollars for."

"You aren't making any sense," Van Arndt said.

"If you knew Jensen as well as I know him, you would know that I'm making a lot of sense," Keno said. "Do you want to hear the idea or not?"

"Yeah," Van Arndt said. "I want to hear the idea."

"It's simple really," Keno said. "All we have to do is snatch his wife. Jensen will do anything to get her back. You want the forty five thousand dollars? Tell Jensen to cash that bank draft and bring the money to us."

"Where is his wife now?"

"Like as not she's at Sugarloaf, Jensen's ranch," Keno said.

"How many are on the ranch?"

"Ah, that's the good part of it," Keno said. "Just before Jensen left on the cattle drive, he fired all the cowboys he had workin' for him. And since he took Pearlie and Cal with him, that don't leave nobody back at the ranch but a bunch of Mexicans, most of 'em too old to do anything. Hell, we can walk in there and take her without no trouble a'tall. Onliest thing is, if we're goin' to do this, we need to do it right now. We need to get back to Sugarloaf before Jensen does."

"All right, Keno, I'll go along with your plan," Van Arndt said. "But there better be no surprises."

"There won't be none if we can get to Sugarloaf afore Jensen does," Keno said.

Turning in his saddle, Van Arndt saw the others riding behind him. The men were dispirited over not being able to steal either the herd or the money.

"Gather round, boys," Van Arndt said. "Keno has come up with a plan that I think may work."

"What plan is that?" Peters asked.

"Tell them," Van Arndt said.

Smiling at his newfound sense of importance, Keno explained his idea of going to Sugarloaf to take Sally Jensen prisoner and hold her for ransom.

"Yeah!" Jeeter said. "And maybe we can have a little fun with her! I'm tellin' you the truth, boys, Jensen's wife is one of the best lookin' women I've ever seen. Yeah, that is a great idea."

"We're not taking her to have fun with her," Keno said.

"What do you mean? You plan to let that just go to waste?"

"Keno is right," Van Arndt said. "If we are going to hold her for ransom, then we can't do nothing with her."

"That don't make no sense at all," Jeeter said. "As long as we've got her, we may as well use her."

"I agree with Jeeter," Shardeen said.

"We ain't goin' to touch her," Van Arndt insisted. "After we get the money, you'll have enough money to buy any whore in Colorado. Hell, you can buy half a dozen whores if you want to."

Peters laughed. "Half a dozen whores! Lord, wouldn't that be a kick now?"

"Yeah," Boswell said. "I don't care how good lookin' the Jensen woman is, she ain't worth half a dozen whores. I say we don't do anything that might cause the whole thing to go sour."

"All right, all right," Jeeter said. "I'll go along with the rest of you. But you wait until you see her. You'll know what I'm talking about then."

"If you boys are through discussing this, it's time we made a few plans," Van Arndt said dryly.

"Yeah, whatever you say," Shardeen said.

"Good. Shardeen, when we get to Gunsight Pass, I want you to climb up to the top and wait on Jensen."

"When I see them, do you want me to come catch up with you?" Shardeen asked.

Van Arndt shook his head. "No," he said. "That would be too late. I want you to hold him up."

"Hold him up? How?"

"Just start shootin' at him," Van Arndt said. "Don't kill him. We wouldn't want to kill the goose that lays the golden eggs now, would we?" Van Arndt asked with a chuckle.

"Let me get this straight. You want me to get into a gunfight with Jensen, but you don't want me to kill him?"

"I didn't say nothing about a gunfight," Van Arndt said. "All I want you to do is get up on top of the pass. When they start through, you shoot at them. Get close enough to make them scramble. Then, all you have to do is keep their heads down for a little while. Then, sneak on out of there and come catch up with us."

"Where will you be? At Jensen's ranch?"

"No. I tell you what, you meet us at the east end of Hardscabble Saddle Pass," Van Arndt said. "By then we'll already have the woman and all we have to do is get through the pass, then wait for Jensen to pay off."

"All right," Shardeen said. He started chuckling.

"What are you laughing at?" Van Arndt asked.

"Half a dozen whores," Shardeen replied. He reached down to rub himself. "Damn, I like that."

"Now, Shardeen, just tell me what the hell you think you can do with six women," Peters said.

"I'm not exactly sure," Shardeen replied. "But damn me if I ain't willin' to give it a try and see how it all comes out."

Chapter Fourteen

Pearlie and Cal met Smoke for supper at the Mama Lou's Café. Supper consisted of steak and beans, with the beans being liberally seasoned with hot peppers. They washed the meal down with mugs of beer.

"Those beans will set you afire," Pearlie said. "But I'll be damned if they ain't about the tastiest things I've ever put in my mouth."

"Ha," Cal said. "I'm sure Miss Sally will love hearin' that some beans you et at a café was better'n anything she can cook."

Pearlie pointed his fork across the table at Cal. "Now, I didn't say no such thing and you know it," he said.

"You said they was about the tastiest things you ever put into your mouth."

"Well, I didn't mean 'ever,'" Pearlie corrected. "I was just pointin' out that they was good beans, that's all."

"Well, you et 'em so damn fast, I don't know how you was able to taste 'em in the first place," Cal said.

"Hey, Smoke, you got that bank draft you said you was goin' to get?" Pearlie asked.

"What bank draft?" Smoke replied, teasing.

"You know what bank draft. The one that says forty-five thousand dollars."

"Yeah, I got it."

"Can I see it? I'd just like to see what that much money looks like."

Smoke pulled a folded piece of paper from his shirt pocket and handed it to Pearlie.

"That's it?" Pearlie asked, his face registering his disappointment. "This little piece of paper is all there is to it?"

"What did you expect it to be?"

"I don't know. I guess I figured it would be some sort of certificate with fancy writin' on it," Pearlie said. "I mean it's forty-five thousand dollars for cryin' out loud. What would it hurt for them to make it look real elegant?"

Smoke chuckled. "Oh, the writing is fancy enough," he said. "It says forty-five thousand dollars. Take a look at it."

Pearlie unfolded the paper and examined it.

"Whooee. That's a lot of money!" Pearlie said. He smiled. "And you're right. It bein' forty-five thousand dollars makes it fancy enough."

"Let me see it," Cal said, and Pearlie passed the paper over to him.

"I've never seen this much money in my life," Cal said.

"You ain't seein' it now," Pearlie said. "All you're seein' is a piece of paper."

"Yeah, but I ain't never even seen a piece of paper with this much money on it," Cal said.

"There's a nice bonus in there for everyone who works at the ranch," Smoke said, taking the draft back.

Pearlie shook his head. "Good, they deserve it," he said. "Juan, Carlos, and those other boys work their tails off for you."

"That bonus includes the two of you," Smoke said. "Especially you two."

"Smoke, you don't have to do that," Cal said. "We're not like all them others. We're more like—" He stopped as if afraid he was about to go too far.

"Family?" Smoke said.

"Well, yeah. I wasn't exactly goin' to come out and say it, but yeah, that's the way I look at it."

"I look at it that way, too," Smoke said. "Maybe that's why I want to do it. Fact is, I plan to give the two of you so much money that you could go out on your own if you wanted to."

"Damn, Smoke, you runnin' us away?" Pearlie asked jokingly.

Smoke laughed. "Hardly," he said. "I just hope that by this, I can show you boys how important you two are to me. And how much I trust you to stay around, even when you don't have to."

"I ain't goin' nowhere till the day they carry me out in a pine box," Pearlie said.

"Me neither," Cal added.

Mama Lou walked over to the table then. "Did you boys enjoy your supper?" she asked.

"Yes, ma'am, we did," Pearlie said. "I was just

tellin' Smoke here how good them beans was. Wasn't I, Smoke?"

"You were in fact," Smoke agreed.

"Are you ready for dessert?"

"Smoke, you think we could get us a piece of that there black and blue pie?"

"Blackberry and blueberry," Smoke said. "That sounds mighty good to me."

"Me, too," Pearlie said.

"Mama Lou, bring us three pieces," Smoke said.

"And, uh, could you maybe make 'em large pieces?" Pearlie asked.

"I'll see what I can do," Mama Lou said, smiling as she took the empty plates away from their table.

"Ahem," Cal said, clearing his throat. Reaching up to the brim of his hat, he repositioned it.

"What time you want to pull out in the morning, Smoke?" Pearlie asked, purposely ignoring Cal.

"We'll leave just before daylight tomorrow morning," Smoke said. "A good steady ride will get us back home by mid-afternoon."

"It'll be good to get back," Pearlie said. "Oh, by the way, did you send Miss Sally a telegram tellin' her that we got here and how much money you got and everything?"

"I sent the telegram first thing," Smoke said. "I'm pretty sure she has received it by now."

Pearlie smiled broadly. "Good," he said. "That means for sure we will have some fresh bear sign waitin' for us when we get back," Pearlie said.

"What makes you think that?" Cal asked.

"Because she'll be so excited that she'll want to

celebrate," Pearlie said. "Don't you think that's right, Smoke?"

"I wouldn't doubt it," Smoke agreed.

"Ahem," Cal said again. Once more, he repositioned his hat.

"What we should'a done is, we should'a brung us along a sack full of them bear sign," Pearlie said, still ignoring Cal's hints.

"Ahem!" Cal said again, "coughing" louder this time than at any previous time.

"Cal, you really do need to do something about that cough, boy, it's beginning to get on my nerves," Pearlie said.

"I ain't got no cough," Cal said.

"Really? Well, you can't prove it by me. Smoke, do you know anything about gettin' rid of a cough? Ole Cal here's been coughin' now for the better part of an hour."

"Why don't you buy you a piece of horehound candy?" Smoke said. "That always works for me."

"Don't worry about it," Cal said. "It'll go away on its own, I reckon."

Cal was clearly agitated that neither Smoke nor Pearlie had noticed his silver hatband. What was the use of getting the thing if no one noticed?

When the pie was delivered, Smoke and Cal began eating, but Pearlie hesitated for a moment.

"What's the matter?" Smoke asked. "Is there something wrong with your pie?"

"Something wrong with my pie?" Pearlie replied. He took a bite. "No, there's nothing wrong with it. It's delicious. Why do you ask?"

"Why do I ask? Pearlie, you are normally the first one to start eating and the last one to finish. But here Cal and I have our pie half finished and you've only taken one bite."

"Yes, well, uh, Smoke, I have something important I want to ask you, and I been thinkin' about it."

"It must be important if it has put you off your appetite," Smoke said.

"Oh, well, it ain't done that," Pearlie replied. "I mean, I can still eat as well as I ever could. But—well, it's about Miss Goodnature."

"What about her?"

"Lucy Goodnature," Pearlie said.

"Yes, Ian's daughter, I know who you are talking about," Smoke said. "What about her?"

"Well, I like her, that's what about her," Pearlie said.

Cal laughed out loud.

"What?" Pearlie asked. "What are you laughin' at?"

"Hell, Pearlie, next thing you know, you'll be tellin' us that you're wearin' a red shirt," Cal said.

"I *am* wearin' a red shirt," Pearlie said. "Which is plain to see if you just take a look." Pearlie was quiet for a moment. "Oh," he said. "Oh, I think I see what you are talking about. Is it really that obvious?"

"It's pretty obvious," Cal said.

"I can see why you like her, Pearlie," Smoke said. "She is a beautiful young woman and, from what I know about her, she is about as nice a young lady as you'll find in the entire state."

"Yes, but her dad owns Crosshatch."

"I know Ian owns Crosshatch. It's a neighboring ranch to Sugarloaf," Smoke said.

"Don't you see what I'm getting at?" Pearlie asked. "How am I going to ask her to marry me if she is the daughter of a rancher and I am just a cowboy?"

"Marry you?" Cal asked, almost choking on a piece of pie. "Has it gone that far?"

"Maybe," Pearlie said. Then, with a sigh, he dismissed the idea. "No, that's foolish."

"Yeah," Smoke said. "Why, that's almost as foolish as a young gunfighter on the run marrying a school-teacher from one of the wealthiest families in New Hampshire."

"That's different," Pearlie said. Both he and Cal knew all the details of Smoke and Sally's courtship and marriage.

"How is it different?" Smoke asked.

"For one thing, you are you," Pearlie said.

"And you are you," Smoke replied. "Look, Pearlie, I don't know what you want. Do you want me to talk you out of it?"

"What? No, no," Pearlie said.

"You are a good man, Pearlie. I think any father of a young woman would be pleased to have you as a son-in-law."

Pearlie smiled broadly. "It's too bad Lucy isn't your daughter. Then I could be your son-in-law."

"Don't push it," Smoke said. "I'm not willing to go that far."

It was obvious that Smoke was teasing, and all three laughed.

"The only thing is, you haven't told me what you

think I should do," Pearlie said, continuing the conversation.

"Pearlie, on something like this, you have to be your own man," Smoke said. "Just know this. Whatever decision you make, I'll be behind you one hundred per cent."

"Me, too," Cal said.

"Are you going to ask her to marry you?" Smoke asked.

Pearlie thought for a moment, then nodded. "Yeah," he said. "Yeah, I think I will."

"When?" Cal wanted to know.

"As soon as we get back," Pearlie said.

"I know that you will probably have Smoke as your best man," Cal said. "But I want to do something in your wedding."

"Actually, I was sort of thinkin' you would be my best man, Cal," Pearlie said. "I was figurin' on Smoke marryin' us."

"Smoke marryin' you?" Cal said.

"Why not? He's a justice of the peace. That means you can marry people, right, Smoke?"

Smoke chuckled. "Yes," he said. "Yes, I suppose it does. I've never married anyone before, but I can do it."

"Would you marry me and Lucy?"

"I would be honored to do it," Smoke said.

"And you'll be my best man, Cal?"

"Yes, of course I will. And I thank you for askin' me."

"Then it's all set. All I need now is for Lucy to say yes. And I'm real glad both of you have agreed to be in the weddin'," he said. "I don't believe anyone has ever had friends as good as you two."

"So," Cal said reaching across the table. "Does that mean you'll share your pie with me?"

"Not on your life," Pearlie said taking another bite of his still mostly uneaten piece of pie. "Friendship only goes so far, you know."

Smoke and Cal laughed.

Chapter Fifteen

Sunrise couldn't be seen because of the range of mountains that lay to the east, but its effect was obvious so that when Smoke, Pearlie, and Cal left Frisco, the sky was the dove gray of a soft dawn. By the time the sun did appear over the mountains, a hot, dry wind moved through the canyon, pushing before it a billowing puff of red dust. The cloud of dust lifted high and spread out wide, making it look as if there was blood on the sun. The three men had ridden in relative silence for the most of the morning. Now Pearlie broke the silence.

"Hey, Smoke," Pearlie said. "Did you know that when we get back, Cal is going to turn the head of every young woman in the county?"

"Is he now?" Smoke asked.

Pearlie chuckled. "Sure 'nough, that's what he's goin' to do. He's goin' to turn the head of every young woman in the county. And he's goin' to break a lot of hearts, too."

"Watch it, Pearlie," Cal cautioned.

"I don't know what you are talking about," Smoke said.

"Well, just take a look at that fancy silver hatband Cal bought back in Frisco, and you'll see what I'm talkin' about."

"Wait a minute!" Cal said. "Pearlie, are you tellin' me you knew about my fancy silver hatband, but you didn't say anything about it?" Cal asked.

"Oh, yeah, I knew about it."

"How come you didn't—" Cal stopped in mid-sentence. "Wait a minute! How'd you know about my turnin' the heads of all the girls in the county?"

"Well, now, Cal, ain't that what that pretty little girl said when she smiled at you and suckered you into buyin' that hatband?"

"She didn't sucker me into it," Cal said. "I went in there to buy it. You was there, wasn't you? You was in the store."

Pearlie chuckled, then mimicked the young girl, speaking in falsetto. "Why, you ain't really spendin' your money. When you buy this silver hatband, it's the same as if you're just puttin' it in a bank."

"I knew it. You was in the store all the time, spyin' on me."

"I wasn't spying, I was just—" Pearlie paused. "Well, all right, I reckon I was spyin' on you just a little bit, but that's only because I didn't want you to go off doin' somethin' foolish."

"Yeah, well, I don't need you motherin' me," Cal replied. He took his hat off and held the band so that it flashed in the sun. "And I don't care what you say, I like it," he said.

"Why don't you show it to Smoke?" Pearlie suggested.

"Smoke's got more important things to do than look at my hatband," Cal answered.

"What's important about just ridin'?" Pearlie asked. "That's all we're doin' now. Come on, show it to him."

"Ah, it ain't nothin'," Cal said.

Pearlie laughed. "The reason he don't want you to see it, Smoke, is 'cause he figures to get all gussied up for all the girls back in Big Rock and he's embarrassed."

"I am not embarrassed," Cal said.

"Then why don't you show it to him?"

There was no closer friendship than the one between Pearlie and Cal, but that friendship did not prevent Pearlie from teasing Cal at every opportunity, and his bantering with the young cowboy now about the silver hatband was an example of that.

"Do you want to see it, Smoke?" Cal asked.

"Sure," Smoke answered.

Cal held his hat out so Smoke could see it it. "This here one is just plain silver," he said. "I could'a got one that had lots of turquoise on it, but that would have been too ostentatious."

"Ostentatious?" Pearlie said. He let out a whooping laugh. "It would have been too ostentatious? Where in the world did you come up with a word like that?"

"Miss Sally taught it to me," Cal said. "Ostentatious means when you are showin' off."

"Well, hell, Cal, what do you reckon you'll be doin' when you go into that dance hall wearin' that shiny band on your hat if it ain't showin' off?" Pearlie asked.

Suddenly, the peaceful banter was shattered when Smoke heard a bullet pop by his ear, then ricochet off a nearby rock to fill the little canyon with its whine. The sound of a rifle shot reverberated down through the canyon.

"Son of a bitch! Someone's shooting at us!" Pearlie shouted.

The three men had been under fire many times before, so they wasted no time asking what was going on or looking at each other in confusion. They knew exactly what was going on, and they knew what to do about it. Simultaneously, they pulled their rifles out of the saddle sheaths, then dismounted and slapped their horses on the rumps to send them out of the line of fire.

"He's up there," Smoke said, pointing to the top of the denuded wall of the red mesa. When Pearlie and Cal looked in the direction Smoke was pointing, they saw a little puff of smoke drifting away.

"Yeah, I see him," Pearlie said.

Even as they were looking, there was another puff of smoke, another bullet striking rock near them, followed a fraction of a second later by the sound of the rifle shot.

"There's only one way we're going to get him out of there," Smoke said.

"I sure hope you ain't about to say what I think you're about to say," Pearlie said.

"We're going to have to climb up there after him."

"Damnit, I knew you was goin' to say that," Pearlie said.

"One of us can climb up after him—the other

two can take up a position in those rocks over there," Smoke said, pointing to a collection of boulders that was located near the base of the cliff.

"One of us is going to have to climb up?" Pearlie asked.

"That's the only way."

"Smoke, you know I can't climb up that wall. I'm afraid of heights," Pearlie said.

"I'll go," Cal said. "I'm a good climber."

Another round whizzed by them.

"No," Smoke said. "I'll go. You and Pearlie get into those rocks over there."

"You sure?" Cal asked.

"I'm sure."

Pearlie took a deep breath, then let it out slowly. "Come on, Cal, it ain't goin' to be all that easy gettin' across there," he said. Without another word, he started running toward the rocks Smoke had pointed out.

"Ooooooh shit!" he yelled as the bullets popped and whined, kicking up dirt all around him. Finally, with a dive that covered the last five yards, Pearlie made it to the rocks. Cal dived in right behind him.

"What kept you so long?" Pearlie teased.

"I stopped to take a leak," Cal said with a little relieved laugh. "What now?" he asked.

"We let Smoke know we made it all right."

"Hell, he was watchin' us. You think he don't know we made it?" Cal asked.

Pearlie stood up, then looked back toward Smoke, giving him a little wave to let him know that they were ready. Smoke nodded back at them.

"All right," Pearlie said. Jacking a round into the chamber of his Winchester, Pearlie raised up and began firing up toward whoever had been shooting at them.

"Who are you shooting at?" Cal asked. "I don't see anyone!"

Pearlie fired again, then cocked his rifle. "It don't matter whether we see anyone or not," he said. He fired again. "All we're doin' now is keepin' the bastard down so as to give Smoke some cover."

"Yeah," Cal said. He jacked a shell into his own rifle. "Yeah, I can see that," he said. Raising up, he fired toward the top of the mesa where he had last seen gun smoke.

Back on the other side of the little open area, Smoke looked around, then saw a possible way up the side of the canyon wall. He followed it with his eyes and saw that it led all the way to the top. Also, except for a few gaps, it appeared to offer cover and concealment for anyone who might climb it. It was obvious that the assailant had not noticed it, or he would not have taken the position he now occupied. That's because if Smoke could successfully negotiate the climb, he would be on top of the mesa . . . behind the shooter.

Smoke realized, though, that "if" was the operative word. It was not at all certain that he would be able to make it all the way to the top.

Smoke began to climb. Although the route had looked passable from the ground, climbing it proved to be very difficult. Smoke had been at it for nearly half an hour, and it didn't seem as if he were any closer to the top. However, when he looked back toward the ground, he could see that he was making progress, for by now he was dangerously high.

All the time he was climbing, he could hear the steady exchange of gunfire between Pearlie and Cal and whoever it was that attacked them.

Smoke clung to the side of the mountain and moved only when he had a secure handhold or foothold . . . tiny though it might be. Sweat poured into his eyes and he grew thirsty with the effort, but still he climbed. Then he came to a complete stop. There was no place to go from there. Although he had seen this gap from his observation on the ground, he had not realized that it would totally impassable.

"Damn," he swore, under his breath, looking around. "Now what?"

From his position behind the rocks, Cal saw Smoke's predicament.

"Damn, he's stopped," Cal said.

"What?"

"Smoke. He's stopped climbin'."

"I don't blame him," Pearlie said. "I wouldn't of got that far."

"He's reached a place where he's run out of foot and handholds," Cal said. "He can't go any further."

"Well, I hope he's got better sense than to keep on tryin'," Pearlie said. "He needs to come down now."

"He ain't goin' to do that," Cal said. "You know

Smoke. He's goin' to keep tryin' till he makes it up, or gets hisself killed tryin'."

"Yeah, that's what I'm worried about, the 'gettin' hisself killed' part," Pearlie said.

"I see a way," Cal said.

"Where?"

"He's goin' to have to come back down a bit, then go up to his right," Cal said. "Only thing is, from where he is now, there's no way he can see it."

"Maybe he'll see it," Pearlie said.

Cal shook his head. "Nope, ain't no way he can see it from there. I'm going to have to point it out to him."

"Point it out to him? Wait a minute, you ain't talkin' about goin' up there with him, are you?"

"No," Cal said. "If I can get him to look at me, I can point to it from here."

"You want him to look at you?"

"Yeah, but he's still tryin' to figure out a way to go on from there."

"Get ready to point," Pearlie said. He raised his rifle to his shoulder and took careful aim.

"Pearlie, what the hell are you doing?"

"Just get ready to point," Pearlie said. He squeezed the trigger.

The bullet hit the wall about two feet away from Smoke. The impact of the bullet carved away tiny stone fragments, some of which peppered his face.

"What the hell?" Smoke said aloud, wondering where the shot had come from. Looking around, he saw a puff of smoke drifting up from the rocks where

Pearlie and Cal had taken cover. Then he saw Cal stand up and wave at him.

For a moment, Smoke wondered what Cal was doing. Then he saw that Cal was making a motion with his hand, indicating that Smoke should come back down a little ways, then go up by a different route. Cal pointed it out to him.

Smoke waved back at him, then started back down the path he had just climbed. After a few minutes, another bullet slammed into the wall beside him and, looking back, he saw Cal pointing again. Looking around, he saw another chute going up, and he knew this was what Cal meant.

Smoke started up this chute, and though the going was very difficult, he was managing to climb again. Above him was nothing but the uninviting rock face of the cliff. Below him was a sheer drop of more than 150 feet to the rocky canyon floor.

Smoke continued his climb, working hard to find the handholds and tiny crevices by which he could advance. Sweat poured into his eyes and slickened the palms of his hands, but still he climbed. He reached for a small slate outcropping, but as he put his weight on it, it failed. With a sickening sensation in his stomach, he felt himself falling.

"Pearlie—he fell!" Cal said in a shocked voice.

Smoke's stomach leaped into his throat as he started to fall and, reflexively, he reached out to grab the first thing he could. It was a juniper tree. With one hand, he managed to grab the tree and stop his fall. He was slammed against the wall, feeling the rocks scrape and tear at his flesh. He flailed against the wall with his other hand until he managed to get a hold.

"It's all right! He caught ahold of that tree!" Pearlie said in relief.

Smoke stayed in place for a moment or two, then, catching his breath, began to climb again. After two minutes of climbing, it began to get a little easier, then easier still, until finally he reached a ledge that showed signs of having been a trail at one time, possibly a trail that had existed until erosion took the bottom part of it away. The trail improved and widened until he could walk upright. Shortly after that, he made it to the top.

Smoke saw the assailant then, no more than twenty-five yards away from him, peering down toward the canyon floor, totally unaware than Smoke had reached the top.

"Enjoying the view?" Smoke asked casually.

"What the hell?" the gunman gasped, spinning around. He stood up.

The two men stood on top of the mesa, silhouetted against the brilliant blue sky. Because the assailant had been using his rifle, he had his pistol holstered. Smoke's pistol was holstered as well, and for a moment the two formed an eerie tableau, a moment frozen in eternity.

"Who are you?" Smoke asked.

"The name is Shardeen."

"Why were you trying to kill us, Shardeen?"

"Wasn't aimin' to kill you. All I wanted to do was hold you up for a while so as to keep you from getting home right away." the gunman said.

"You wanted to keep us from getting home?" Smoke replied, his face mirroring his confusion. "Why would you want to do that?"

"To give Van Arndt time to snatch your woman," Shardeen said. He smiled. "I've done my job. By now, we've done took her, and I reckon you'll pay plenty to get her back."

"Snatch my woman?" Smoke said. "Are you talking about Sally?"

"Is that her name? Sally?" The assailant smiled, though the smile merely exaggerated his bulging eyes, making his visage even more evil. "Well, now, that's a right pretty name. Yes, sir, it is. But then I've heard she's a real pretty woman. So I expect you'll pay purt' near any amount of money we ask for just to get her back now, won't you?"

"It won't make any difference to you whether I pay or not," Smoke said.

The smile left Shardeen's face. "What do you mean, it won't make any difference to me? What are you talkin' about?" Shardeen smiled again. "Oh, wait a minute, I see what you are tryin' to do. You are tryin' to turn me against Van Arndt by makin' me think he won't give me my share, aren't you? Well, it ain't a'goin' to work."

"It won't make any difference to you whether I pay or not because you'll be in jail," Smoke said.

"In a pig's eye, I'll be in jail. You know better than to try something like that. Don't forget, we've got your woman."

"You're coming to Big Rock with us," Smoke said. "I wouldn't be surprised if Sheriff Carson didn't have some paper on you."

"Haw! You're plannin' on turnin' me in for the reward, are you?" Shardeen asked. "Tell me, Mr. Jensen, are you deaf? The reason I asked is, I told you, we have your woman. Now just think about it for a moment. What do you think is going to happen to your woman if I wind up in jail?"

"You let me worry about that," Smoke said.

"Yeah? Well, worry about this. Van Arndt will kill your woman if you don't cooperate with him. Only, before he kills her, he'll pass her around amongst all the others so ever'one will get their turn with her, if you know what I mean. Now, are you still hell-bent on takin' me into jail?"

"Yes, I am. Come on, let's go."

"Mister, you don't even have your gun out, and you're telling me to come with you?"

"You can come to jail with me now, or die right here," Smoke said. "It's up to you."

"I ain't a'goin' nowhere with you, you son of a bitch!" Shardeen said as he made a desperate grab for his pistol.

"You don't want to do that!" Smoke warned.

Shardeen's gun didn't even break leather before Smoke's gun was out and booming. Smoke's bullet hit Shardeen in the chest, and the assailant stood there for a moment, looking on in total surprise. He tried to take a step forward, lost his balance, then fell. Holstering his pistol, Smoke moved quickly to him, then stood, looking down at him.

"Damn, that hurts," Shardeen wheezed, his voice breaking with pain.

"Where are they taking Sally?" Smoke asked.

"Smoke! Smoke, you all right?" Smoke heard Pearlie's voice calling anxiously.

"Where are they taking her?" Smoke asked again, but even as he was asking the question, he knew that it would go unanswered. The gunman was dead.

"Smoke! Smoke, are you all right?" Pearlie called up again.

Smoke walked over to the edge to call down. "I'm all right, Pearlie. You and Cal round up our horses. I'll be right down."

It took Smoke a lot less time to reach the ground than it had taken him to climb. When he reached the ground, Pearlie and Cal walked over to him. Cal was holding the reins to Smoke's horse.

"Who was that up there?" Cal asked. "What was all that about?"

"The man's name was Shardeen," Smoke replied. "Have either of you ever heard of him?"

"I haven't," Pearlie said, shaking his head.

"Me neither."

"Well, if he wasn't lying, we have to get home, and we need to get there as fast as we can."

"Why?" Pearlie asked.

"According to Shardeen, Van Arndt is going after Sally," Smoke answered.

There were no more questions. All Smoke needed to say to galvanize the others into action was that Sally was in danger. In an instant, the three men were mounted. Then they rode out of the canyon, having to fight hard against the impulse to break into a gallop.

Chapter Sixteen

Sally was on the porch pumping water when she saw the buckboard pull into the yard. Lucy Goodnature was driving.

"Lucy," Sally called out to her. "What a delightful surprise."

"Is it true?" Lucy asked.

"Is what true?"

"Is it true that Pearlie is getting back today? I saw Hodge Deckert in town and he said he had delivered a telegram to you yesterday, saying that Mr. Jensen would be back home today."

Sally laughed. "Well, I guess it's no secret," she said. "Yes, Smoke is due back today."

"And Pearlie will be with him?"

"Well, as far as I know he will be," Sally said. "Would you like to wait here for him?"

"Oh, yes, ma'am, I would love to wait for him," Lucy said. "That is, if you don't mind. If I wouldn't be in the way."

"Of course I don't mind. You wouldn't be in the

way at all," Sally said. "Carlos, would you take care of Lucy's rig? Lucy, I'm baking bear sign for when the men return. Maybe you would like to help me?"

"Oh, yes, I can't think of anything I would rather do." Lucy held out her hand for Carlos to help her down. "*Gracias*, Carlos," she said.

Carlos touched the brim of his hat. "It is my pleasure, Señorita," he replied.

As Lucy climbed down from the buckboard, Maria came running across the yard.

"Señorita Lucy!" Maria called. "*Hola!*"

"*Hola*, Maria," Lucy replied.

"Do you see my new dress?" she asked, twirling around once to model the dress Sally had bought her.

"Oh, how beautiful," Lucy said. Then, smiling at the little girl, she held up her finger and began waving it.

"Oh, wait, I shouldn't be talking to you," she teased.

"Why should you not talk to me?" Maria asked.

"I should not talk to you because you are my competition. I think you are Pearlie's girlfriend."

"No, Señorita, I am not Señor Pearlie's girlfriend. We are just friends!" Maria said, sincere in her denial.

"Are you sure you are just friends? Do you promise that you aren't trying to steal him from me?"

Although Lucy's accusations were softened by a big smile, Maria was taking them seriously.

"I promise I will not try to steal Señor Pearlie from you," Maria said, crossing her heart. "He says he wants to marry me, but I think he is teasing because he knows I am too young. I think it is you he wants to marry."

"Do you think so?"

"*Sí*, I am sure of it," Maria said.

Lucy laughed. "From your lips to God's ear, little one," she said.

"Maria!" Maria's mother called. "Don't be bothering the nice ladies."

"I'm not bothering them, *mamacita*," Maria replied. "I am just talking to them."

"Don't you have some chores to do?" Consuello asked.

"*Sí,*" Maria called back to her mother. "I must go," she said to Lucy and Sally. Then, turning, she ran back across the yard.

"What a delightful child," Lucy said. "I hope that someday I can have—" she paused. "Oh, I shouldn't be so foolish," she said.

"Nonsense," Sally replied. "Why is it foolish to hope to someday have a child as delightful as Maria? She would bring joy to any mother's heart."

"Yes, she would, wouldn't she? I believe you said there was something I could do to help you with your baking?"

"Yes, come on into the kitchen. I'm just ready to take the first batch out," Sally told her.

Sally's kitchen was redolent with the sweet, hot dough and cinnamon aroma of freshly made bear sign. Using several layers of cloth as a hot pad, Sally took a pan out of the oven.

"All right, Lucy, we're ready to put the next pan in," she said, pointing to another baking pan.

The baking pan Sally had mentioned was sitting on the table, filled with puffs of dough and liberally dusted with powdered sugar and cinnamon. Lucy picked it up, then stepped over to the open oven.

"Which rack should I put it on?" Lucy asked. "Top, middle, or bottom?"

"The middle rack is fine."

"I can't thank you enough for allowing me to visit so I could be here when Pearlie returns," Lucy said as she slid the new pan into the oven. "And I thank you also for allowing me to help you with the bear sign, even though I know I am probably more of a bother than I am a help."

"Nonsense. Every time you have come over here you have been a big help and I have appreciated it," Sally replied.

"I know Pearlie likes your bear sign. He has mentioned them to me."

"Ha!" Sally said, closing the door to the oven after Lucy put the new tray in. "Is that what you think? That Pearlie likes them? Honey, *like* isn't the word. Why, I do believe that man could eat every bear sign on that tray and then ask for more," she said, laughing, as she pointed to the ones that had just been removed.

The pastries Sally pointed to had swollen much larger during the baking process and were now golden brown and glistening.

"Oh, these are so beautiful and they smell so good, I can see why Pearlie loves them so," Lucy said as he examined the tray. "I can barely resist trying one myself."

"Well, what makes you think you have to resist?" Sally asked. "One of the best things about being the cook is that it is sometimes necessary to taste something just to make certain it is coming out as it should. Go ahead, eat one."

"Oh, should I?"

"Of course. One of us will have to test them out, to see how good they are. It may as well be you."

"Well, couldn't both of us test them?" Lucy asked.

Sally laughed. "I like the way you think," she said as she reached for the tray.

Lucy picked one of the pastries up and took a bite, then closed her eyes and made an expression of pure joy.

"Oh," she said. "Oh, Sally, this is the most delicious thing I have ever put in my mouth."

"Thank you, dear, I appreciate the compliment," Sally replied. She took a bit. "Uhmm, I know I shouldn't talk about my own baking, but these are particularly good."

"No wonder Pearlie likes them."

Finishing the pastry, Sally licked her fingers, then turned toward the stove. "I had better check the fire." Using a lifter, she picked up one of the eyes and looked down inside at the burning embers. That was when she heard the door open behind her.

"Sally?" Lucy said. Although she spoke only one word, there was something about the strained tone of Lucy's voice that alarmed Sally, and when Sally turned, she saw that three men had come into the kitchen. All three were holding guns.

"Keno," she said, recognizing the cowboy who had ridden for them in the season just passed. "What are you doing here?"

"I'll just bet you thought you'd never see me again, huh?" Keno said.

"Let's just say that it was my fervent hope that I would never see you again."

"Ha. Next you'll be saying that you should have kilt me back in Longmont's saloon, when you had the chance."

"You are right, I should have. But what can I say? We all make mistakes from time to time. Letting you live was one of mine," Sally said. Despite the fact that she was in obvious danger, her voice was agonizingly calm.

One of the three men who had entered the kitchen had pink eyes and skin that was as white as chalk. Sally knew about the albino named Reece Van Arndt, knew that Smoke had had a run-in with him a few years earlier, and remembered Sheriff Carson's warning that he had been released from prison. And although Sally had never seen Van Arndt, this man certainly fit Van Arndt's description.

"And who is this beautiful young lady?" Van Arndt asked, nodding toward Lucy.

"This here is Lucy Goodnature," Keno said. "She's the daughter of a neighboring rancher and, if you ask me, she is a stuck-up little bitch. Pearlie is sweet on her, and from what I can tell, she's sweet on him."

The man with the white skin reached over to touch Lucy, and Lucy reacted with a little gasp of fear.

"Leave the girl alone, Van Arndt," Sally said sternly.

Van Arndt looked toward Sally in surprise, then he smiled. "Well, now, you called me by name. I see that you have heard of me."

"Oh, yes, I have heard of you."

"I am surprised, and I am flattered."

"I wouldn't be flattered if I were you. Not if you knew what I've heard."

Van Arndt chuckled. "And what have you heard, my dear? Have you heard that I am a desperate outlaw?"

"No. I have heard that you are a miserable excuse of a man with less redemptive tissue than a maggot on a gut wagon," she said.

"A maggot on a gut wagon," Miller repeated, laughing out loud. "That's funny. I ain't never heard that expression before."

"Shut up, Miller!" Van Arndt said, glaring at the third man. He turned his attention back to Sally.

"Now, now, now, Mrs. Jensen, is that any way to treat houseguests?" Van Arndt asked. He sniffed. "What is that delicious aroma? Oh, pastries, I see. Aren't you going to serve your guests?"

"You are not my guest, Van Arndt," Sally said. "None of you are, and I'm going to ask all of you to get out of my house now."

Van Arndt shook his head and clucked. "Isn't that just like a woman, givin' orders when she's holdin' the short end of the stick?" Van Arndt took one of the bear sign and took a bite.

"Oh, delicious," he said.

"Those are not for you," Sally said resolutely.

"Now, tell me, little lady. Just how are you going to stop me?" Van Arndt asked. "Keno, take her outside and tie her up. Miller, you take the other one out."

Taking another bite of the pastry, Van Arndt turned and left the kitchen, so that only Keno and Miller remained behind with Sally and Lucy.

Keno put his pistol in his holster, then stepped across the kitchen toward Sally.

"You know, when I look at you, I remember how you stood out on the porch and lorded over all of us at the barbeque. You were the ranch owner's wife, I was just one of the low-life cowboys," Keno said.

"No," Sally said. "The cowboys were all decent men. You were just a lowlife."

"Is that so?" Keno replied. "Well, now, Mrs. Jensen, I reckon you aren't so high-and-mighty now, are you? Come on, you are going to take a little trip with us."

He smiled, and when he did, the broad, ugly smile displayed a mouth full of broken and discolored teeth.

Sally waited until he was very close, then, suddenly and unexpectedly, she shoved the hot stove lid, which was still hanging from the end of the lifter she was holding, into his face.

Keno screamed and put both his hands to his face. As he did so, Sally dropped the lifter and pulled Keno's pistol from his holster and shot the one called Miller. Miller went down and Sally ran to the door, intending to shoot Van Arndt as well, but she stopped as soon as she reached the door.

There, in the backyard of her house, were four men. All four were armed, but it wasn't their superior numbers that stopped her. What had stopped her was the fact that Van Arndt was holding his pistol to the head of the little girl, Maria. Maria's father and mother were standing by looking on as well, their faces reflecting their fear.

"Put the gun down, Mrs. Jensen," Van Arndt said.

When Sally hesitated, Van Arndt cocked his pistol and pressed it harder into Maria's head. "I said put the gun down, unless you want to see me blow this little girl's brains out," he repeated.

"No, don't!" Sally shouted anxiously.

Maria whimpered in fear, but said nothing.

"Please, don't hurt the girl," Sally said. "She is an innocent child, she has done nothing to you."

"This is the last time I am going to ask you. Put—the—gun—down," Van Arndt said again, this time in slow, measured words.

Slowly and carefully, Sally put the pistol on the ground in front of her.

"Maria, don't be frightened," she said to the little girl. "It will be all right. Carlos, Consuela, we are all going to do exactly what they tell me to do. It will be all right. Don't be frightened."

"*Sí, Señora,*" Carlos replied. Carlos was trying to remain calm, but his voice was tight with fear.

"You bitch!" Keno shouted, running out of the house then. His face was red from the hot stove lid. "I'm going to kill you!" He started toward Sally.

"Keno, leave her be!" Van Arndt shouted. "She is no good to us dead!"

"But look at what the bitch did to me!" Keno said angrily, holding his hands up to his red and puffy face.

"That was your own fault," Van Arndt said.

"It hurts," Keno said.

"Go back in the kitchen, find some lard, and smear it on your face," Van Arndt said.

Keno turned back toward the kitchen.

"And check on Miller."

"Miller is dead," Keno called back. "This bitch killed him."

"No, you killed him," Van Arndt said. "The woman wasn't armed, you were. I gave you a simple thing to do and you wound up getting Miller killed and your face burned."

"She—she tricked me," Keno said.

"Uh-huh," Van Arndt said. He looked at one of the other men. "Boswell, since Keno couldn't do it, you tie her up. Tie the other one up, too. We'll take both of them."

"What the hell are we taking both of them for?" Boswell asked.

Van Arndt pointed toward Lucy. "This one will be our insurance," he said.

"Sally!" Lucy called out in fright. Lucy was now standing out on the porch.

Boswell walked up to Sally and dropped a noose around her, then he circled the rope several times, pinning her arms to her side.

"What do you mean you will take us with you? Take us where?" Sally asked. "What do you want with us?"

"Don't ask so many questions," Van Arndt said. "You got a horse in the barn?" Van Arndt asked.

"Yes, of course I do."

Van Arndt looked at Carlos. "You," he said. "Get the woman's horse. Saddle it, and bring it out." He looked over at Lucy. "Get her horse, too."

"She came over in a buckboard, Señor," Carlos said. "She has no horse."

"Then find her one," Van Arndt said angrily.

"*Sí, señor.*"

"What do you want with us?" Sally asked again.

"What do I want with you? Right now, I want you to shut up," Van Arndt said.

"I'll go with you, but you don't need Lucy. Also, let the little girl and her family go. I've done as you asked," Sally said.

Van Arndt stepped up to Sally and slapped her hard. Her cheek turned red, and a little dot of blood appeared at her lips.

"You don't listen very well, do you? You have not done what I said. I said I want you to shut up and you haven't. Now, shut up!" Van Arndt demanded.

By now, several of the permanent ranch hands were standing around in the yard outside the house they called the Casa Grande. Having been drawn by the initial gunshot and the commotion, they had come from their individual quarters, or from where they had been working. The hands, all Mexican, were gathered in a little cluster in the yard behind the house. They looked on in fear and in frustration over the fact that there was nothing they could do for Sally, Lucy, or the little girl who was still being held at gunpoint.

Keno came back outside then, with his red face covered with lard. "I put the lard on it like you said, but it didn't help none. My face still hurts," he complained.

"Ha, ha," Jeeter said, pointing to Keno. "Damn, I wish you could see yourself, Keno, with your face all red and shining like that. You look like shit."

"Jeeter, see if any of these Mexes are armed," Van Arndt said.

"If they are, you want me to take their guns?" Jeeter asked.

"No," Van Arndt replied.

"No?"

"If you find a gun on any of them, I want you to kill him."

Jeeter laughed, a lilting, almost insane laugh. Then he ordered the Sugarloaf ranch hands to spread out so they could be searched.

"Come on, Boswell, help me look," he said.

Boswell, who had finished tying Sally and Lucy, walked over to join Jeeter, and the two of them checked everyone very thoroughly. Despite the thoroughness of their inspection, they did not find a weapon on anyone.

"There ain't nobody carryin' a gun, Van Arndt," Jeeter said. There was the hint of an edge of disappointment in his voice. It was as if he had wanted one of them to have a gun so he could carry out Van Arndt's order to kill him.

"All of you," Van Arndt said, making a waving

action with his pistol. "Get over there by the house. I want you to sit down in one long row."

For just moment after Van Arndt gave his order, the employees just looked at each other, as if unsure what to do next.

"What should we do, Señora?" Juan asked. Juan was the oldest of all the Mexican employees.

Suddenly, and without warning, Van Arndt turned his pistol toward Juan and pulled the trigger. A little mist of blood flew out from the side of Juan's head.

"No!" Sally shouted, her cry joined by the loud shouts and cries of the others.

Van Arndt's bullet had hit Juan in his earlobe, and the old Mexican was now holding his hand to it, as he winced in pain. The ear was bleeding profusely and some of the blood was dribbling through Juan's fingers.

"Don't look to the woman for directions," Van Arndt said. "I'm in charge here. Now I said for all of you to get over by the house and sit in one long row. Do it now, or I'll shoot again. And next time it won't be just an ear."

The others, galvanized by Van Arndt's cruelty in both action and words, now hurried over to sit down as ordered. Consuela reached out for Maria, intending to take her daughter with her join the others, but Van Arndt held out his hand to stop them.

"No," he said. "The little girl stays here with me. Peters," he called to one of his men.

"Yeah, Van Arndt?" Perhaps under normal circumstances, the puffy, purple scar that ran from Peter's left eye down to his mouth, disfiguring part of his lip, would not have been as noticeable. But in the hell that Van Arndt was creating, the disfigurement just made him more hellish, adding to the horror of the moment.

"See what the hell is keeping that Mexican I sent after the horses. He should have both of them saddled and out here by now."

Peters started toward the barn, then stopped. "Here he comes now," he said.

Looking toward the barn, Sally saw Carlos leading two saddled horses. One was hers, and the other was from the string that they kept for temporary cowboys. Carlos walked up to Van Arndt and tried to hand him the reins.

"Don't give 'em to me, you stupid Mexican," Van Arndt said. "I'm not ridin' that horse."

Van Arndt waved for Peters to come over and take the reins. Carlos started toward his wife and child.

"Just a minute, you," Van Arndt called to Carlos. Carlos stopped.

"Your name is Carlos, is it?" Van Arndt asked.

"*Sí, señor.*"

"Well, Carlos, is there anything you want to tell me?"

"I do not understand," Carlos said.

"Oh, you understand all right," Van Arndt replied. "Did you hide something on this horse?"

Carlos didn't answer.

Van Arndt walked over to Sally's horse. First, he checked the saddlebags. Then he began running his hand around the blanket, then around and under the saddle itself.

"Well, now," Van Arndt said with an evil grin. "What do we have here?"

Van Arndt pulled out a derringer and held it up for all to see.

"You hid this here, didn't you, Carlos?"

Carlos remained silent.

"You hid this gun under the saddle blanket, didn't you, Carlos?" Van Arndt asked again, loudly and angrily.

"*Sí, señor,*" Carlos replied, he spoke words so quietly that they could barely be heard.

"What did you say?" Van Arndt demanded. "Come on, let me hear it. Let everyone hear it. Did you hide this gun under the saddle blanket?"

"*Sí, señor,*" Carlos said again, louder this time, and in a voice that cracked with fear. "I hid the gun under the blanket."

"Yeah, that's what I thought, you sneaky son of a bitch," Van Arndt said. He looked over at Sally, his widening smile making a large, dark scar across a face that was as white as if it had been coated with flour. He clapped his hands together lightly.

"Well, my dear," he said. "You are to be commended for inspiring such loyalty as has been demonstrated here. The Mex there tried to sneak this pistol to you even though he was well aware that if he got caught doing it, he could be killed."

Van Arndt looked over at Carlos. "That is right, isn't it, Carlos? You did understand, did you not, that if you tried to give your mistress this gun, that you could be killed?"

Carlos made a barely imperceptible nod of his head. *"Sí, señor,"* he said.

"Well, that is very brave of you, Carlos," Van Arndt said with a condescending smile. "You knew it could get you killed, but you did it anyway." Van Arndt dipped his head in a small bow. "You have my respect for that."

"I—uh—*gracias, señor,*" Carlos replied, not quite sure where all this was going.

"I congratulate you on your courage, Carlos. But you have just made it clear to all of us that you knew the danger of doing such a thing."

"Van Arndt, leave him alone," Sally said. "Whatever bone you have to pick is with me or my husband. None of my employees are a part of this, and neither is this girl." She nodded toward Lucy.

"Oh, but Carlos made himself a part of this when he tried to sneak this gun to you," Van Arndt said. Again, he held up the derringer. "And I think it is very important that everyone understand that he knew exactly what he was doing, just so there will be no misunderstanding over what I must do now."

"Que?" Carlos said, suddenly realizing that the conversation had taken a very dangerous turn.

Suddenly, and without warning, Van Arndt turned the gun toward Carlos and squeezed the trigger on the derringer. There was a loud report as fire and smoke billowed out from the barrel of the little pistol. The recoil kicked up Van Arndt's hand.

Though the pistol was small, the bullet it fired was of a large caliber and heavy. The ball hit Carlos in the forehead and he pitched back, dead before he even hit the ground.

"Carlos!" Consuela screamed in horror, running to kneel beside her stricken husband.

Several others called out in fear and fright as well.

"You son of a bitch!" Sally cursed.

Van Arndt put his foot into the stirrup, then swung up into the saddle of his horse. "Keno, get Mrs. Jensen and the other woman onto their horses," he ordered. "It is time for us to leave this place."

"Gladly," Keno said. By now his face looked somewhat like a glistening ham. He grabbed Sally and pulled her over to her horse. Because her arms were tied to her sides, she could not get mounted without help, so Keno lifted her foot into the stirrup, then put his hand on her butt and pushed her up until she was in the saddle. He chuckled as he did so.

"You know what? I wouldn't be surprised but what you sort of enjoyed my hands playin' around on your ass like that," he said.

"You go to Hell," Sally replied with a snarl.

"Oh, I am sure I will go to Hell," Keno said. He turned to Lucy. "Now, little lady, it's your time. But don't worry, I promise to be gentle."

"No, please!" Lucy said, cringing away from him. "Why do you want me to go with you?"

"Leave her alone," Sally said. "Van Arndt, I beg of you, leave the girl here. She has no part of this."

"You stay out of this," Van Arndt said to Sally. He pointed at Lucy. "Look, here, girlie, you either come with us like I am telling you to, or I will personally shoot you dead and leave you behind. It's up to you. Which shall it be?"

"I'll—I'll come with you," Lucy said with a whimper.

"I thought you might see it my way," Van Arndt said.

By the time Sally and Lucy were mounted, the men who were riding with Van Arndt were mounted as well.

"Now, Mrs. Jensen, you and the girl here will do everything we ask of you without giving us any trouble," Van Arndt said. "If you don't, I will kill the girl first, then I will kill you. And, just to show you that I am serious, here is a little demonstration of how serious I am."

From the saddle, Van Arndt pointed, not the derringer, but his own pistol at Maria.

"No!" Sally shouted when she realized what Van Arndt was going to do. "My God, Van Arndt! Please, no!"

Van Arndt pulled the trigger and the little girl went down, the new dress she was so proud of now covered with red from the bleeding wound in her chest.

Consuela, who was still crying over her dead husband, screamed again, then passed out over her daughter's body.

"I hope this gets your husband's attention," Van Arndt said.

Sally, who had been shocked into silence by the enormity of Van Arndt's crime, did not answer.

"Let's go," Van Arndt said, and the men, with the two women as their prisoners, rode away from the ranch house. As best she could, with her restraints,

Sally twisted around in her saddle to look back at the grisly scene they were leaving behind them. Tears streaked down her cheeks as she saw the crumpled form of the little body. Maria was still wearing the dress Sally had so recently bought for her.

"Hey, Van Arndt, why are we takin' both of them?" Jeeter asked as they rode off. "Seems to me like havin' two of them will just slow us down."

"The girl is our ace in the hole," Van Arndt replied.

"Ace in the hole? What do you mean?"

"You don't have a lick of sense, do you, Jeeter?" Van Arndt asked.

"Yeah, I do. I've got plenty of sense," Jeeter said defensively.

"You seen what the Jensen woman did back at the house, didn't you? If you've forgot already, just take a look at Keno's face, then think about Miller lyin' back there dead."

"Yeah, but what does that have to do with why we are takin' both of 'em?"

"I figure the Jensen woman is less likely to try anything if we have the girl, too."

Grimly, Sally realized that Van Arndt was right. If she was by herself, she was confident that she would find a way to escape. But, as long as they had Lucy, too, her options would be very limited.

"Yeah," Jeeter said. "Yeah, I see what you mean. Besides which, I reckon before all this is said and done, we'll have some fun with her." Jeeter chuckled. "Yeah," he said. "I reckon I'm goin' to appreciate that."

"Lucy, I'm so sorry you got caught up in all this," Sally said.

"It isn't your fault," Lucy replied, her voice shaking with the terror of the moment. "I'm the one who came over today."

Chapter Seventeen

It was late afternoon by the time Smoke, Pearlie, and Cal arrived at Sugarloaf. They saw several people standing around outside the house, and the tension was almost palpable. As Juan approached them, Smoke saw that the old Mexican was wearing a bandage wrapped around his head. There was a spot of red over his right ear where it had bled through.

"What happened to your ear?" Smoke said as he dismounted.

"My ear is nothing, Señor," Juan said as, almost unconsciously, he put his hand over it. "Carlos and little Maria are dead. Murdered. And Señora Jensen the *bandidos* took."

"Van Arndt," Smoke said, speaking the name almost as an oath.

"Sí, Van Arndt. They took the señorita, too," Juan said.

"Took the señorita? What señorita? Who are you talking about?" Smoke asked.

"Señorita Lucy," Juan said.

"What?" Pearlie asked quickly. "They took Lucy?"

"*Sí, señor.*"

"I don't understand. How did they get her?"

"She had come to greet you when you came home, Señor Pearlie."

"Damn," Pearlie said. "Damn, damn."

"Juan, do you have any idea where they went? Did you hear any of them mention where they were going?"

Juan shrugged his shoulders. "I heard nothing, Señor Smoke," he said. "But when they left, they were going in that direction." He pointed.

"It looks like they are headed for either Hardscrabble or Red Table Mountain," Pearlie said.

"Yes," Smoke answered. Looking around, he saw Consuela being comforted by some of the others, and he walked over to her.

"Señora Rodriguez, I am so sorry about Maria and Juan," he said. "I wish there was something I could say or do that would comfort you."

"Consuela had no family but Carlos and Maria," one of the others said. "Now she has no place to go."

"She doesn't need to go anywhere. She is welcome to stay on Sugarloaf as long as she wishes," Smoke said.

Smoke embraced Consuela, felt her crying against him. He held her for a long moment. Then she moved away.

"You must find Señora Jensen," she said. "Find the men who did this evil thing. Find them and punish them."

"I will find them, " Smoke said. "And I promise you, they will be punished."

Smoke walked back over to Juan. "Tell me, Juan, I think I know why Van Arndt took Sally, and maybe even Lucy. But why did he kill Carlos and Maria?"

"He kill Carlos because Carlos hid a gun on the horse of Señora Jensen. Van Arndt found the gun," Juan said.

"Damn," Smoke said. He shook his head. "That was very courageous of Carlos. But what about the little girl? Why on earth would Van Arndt kill a little girl like that? What possible danger could she have been to him?"

"He said if he kill the little girl, he will get your attention," Juan replied.

"Is that it? He killed Maria just to get my attention? Well, I'll say this for the son of a bitch. He's gotten my attention all right."

"There is another one," Juan said.

"Another what?"

"*Cadáver,*" Juan said. "Another body, Señor," he added. "There is another body."

"One of our people?"

"No, Señor, he was one of the evil ones," Juan said. "Señora Jensen killed him."

"You say Sally killed him?"

"*Sí, señor,*" Juan replied. He put his hand to his face. "To Keno, the one who worked here before, Señora Jensen burn his face, very bad, with a hot plate from the store. Then she took the pistol from Keno and she killed another man."

Smoke nodded his head. "Good," he said. "Good for Sally. Where is the man she killed?"

"He is out in the pigpen, Señor. I did not want

his body near those of Carlos and little Maria. I hope I did not do wrong."

Smoke shook his head. "You didn't do wrong," he said. "As far as I'm concerned, the pigpen is just the place for him," Smoke started toward the pigpen, with Pearlie and Cal close on his heels.

"What do you think this is all about, Smoke?" Cal asked.

"Well, if the fella lyin' up there on top of the canyon wall is to be believed, this man Van Arndt is holding Sally for ransom," Smoke said.

"But if he's holding her for ransom, doesn't that mean he is going to have to send you a note or something to let you know where to take the money and how to get Sally back?"

"Yes."

"Then what?"

"Then we find Van Arndt, and we kill him," Smoke said casily.

Sally and Lucy were riding in the middle, while three of their captors were riding in front and three were riding behind. They stopped just before starting up Hardscrabble Saddle Pass.

"Where the hell is Shardeen?" Van Arndt asked with a growl. "I told the son of a bitch to meet us here."

"Maybe he's gone on ahead," Boswell suggested.

Van Arndt shook his head. "Nah, he wouldn't do that. But I don't know where he is. All the hell he was supposed to do was slow down Jensen, then head right to here."

"Did you say he was supposed to slow down Smoke?" Sally asked. She laughed. "Slow down Smoke?" She laughed again. "Do you have any idea how funny that is?"

"What the hell are you laughing at?"

"I'm laughing at the idea that you actually thought you could do anything that would slow down Smoke. I'll tell you right now, Van Arndt. If you sent your man to try and slow Smoke down, you may as well just forget about him, because you aren't ever going to see him again."

"Yeah, well, he must've done it," Van Arndt said. "Jensen didn't show up while we were at the ranch now, did he? Peters."

"Yeah?"

"I want you to ride on back to the ranch. I am pretty sure that Jensen is there by now. If he isn't there yet, you wait. When he shows up, tell him that if he wants to see his wife alive again, it's going to cost him forty-five thousand dollars."

"You want me to tell him that—in person?" Peters asked. "What the hell do you want me to do that for? Why don't we just send him a note?"

Van Arndt shook his head. "Huh-uh, a note won't work," he said. "We need to be absolutely certain that he gets the information. Don't worry, he's not dumb enough to do anything to you as long as we have his wife."

"Am I supposed to get the money from him?" Peters asked.

"Haw! You'd sure like that, I s'pose," Van Arndt said. "Nah, tell him to get the money together and send it, by mail, to Clay Thomas, general delivery, Denver."

"Clay Thomas?" Keno said. "Who the hell is Clay Thomas? Why should he get the money?"

"There ain't no Clay Thomas, you dumb shit," Van Arndt said. "That's just a name I'm usin'." Then, to Peters, he continued his instructions. "Tell him when we have the money, we'll let his wife go."

"What about the girl here?" Peters asked. "Should I tell him we have her?"

"I'm sure he will know."

"Are we goin' to ask more money for her?"

Van Arndt chuckled. "No, we aren't. Tell him we've got this girl as well as his wife, and if he cooperates with us, we'll throw her in for free." Van Arndt chuckled. "She will be a token of our good faith, so to speak."

"All right," Peters said, turning away from the others.

"There's an old abandoned mine on the other side of the pass," Van Arndt said. "We'll meet you there when you come back."

"There are two abandoned mines over there. Which one are you talking about?" Peters asked.

"You don't need to be worrying any about that, Peters, since you won't be coming back," Sally said.

"What?"

"Don't pay any attention to that bitch," Van Arndt said. "Just do what I told you."

"Peters, just ask yourself this question," Sally said. "Did Shardeen come back?"

Van Arndt rode back to Sally, then slapped her hard.

"I thought I told you to shut up," he said.

Peters lingered for a moment longer.

"I don't know, Van Arndt, maybe the woman has a point," Peters said. "I mean, when you think about it, just where is Shardeen anyway?"

"How the hell do I know?" Van Arndt replied. "Knowing him, the dumb son of a bitch is probably lost. Get on with you now. Or else ride away from your share of the money."

"No need for that. I'm goin', I'm goin'," Peters said. He turned and started back down the trail.

Van Arndt watched Peters for a few minutes until he was satisfied that Peters was following his orders. Then he turned to the others. "All right, let's go," he called out to them. "I want to be through the pass before dark."

The little party began riding again and as before, Sally and Lucy were in the middle of the file. Only this time, with Peters gone, there were only two riders in front of them and three behind. Jeeter was just in front of her, Keno was just behind her.

Jeeter's horse lifted its tail to defecate. Sally looked down at the horse apples and saw that they—like the droppings of the other horses—showed grass and hay. Her horse and the horse Lucy was riding were fed oats. Smoke would pick up on that.

She knew that Smoke would be coming after her, so she started making a concerted effort to slow them down. Gradually, the distance between her horse and Jeeter's horse began widening.

Turning around, Van Arndt noticed that the distance was widening. "Keep up with us. If you don't keep up with us, I'll tie the both of you belly-down across the saddle and lead your horses," Van Arndt growled.

"It's difficult to ride with our arms tied to our sides like this," Sally said. "We're having to hold on with our knees."

"Believe me, woman, it will be a hell of a lot harder if you are belly-down on your saddle, and that is exactly what I'm going to do to you if you two don't keep it up like I said," Van Arndt said with a snarl.

Sally had purposely dropped back, doing everything she could do to hold them up. Now she had no choice but to comply.

As they passed close to a dirt wall to the right of the trail, Sally held out her right stirrup, doing so just far enough for it to leave a long gouge in the dirt. She did it naturally and easily, without her horse losing step, so that none of the three riders who were behind her noticed anything untoward.

As the little group moved on, the trail was empty, except for horse droppings—and the gouge in the dirt wall. In the west, the sun dipped lower and the shadows lengthened.

Sally heard Lucy sniffing, and she knew that the young woman was trying hard to fight her fear.

"Lucy, it will be all right," she said. Even as she said the words, though, they rang hollow in her ears, because she recalled having said the same thing to Carlos and Maria. But this time she meant it. Somehow, someway, she would make it be right.

Chapter Eighteen

"Smoke, there's a rider comin' in," Pearlie said.

Turning away from his conversation with Juan, Smoke saw the rider passing under the arch of the gate.

"Señor Smoke!" Juan said. There was a look of fear on his face.

Smoke held his hand out soothingly. "It's all right, Juan," he said.

"That rider. He was one of them. One of the evil ones."

"Yes, I figured he might be."

The rider approached calmly, almost arrogantly. When he reached the area where Smoke and the others were standing, he dismounted, then took the makings from his pocket and started rolling a cigarette.

"Who are you, and what do you want?" Smoke asked.

"Don't get so anxious," the rider said as he continued to roll his cigarette. "I been a'wantin' me one of these here smokes for the last half hour or so."

Holding the paper up to his mouth, he licked

along the edge, then pressed the cigarette together. After that, he took out a match and fired it up by popping it on his thumb. He lit the cigarette and took a long puff, then let it out with a satisfied sigh.

"Who are you?" Smoke asked again.

"The name's Peters. But then, I reckon you know who I am," he said. He pointed toward Juan. "Unless I miss my guess, the old Mex there has told you I am one of the men that snatched your woman."

"He said you were one of the ones who killed Maria and her father," Smoke said.

"Yeah, well, as far as the killin' is concerned, it was Van Arndt that done that. He's a pistol, he is. He said that by him killin' the little girl like that, it would show that we are serious when we tell you we'll kill your woman if you don't do what we tell you to do." Peters laughed out loud. "And I reckon he was right, 'cause here we are negotiatin'."

"No, we aren't," Smoke said.

The laughter changed to a chuckle.

"We ain't what?" Peters asked.

"We aren't negotiating," Smoke said.

"Well, I guess you're right at that," Peters said. "I mean, seein' as there ain't goin' to be no palaverin' to it. I'm just goin' to tell you flat out what we want."

"I don't care what you want," Smoke said.

"What we want is forty-five thousand dollars. Van Arndt says that you are to mail the money to Clay Thomas, general delivery in—" Peters stopped, as if not sure of what he had just heard Smoke say.

"What did you just say?"

"I said I don't care what you want."

"Mister, maybe you don't understand what's goin' on here. We've got your woman. Truth to tell, we've got another woman besides. What do you mean, you don't care what we want?"

"Seems like a simple enough statement," Smoke said. "I don't care what you want."

"Look here, don't you want us to give you your woman back?" Peters asked, surprised and confused by the way the conversation was going.

"You won't be giving me anything," Smoke said. "I intend to take her back."

Peters shook his head. "Mister, there ain't no way you are goin' to get her back. Not without dealin' with Van Arndt, you won't," he said.

Smoke didn't respond.

"So, uh, what is your answer?"

Still, Smoke had said nothing, and now Peters was growing visibly confused by Smoke's lack of communication. Clearly, this was not going the way Van Arndt told him it would go.

"Come on, Jensen, I have to tell Van Arndt something," Peters said. "I can't go back to him and tell him you didn't say anything a'tall."

"You don't have to worry about that," Smoke said.

"What do you mean I don't have to worry about that?" Peters asked. His eyes narrowed as he tried hard to understand just what was going on here.

"I mean you don't have to worry about telling Van Arndt anything, because you aren't going back," Smoke said.

"Damn! That is the same thing she—" Peters stopped.

Smoke laughed. "That's what Sally told you, isn't it?"

Peters pointed at Smoke. "See here, I ain't goin' to let you work on my mind like that. I damn sure am going back."

Smoke shook his head. "No, you aren't," he said.

"We—we've got your wife! Don't you understand that?" Peters asked. By now, there was nearly as much panic in his words as there was anger.

"And I've got you," Smoke said.

"What do you mean, you have me?"

"Van Arndt has Sally, I have you," Smoke said. "And the only way Van Arndt is going to get you back alive is by giving me Sally."

Peters chuckled, a nervous laugh; then, seeing by the look in his eyes that Smoke was serious, he shook his head. "You're—you're crazy," he said.

"What's the matter, Peters? Are you afraid that Van Arndt won't negotiate for you?"

A little bead of perspiration broke out on Peters's upper lip; then, with a loud yell, he went for his pistol.

Smoke had not expected Peters to draw his pistol, certainly not here where he was facing not only Smoke, but Pearlie and Cal as well. As a result, Peters actually had his pistol out before Smoke started his own draw.

Seeing that he had beaten Smoke to the draw, Peters allowed a broad smile to play across his lips as he brought his pistol to bear. Then, even before he could pull the trigger, Smoke's gun was out and firing.

The smile on Peter's face changed to a grimace of surprise and pain as the heavy bullet plunged into his chest.

"How the hell—how the hell did you do that?" he asked in a strained voice. He fell very near his cigarette, which was still lit. Pearlie walked over to the cigarette and stepped on it, grinding it out beneath his boot.

"What a waste of good tobacco," Pearlie said.

"It was wasted the moment someone like him started to smoke it," Cal said.

Pearlie chuckled. "Yeah," he said. "Yeah, I guess you are right at that."

"I wonder if we could have talked him into leadin' us to Sally," Pearlie said. "Maybe you shouldn't have killed him, Smoke."

"There wasn't time not to kill him," Smoke replied, and it was not necessary for him to explain the strange comment to his friends.

The last thought of which Peters was aware was the almost casual way everyone was treating his dying.

Cal walked over to Peters's horse, then lifted one of its feet. Using his knife, he scraped at the iron-shod hoof, then looked at the residue.

"What have you got, Cal?" Smoke asked.

"Looks like crushed yellow rock," Cal said, holding the knife blade out for Smoke to examine.

"Yeah," Smoke said. He examined the residue more closely. "The only place you'll find dirt like that is Hardscrabble Saddle Pass."

"I'll get us some travelin' food," Pearlie said, starting toward the house.

"I'll get some extra ammunition," Cal said, following Pearlie.

"Señor," Juan said. "About Carlos and Maria.

Consuela wants to know if she can bury them here on your ranch."

"Yes, of course she can," Smoke said. He took some money from his billfold and handed it Juan. "Go into town and buy the caskets for both of them from Mr. Welch. Get the very best he has."

"*Gracias, señor.* And this hombre, and the one in the pigpen?"

"Take these two bodies into town as well and give them to Sheriff Carson. Tell him what happened, and tell him that Pearlie, Cal, and I are going after Sally."

"*Sí, señor.*"

On the trail in Hardscrabble Saddle Pass

Checking to make certain she wasn't being seen, Sally left another long scar on the cut beside the trail. When she looked over at Lucy, she saw the young woman still fighting hard to hold back the tears, and to a degree she was succeeding.

"How are you doing, Lucy?" she asked quietly.

"I have never been so frightened in my entire life," Lucy said.

"It is a frightening experience, I'll grant you that," Sally replied.

"But you aren't afraid at all," Lucy said. "I don't understand. How is it that you are not afraid?"

"Oh, I'm afraid all right," Sally said. "It's just that I don't intend to give these bastards the satisfaction of knowing I'm afraid."

"What do you think they are going to do with us?"

"As long as they think they can extort money from Smoke, they won't do anything to us," Sally said. "That will give Smoke time to rescue us."

"Will Smoke pay money to get us free?"

"Smoke will rescue us," Sally repeated without being specific.

"I wish I had your courage and confidence," Lucy said.

"Smoke will get us out of this," Sally said. "Just hang on."

"I'll try," Lucy said.

Smoke had learned his tracking skills from a master tutor. The classes began during his days of living in the mountains with the man called Preacher.

"He's a good one to learn from," another mountain man once said to Smoke, speaking of Preacher. "Most anyone can track a fresh trail, but Preacher can follow a trail that is a month old. In fact, I've heard some folks say that he can track a fish through water, or a bird through the sky. And I ain't one to dispute 'em."

Now, as Smoke started on the trail of Van Arndt and the others, the words of his tutor came back to him.

"Half of tracking is in knowin' where to look," Preacher told the young Smoke. *"The other half is looking.*

"Reading prints on a dirt road is easy. But if you know what you are doing, you can follow the trail no matter where it leads. Use every sense God gave you," Preacher explained. *"Listen, look, touch, smell. Taste if you have to."*

"Smoke, you been noticin' them horse turds?" Pearlie asked. "They's a couple of horses droppin' oat turds, the others is grass turds."

"Yeah, I seen that, too," Cal said.

"You boys have good eyes," Smoke said. "There's also that," he said, pointing.

"What?"

"Look at the cut alongside the trail," Smoke said. "You see that long scar there?"

"Yeah, I see it. What about it?" Cal asked.

"Look on the trail below the scar," Smoke said. "There is fresh dirt from the scar."

"I'll be damn, I do see that," Cal said. "What do you reckon that is?"

"Well, seeing as that is the fourth one I've seen, I believe Sally has been leaving it for us," Smoke said.

"Yeah," Pearlie said. "Yeah, I think so, too. How is she doing that, do you reckon? I mean, how's she doin' that without bein' seen?"

"Sally is pretty resourceful," Smoke said. "She can find a way to do just about anything she puts her mind to."

"She's leavin' us a trail so we can track her," Pearlie said.

"Yes," Smoke agreed. "But she's also letting us know that she is still all right."

"Hey," Boswell said as they left the pass. "Where are we goin'? The mine is this way."

"Yeah, I know," Van Arndt said.

"Well, didn't you tell Peters to meet us at the mine?"

"I expect Peters is dead by now," Van Arndt said. "Same as Shardeen."

"What do you mean you expect Peters is dead? You told him that as long as we had Jensen's woman, nothing would happen to him."

"Yeah, I did, didn't I?" Van Arndt said. He chuckled.

"Are you sayin' you know'd all along he'd more than likely get hisself kilt?" Boswell asked.

"I figured that, yeah."

"Then why did you send him?"

"Would you rather I have sent you?" Van Arndt asked.

"What? Hell, no."

"Then think about it, Boswell. I had to send someone," Van Arndt replied. "Otherwise, how would Jensen know we had his woman?"

"You never had no intention of goin' to that mine, did you?"

"Nope."

"Then why did you tell him that?"

"Suppose Peters got a little gabby before Jensen killed him," Van Arndt said. "Suppose he started talking—you know—to save his own hide and he told Jensen about the mine."

"Do you think he would really do that?" Boswell asked.

"Do you think for one minute that he wouldn't?"

"Yeah, I—I guess you are right," Boswell said.

"Are you that dumb, Boswell?" Sally asked.

"What?"

"Don't you see what Van Arndt has done? He has

already gotten rid of two of you. There are only three of you left now. If I were one of you, I'd be worrying about which one he is going to sell out next."

"We'd better keep an eye on this bitch, Van Arndt," Keno said. "She's a smart one, all right. She's trying to get us to arguin' amongst ourselves now. Hell, it don't bother me none that Shardeen and Peters has got themselves kilt. It's just more money for the rest of us."

Sally laughed. "I thought you were smarter than that, Keno. You know Smoke pretty well. You know there isn't going to be any money. Smoke will not pay one thin dime."

"Is that right, Keno?" Jeeter asked. "Will Jensen really not pay anything to get his wife back?"

"Don't worry about it," Keno said. "Jensen sets more store by his woman than anyone I've ever met. I promise you, he'll pay whatever it takes to get her back. Ain't that right, Van Arndt?"

"It doesn't matter whether he pays the ransom or not," Van Arndt said.

"What? What do you mean it don't matter?" Keno asked. "Of course it matters?"

"No, it doesn't," Van Arndt said.

"What the hell are you talking about? If Jensen don't pay any ransom, then what for are we a'doin' all this? I mean, why did we take his woman?"

"As bait."

"Bait?"

"Yeah, as bait," Van Arndt said. "Jensen is going to come after her, and when he does, we're goin' to kill him."

"Van Arndt, I don't like the son of a bitch any more than you do," Keno said. "But I wouldn't have gone into all this if I hadn't thought we was goin' to make some money."

"Oh, we are goin' to make money all right," Van Arndt said.

"How? I mean, if he isn't goin' to pay us any ransom, how are we goin' to make any money?"

"You let me worry about that," Van Arndt said.

Just after sundown, Van Arndt called a halt in order to allow them to eat a few bites of jerky and to take a few swallows of water.

Keno chewed on the leathery jerky, then took a drink of tepid water from his canteen. He spit some out in disgust, and wiped his mouth with the back of his hand.

"This damn water tastes like horse piss," he complained. "And the jerky tastes like dog turds. I know damn well there's got to be a town near here. Yeah, Mitchell is near here. Listen, Van Arndt, why don't we go into Mitchell?"

"Why would we want to do that?" Van Arndt asked.

"Well, I was just thinkin'. If we went into Mitchell, we could maybe get us somethin' fit to eat an' decent to drink," Keno said.

"You was thinkin', was you? What makes you believe you have enough brains to think?"

"You got no right to talk to me like that, Van Arndt. Who's idea was it to snatch Jensen's wife in the first place? I mean we didn't do that well takin' Jensen's herd or stealin' him money, did we?"

Van Arndt looked over at Keno, then he sighed. "Look, just do things my way for a little while longer. We can't go into Mitchell now, not while we're draggin' a couple of women prisoners along with us. We're not far from Salcedo. That's where we're headed."

"Salcedo? Where the hell is Salcedo? I ain't never heard of it," Keno said.

Van Arndt chuckled. "Not many have heard of it," he said. "That's why it's the place we need to be."

"You know anybody in Salcedo?"

"Yeah, I know someone there. I know the marshal there."

"Ha," Keno said. "Like that's going to do us any good."

"It may."

"You want to tell me how, knowin' the marshal in this town—Salcedo—is goin' to do us any good?"

"The marshal of Salcedo is my brother," Van Arndt said.

"Your brother? No shit? The marshal is your brother?" Keno said. He laughed. "Son of a bitch, you had it mind all along to go there, didn't you?"

Van Arndt screwed the cap back on his canteen, then hooked it back onto his saddle. "Yeah, I did," he said. "Mount up."

Chapter Nineteen

The street was dimly illuminated by squares of yellow light that spilled through the doors and windows of the buildings. High above the little town, stars winked brightly, while over a distant mesa the moon hung like a large silver wheel.

"What do you say we get a drink?" Keno suggested.

"Not till we get these women took care of," Van Arndt said.

"What do you mean took care of? Took care of how?" Jeeter asked.

"I mean find someplace to keep 'em," Van Arndt said.

"You got someplace in mind?"

"Yeah," Van Arndt said.

"Where?"

"We're goin' to put 'em in jail."

"Jail? Are you kidding me?"

Van Arndt chuckled. "I told you, my brother is the marshal here."

"Ha!" Keno said. He rode up alongside Sally, then

leaned over. Although the red could not be seen in the moonlight, his face did shine from the smear of lard.

"Well, now, how about that, Mrs. High-and-mighty Sally Jensen?" Keno asked. "I'll just bet you ain't never been in no jail before now, have you?"

Sally didn't answer.

"Van Arndt, I know you said your brother was the marshal here," Boswell said. "And maybe he will go along with puttin' these here women in jail. But what about the rest of the folks in town? How are they goin' to take it?"

"When they learn these two women are a couple of whores who tried to steal from us, why, they'll take it just fine," Van Arndt said.

"Whores?" Lucy cried out. "You are going to say that we are whores? No, please! I couldn't stand the shame of such a thing."

Keno laughed. "You're really somethin', you know that? If things don't go the way they're supposed to, both of you women is going to be kilt, and all you are worried about is whether or not you are being called a whore."

They reined up in front of a small adobe building. A board was attached to the front of the building on which the word JAIL had been crudely painted. A dim light flickered from inside.

Van Arndt dismounted, then looked at the others. Not one of the others had dismounted.

"Come on," he said. "Get down."

"Van Arndt, I tell you the truth, I ain't all that

happy about walkin' into a jailhouse on my own," Boswell said.

"I told you, there ain't nothin' to worry about. Get down. Soon as we get the women took care of, we'll go get us somethin' to drink."

Keno smiled. "Hell, I don't know about you boys, but that sounds good to me," he said as he swung down from his horse.

The men tied off the horses, then went into the jail. At first they didn't see anyone.

"Damn, is the place empty?" Jeeter asked.

"Nah, there he is," Van Arndt said.

Van Arndt pointed to the back of the room. There, someone was sitting in a chair that was tipped back against the wall. His hat was pulled down over his eyes, and his feet were up on the desk. He was snoring loudly.

"Is that your brother?" Jeeter asked.

"Nah, he must be the deputy. Hey, Deputy!" Van Arndt said, loudly. "Deputy, wake up!"

Startled, the deputy jumped, then he raised his hat and opened his eyes in surprise. Blinking a couple of times, he looked up at all the people standing inside. His eyes grew wider when he saw that the men had two women with them, both of whom were bound by ropes.

"Who the hell are you?" the deputy asked.

"Where's the marshal?" Van Arndt asked.

"More'n likely he's down at the saloon. Who are you?"

Without answering, Van Arndt nodded toward the jail cells. "You got a key to the jail?"

"Yeah, over there," the deputy said, pointing to a key on a ring hanging from a hook on the wall.

"Good. I want these two whores locked up for stealin'," Van Arndt said, walking over toward the key ring.

"I can't do that," the deputy replied.

"Why not?"

"On account of because this here jail has only got one cell and there's a prisoner in it already," the deputy said. "I can't put women in with a man prisoner."

"Hell, that's not a problem," Van Arndt said. He took the key down from the hook, then opened the cell door. "Hey, you, prisoner," he called out to a man who was sleeping on one of the four bunks. "You're a free man. Get out!"

"What the hell are you doin'?" the deputy asked. "You can't do that. This man is a burglar. We're waitin' on a visit from the circuit judge."

"I just found him not guilty," Van Arndt said. "Hey, you," he yelled at the prisoner. The prisoner, though awake now, was still confused by what was happening. "What's goin' on?" he asked. "Who are you?"

"I'm the judge and I just found you not guilty. You are a free man. Get out of here now."

"Yes, sir!" The prisoner replied. Grabbing his hat, he stepped out of the cell. He stopped when he saw the two bound women.

"Who is this?" he asked.

"It don't matter none to you who it is," Van Arndt said. He pulled his pistol and cocked it. "Get out now."

"I'm goin', I'm goin'," the man said, hurrying for the door.

Van Arndt turned to the deputy. "What's your name, Deputy?"

"Laney. Jerry Laney."

"Well, Laney, it's like I said, you don't have a problem. Now, get these two whores in that cell."

"Help us, please!" Lucy said to the deputy. "We aren't whores and we didn't steal anything. These men have taken us prisoner. They are holding us for ransom."

"What?" Laney asked. He turned toward Van Arndt. "What is she talking about?"

Van Arndt laughed. "How long you been a deputy?"

"About two years," the deputy answered.

"You ever put anyone in jail who didn't say they was innocent?"

"No, I don't reckon I have," he said. "But then I ain't never put no women in jail before."

"A woman ain't no different from a man," Van Arndt said. "Catch 'em in the act and they'll lie about it, same as a man will."

"Yeah, I guess so," the deputy said. "It's just, I'm not all that sure about this."

"I tell you what, if you don't feel right about it, just go ahead and lock 'em up now, then come on down to the saloon with us. You can talk to my brother about it."

"Talk to your brother about it? What does he have to do with anything?"

"He has everything to do with it. My brother is the marshal of this town."

The deputy paused for a moment, then nodded. "Oh. Well, why didn't you say so in the first place? All right," he said. "Let's go talk to him."

"You are making a mistake, Deputy Laney. A big mistake," Lucy said. "My name is Sally Jensen. My husband's name is Smoke Jensen. These men have kidnapped us and are holding us for ransom. If you go along with them, you will be guilty of collusion."

"Guilty of what?" the deputy asked.

"Collusion. It means you are just as guilty as they are."

"Look here, I didn't kidnap you," Laney said.

"If you help these men now, then it will be the same as if you did," Sally said.

"Look, miss, I'll talk to the marshal about it," Laney said. "I'm just the deputy here."

"Good idea," Van Arndt said.

"You will at least untie us now, won't you?" Sally asked.

"Untie 'em, Keno," Van Arndt ordered.

Keno untied Lucy first, taking his time with it and allowing his hands to move all across her body as he did so. She shivered in revulsion, and he laughed at her.

"Honey, you just wait," Keno said. "Before all this is over, I'm going to show you what a real man can do."

When he finished with Lucy, he turned to Sally.

"It's your turn, Sally," he said. He chuckled. "You don't mind if I call you Sally, do you?"

"Call me whatever you want," Sally replied. "Your days are numbered."

"Ha!" Keno said. "We'll just see about—" He

reached for Sally, but stopped when he saw her remove the rope herself and hand it to him.

"What the—? How did you do that?" Keno asked. He turned to Van Arndt. "Van Arndt, did you see what she just done?"

"Get them in the cell and let's go," Van Arndt said.

"But did you see what she did?" Keno asked again. "She got herself untied. Have you been untied all along?" he asked Sally.

"What difference does it make whether she was or wasn't?" Van Arndt asked. "She's here, ain't she? Now, get 'em both in the cell like I told you to."

"All right, get in there," Keno said, moving them toward the single cell. The deputy, who had taken the key from Van Arndt, closed the cell door with a clang.

"Deputy, you seen what a slippery bitch she is, so make damn sure the cell door is locked," Van Arndt said.

"Yeah, I will," the deputy said, turning the key in the lock, then holding the key up for Van Arndt to see. "It's locked."

Not trusting him, Van Arndt walked over to the cell door and tried to open it. When he was satisfied that it was securely locked, he turned to the others.

"It's always good to double-check," he said. "What do you say we go have that drink now?"

"You ladies don't get into any trouble while we're gone," Keno called back to them with a high-pitched laugh as the men left the jailhouse.

"Oh," Lucy said. "Oh, Sally, what's going to happen to us? I am so frightened."

"We'll be all right," Sally replied. "Just keep your courage up."

Lucy held her hands out to look at them. "I can't feel my hands," she said. "I can't even feel my arms."

"That's because the rope cut off your circulation," Sally explained. "Don't worry about it, the circulation will come back. Here, sit on the bed, let me see what I can do to help it."

Lucy sat on the bed and Sally began rubbing on her arms. Lucy was quiet for a long moment before she spoke.

"He was right, wasn't he?" she said.

"Who was right about what?"

"Van Arndt was right," Lucy said. "He said bringing me along would keep you from escaping. You got free from the ropes. That means you could have escaped it if hadn't been for me."

"Nonsense," Sally said. "Just because I got free from the ropes doesn't mean I could have escaped."

"But you could escape if it weren't for me, couldn't you? I'm holding you back."

"No, you aren't," Sally said. "Believe me, honey, if I see the opportunity to escape, I am going to do it. And when I do, I'm going to take you with me."

"Oh, I don't know. I don't think I could do anything like that."

"Sure you can," Sally said. "Most people have a lot more strength and courage than they realize."

"Sally, are you afraid?" Lucy asked.

"Yes, of course I am afraid. One would be a fool not to be afraid."

"Thanks," Lucy said.

"Thanks?" Sally laughed. "You are thanking me for being afraid?"

"Yes. Somehow, I don't know why, but somehow knowing that you are afraid, too, helps."

When Van Arndt and the others went into the saloon, Van Arndt looked around the room for a moment. At this time of night, the saloon was filled with customers, most of whom were rough-looking characters. Many, Van Arndt knew, were on the wrong side of the law, and they came to Salcedo because they were able to work out an arrangement with the marshal.

The women who worked the bar were from the very lowest strata of whores and bar girls. Their looks and health had been so ruined by the dissipation and diseases of their trade that a place like this was absolutely the last rung on the ladder for them.

Van Arndt saw the man he was looking for sitting at a table in the back of the room, drinking a beer.

"There's my brother over there," he said. "You three go up the bar and have a drink. I think the deputy and I need to talk to him for a few minutes."

Keno, Jeeter, and Boswell stepped up to the bar and the barkeep slid down the bar toward them.

"What can I get you gents?"

"Whiskey," Keno said. "Leave the bottle."

"What kind?"

"The cheapest. We are here to get drunk, we ain't here to give a party."

The bartender took a bottle from beneath the

counter. There was no label on the bottle and the color was dingy and cloudy. He put three glasses alongside the bottle, then pulled the cork for them.

Keno poured a glass, then passed the bottle down to the others. He took a swallow, then almost gagged. He spit it out and frowned at his glass.

"Goddamn!" he said. "This tastes like horse piss."

Jeeter took a smaller swallow. He grimaced, but he managed to get it down. Boswell had no problem with it at all.

"It's all in the way you drink it," Boswell explained. "This here whiskey can't be drunk down real fast. You got to sort of sip it."

Keno tried again, and this time he, too, managed to keep the whiskey down.

"Yeah," he said. "I see what you mean."

The three men refilled their glasses, then turned to look back at the table where Van Arndt was having an animated conversation with a man who was wearing a badge. The deputy was there as well, but he didn't seem to be talking.

"Can you imagine Van Arndt having a brother who is the law?" Keno asked with a chuckle.

"He ain't his full brother," Boswell said.

"He ain't?"

"Nope. They got the same mama, but they don't have the same papa. The marshal's name is Craig. Don't many people know that Van Arndt is his brother. I reckon if folks knew that, it could cause him some trouble."

"I'll be damn."

"I hope they get along all right," Keno said.

"They get along fine," Boswell said.

"You've met him, have you?" Keno asked.

"Yeah, a few times," Boswell said.

"What about the deputy? You ever met him before?"

"No, I ain't never met the deputy," Boswell said.

"He might give us some trouble," Keno suggested.

"Why do you say that?"

"I just got that feelin' is all. I mean, look at him over there. Looks like he's givin' the marshal an earful."

"I wonder what they are talkin' about," Jeeter said.

"I don't feel right about this, Marshal," Laney was saying. "The woman says she is Smoke Jensen's wife, and she says she's been kidnapped and is being held for ransom."

"Are you crazy, Reece, putting Smoke Jensen's wife in my jail?" Marshal Harlan Craig asked.

"Who said she is Jensen's wife?" Van Arndt answered.

"She says she is Jensen's wife," Laney said.

"I told you, Deputy, they ain't nothin' but just a couple of whores that tried to steal from us. She just told you she was Jensen's wife. I can't believe that you believed her."

"Is that true?" the deputy asked.

Van Arndt looked at the deputy for a moment. "Yeah," he said. "They're whores. Look, Laney, why don't you step up to the bar and have a drink with them other boys while me and my brother talk? We got some business to discuss—family business," he added pointedly.

The deputy looked at Craig. "Marshal?" he asked.

"Go ahead, Jerry," Craig said. "If it's family business, then my brother and me need to talk in private for a few minutes."

"All right, but I'll be just over there if you need me," the deputy replied.

When the deputy stepped up to the bar beside the others, Keno looked down toward the bartender.

"Bring us another glass for the deputy," he asked. He turned back toward Laney. "We might as well get acquainted with a friendly conversation."

"I'm all for a friendly conversation," the deputy replied. "But if it's all the same to you, I'll have a beer."

The barkeep nodded, but said nothing. He drew a mug of beer from the barrel, then set the foaming liquid in front of the deputy.

"What are they talking about?" Keno asked, nodding toward the table.

The deputy blew some of the foam away from the head before he replied.

"I don't have the slightest idea what they are talking about," he said. "They said they had some family business to talk about. Then they sent me away." He punctuated his statement with a long drink of beer. "I want to ask you boys a question," he said.

"What's that?"

"The women you brought in. Is one of them really Smoke Jensen's wife?"

Keno laughed. "Yeah, she's Jensen's wife," he said. "Can you imagine that? Jensen's wife in jail?"

"Son of a bitch," Laney said. "This is bad. This is really bad."

* * *

"Have you lost your mind?" Marshal Craig asked. "What the hell you are doin' with her? And why did you bring her to my town and my jail? Do you really expect Smoke Jensen to pay a ransom for her?"

"I'm not actually holding her for ransom," Van Arndt said. "I mean, that's what I thought I was goin' to do when I took her, but the more I thought about it, the more I knew it wasn't goin' to work out. That's when I come up with the other plan."

"What other plan?"

"I'm usin' Jensen's wife as bait."

"What?"

"You know what bait is, don't you?" Van Arndt said. "You use bait to set a trap. Well, sir, that's what I've done. I've set a trap for Jensen. Once he finds out I've got his wife, he'll come for her."

"Oh, he'll come for her all right. That is, if he knows you have her."

"He knows. I sent Peters to tell him that we are holding her for ransom."

"How did he react to that?"

Van Arndt chuckled. "Most likely, Jensen killed Peters."

"What the hell, Reece, have you gone plumb loco? You're doin' all this just to kill Jensen?"

"Yeah, but there's more to it than just killin' him. There's also the money part of it."

"What money? And how much money are you talkin' about?" Craig asked as he lifted the beer to his lips.

"Oh, I'd say about a hundred and twenty-five thousand dollars," Van Arndt said easily.

Craig had just taken a swallow of his beer, and he suddenly spewed it out as he gasped.

"What? Did you say a hundred and twenty-five thousand dollars?"

"At least that much."

"All right, you've got my attention. Go on with your story."

"Jensen has one of the biggest ranches in the entire state. With him, his wife, and his two hands dead, there will be no one left behind at the ranch. I plan to move in and take over."

"Don't be foolish," Craig said. "You can't steal a ranch."

"No, but we can cut out about five thousand head from his herd."

"You are absolutely loco. You're just goin' to steal five thousand head of cattle, are you? And do what with them?"

"It's after spring roundup," Van Arndt said. "More than likely there are ten or fifteen big herds being moved, maybe more. One more big herd ain't goin' to arouse no suspicion at all. We'll drive 'em up to Harney in Wyoming and sell them there. They're paying twenty-five dollars a head. Five thousand head and twenty-five dollars a head, you figure it out for yourself."

"That is a lot of money," Craig said, beginning to show a little interest in the plan. "But how are you going to get the cattle in the first place?"

"He has thirty thousand head wandering all over

fifteen thousand acres of grassland," Van Arndt explained. "With Jensen, his wife, and his two hands gone, there won't be nobody left at the ranch but a few old Mexicans, and they'll be so confused by everything that they won't know whether to pick their nose or scratch their ass. I'm telling you, there won't be anyone left to keep an eye on things at Sugarloaf. We'll have the cattle gone and sold before anyone misses them."

"Yeah, well, there is one little problem with your whole idea," Craig said.

"What is that?"

"Smoke Jensen is a well-known man in these parts. Killin' him is going to put ever' lawman between Canada and Mexico on the hunt."

"No, there won't be anyone lookin' for us."

"How do you figure that?"

"At one time Jensen was a wanted man, and the whole state was plastered with wanted posters for him. Dead or alive. Am I right or wrong?"

"You are right, but all those dodgers were pulled back a long time ago."

"Say there was somebody, a bounty hunter say, who come across one of those wanted posters and didn't know that they had been pulled back? And suppose that bounty hunter kilt Jensen and the other members of his gang? Would that be murder? Or would that just be an awful mistake?"

"Well, things like that have happened before. I recollect that a feller by the name of Flat Nose Parker was shot and killed by a bounty hunter after Parker had already be tried and found innocent. The bounty hunter wasn't charged because the thing is, you can't always be sure there ain't no reward posters left out there," Craig said.

"Yeah, that's pretty much what I was thinkin'," Van Arndt said. "Do you have any old dodgers with Smoke Jensen's name on them?"

Craig stroked his cheek for a moment, then broke into a big smile. "Yeah," he said. "Yeah, as a matter of fact, I do."

"Then who is to say that killin' him isn't an honest mistake by someone who didn't know the paper had all been pulled?" Van Arndt asked.

"Maybe," Craig said.

"Ha! It's damn more than maybe, and you know it," Van Arndt said. "You know the idea will work, don't you?"

"Yeah, it just might work at that," Craig said. "By the way, Jerry said you had two women in the jail. Who's the other one?"

"Her name is Lucy Goodnature. She's the daughter of Jensen's neighbor."

"What do you have her for? That is just going to make things more complicated."

"I hadn't planned on takin' her," Van Arndt said. "It just so happened that she was over at Smoke Jensen's ranch, visitin' when we showed up. I didn't have no choice but to take her. But it's worked out real good."

"How so?"

"As long as we have her, Jensen's wife ain't goin' to try and escape."

"Yeah, I see your point," Craig said. He was silent for a moment, then he said, "Half."

"Half? Half of what? What are you talkin' about?"

"I want half the money," Craig said.

The smile left Van Arndt's face. "What the hell makes you think I'm goin' to give you half the money?"

"You'll give me half the money, or you'll take the women somewhere else," Craig said.

"Now that ain't no way fair, Harlan, and you know it," Van Arndt said. "I mean, yeah, I'm countin' on your help and I was plannin' on cuttin' you in on some of the money. But what the hell kind of way is that to treat your own brother, to ask for half like that?"

"I'm your half brother," Craig said. "When you think about, it seems only right to give half the money to your half brother," he added, laughing at his own joke.

"We may only be half brothers, but we have the same mama," Van Arndt said.

"Half the money," Craig repeated.

"I'm the one that took all the risks," Van Arndt said.

"What the hell are you talkin' about?" Craig asked. "There ain't been no risk took at all yet. The real risk don't start until Jensen catches up with you. Then you are going to need me. Half the money."

"All right, half," Van Arndt agreed. "But you damn sure better be there when I need you."

"I'll be there," Craig promised.

Chapter Twenty

Deputy Laney looked over at the table where Van Arndt and Craig were still engaged in conversation. "Van Arndt told me that the woman was lying, that she wasn't Jensen's wife. Why would he tell me that?"

"Maybe he figured it was none of your business," Boswell said.

"I'm the one who put the women in jail," Laney said. "That makes it my business."

"Yeah, well, don't worry about it," Jeeter said.

"Why do you have them? What are you going to do with them?"

"I tell you what I'd like to do with the young one," Jeeter said, rubbing himself, then laughing.

"What do you mean the young one?" Boswell asked. "Jensen's wife is just as good-lookin'. Hell, she might even be better-lookin'."

"Yeah, but she's too damn feisty," Jeeter said. "Messin' around with her would be like tanglin' with a mountain lion. No, sir, the young one for me."

"This here whiskey is makin' me sick," Keno said,

butting into the conversation. "I'm goin' out back to puke."

"Haw!" Jeeter said. "Some man you are!"

Keno waved him off, then stumbled toward the back door.

"What the hell is wrong with Keno?" Boswell asked.

"Ah, don't worry none about him," Jeeter said. "I reckon he's woke up in a puddle of his own puke more than once. Besides, with him gone, there's more whiskey for us."

"You got that right," Boswell said with a smile, holding his glass out for Jeeter to refill it.

Again, Jeeter offered whiskey to the deputy, and again the deputy declined, preferring beer instead. The deputy continued to keep his eye the table where Marshal Craig and the strange-looking, very white man who was his brother were talking.

"I wonder just what the hell they are talking about," the deputy said.

"Ha. Knowing Van Arndt, he's done got his little brother twisted around his finger by now."

"Yeah," Laney said. "That's what I'm afraid of."

Jeeter laughed. "You're a funny one, you know that?"

As soon as Keno reached the alley behind the saloon, he looked back toward the door to make sure that no one was following him. When he was certain he was alone, he smiled broadly and started quickly up the alley toward the jail.

The whiskey had not really made him sick; he

had merely used that as an excuse to get away from the others so he could do what he planned to do.

When Keno reached the jail, he stepped inside and looked back toward the single cell. The two women were sitting on the same bed, talking quietly. They looked up when Keno came into the room.

"Keno," Sally said. Looking beyond him, she saw that nobody else was with him. "Where are the others?"

"It don't matter none where the others are," Keno replied. "I don't need them to take care of my business."

"To take care of your business? What business would that be?" Sally asked.

"I tell you what, Sally, whatever my business is, it ain't nothin' you need be a'worryin' none about it," Keno said. "Fact is, what I got to take care of don't have nothin' to do with you."

Keno walked over to the wall and took the key down from the hook. Stepping up to the cell, he held the key up and smiled at Lucy.

"This is the little lady I'll be dealin' with. Tell me, Lucy, do you remember when you wouldn't dance with me at the dance?" he asked.

Lucy didn't respond.

"Oh, I'm sure you remember," Keno said. "I asked you just real nice to dance with me, but bein' as you are the daughter of a rich rancher and me bein' only a cowboy, you wouldn't have nothin' to do with me."

"You aren't a cowboy," Lucy said. "Cowboys are honorable men. You are nothing but an outlaw.

And I believe I told you that I didn't want to dance with you because I don't like you."

"Uh-huh. Well, here's the thing, girlie. You're goin' to dance with me now, only it ain't exactly goin' to be dancin' if you get my meanin'." Keno laughed a low, guttural laugh. "Yes, ma'am, me an' you is goin' to have us some fun."

Keno stuck the key into the lock; then, pulling his pistol, he opened the door to the cell and stepped inside.

"Does Van Arndt know you are here?" Sally asked.

Keno turned his pistol toward Sally. "It ain't none of your concern whether Van Arndt knows I'm here or not," he said. "What I want you to do is stand over there up against them bars. If I see you so much as move one inch, I'll kill this girl and have my fun with you."

Obeying Keno's instructions, Sally stepped up against the bars right alongside the open cell door.

"That's more like it," Keno said.

When Lucy saw Keno coming toward her, her fear became palpable, and she felt a bile in her throat. "No," she said in a choked voice. "No, please don't. Van Arndt said I was for insurance."

"Hell, honey, he just said that 'cause he wanted first crack at you hisself, that's all. Only thing is, I figure on takin' my turn with you before anyone else."

"No," Lucy whimpered. "Please, no."

Lucy squeezed her eyes shut, trying unsuccessfully to prevent the tears from sliding down her cheeks. Her entreaties fell upon deaf ears, however, for she felt him approaching, then smelled his foul breath and body stench as he reached for her.

"Go ahead and cry if you want to, girlie," Keno said. "I like it when you cry."

Behind Keno's back, Sally tore off a piece cloth from her dress, then stuffed it into the lock plate of the cell door opening.

"Step outside," Keno said, waving with his pistol. Turning his head, he saw Sally standing very still by the bars. "Well, aren't you being a good girl now?" he asked.

Whimpering, and shivering with fright, Lucy stepped through the open door. Keno closed the cell door, turned the key in the lock, then hung the key back on the wall hook.

"I'll tell you what, Sally, you can watch us," Keno said, tossing the remark over his shoulder. "Maybe you'll learn a trick or two you can teach Smoke." Keno laughed, then pushed Lucy over to the desk. "Bend over that desk, girl," he said. "Me and you is goin' to have us a fine time."

When Lucy hesitated, Keno spoke more harshly. "Damn you, I told you to lean over." He pushed her belly-down over the desk, then hiked her dress up over her waist.

"Yes, sir, this is goin' to be fine," Keno said.

Behind Keno, and unnoticed by him, Sally took a pin from her hair and stuck it in between the door lock and the lock plate. As she had hoped, the cloth she had stuffed into the lock plate had prevented the bolt from seating. She was able to push it back with the hair pin. Then, slowly, she opened the door.

Keno, who had been holding his pistol up to this point, now put it down on the desk so he could free both hands. He started to unbuckle his belt.

Sally stepped out of the cell and, walking very quietly, moved up behind him. She reached out and picked up his pistol, then, holding it by the barrel, brought the pistol butt down hard on the back of Keno's head.

Keno fell to the floor like a sack of potatoes.

"Oh!" Lucy said aloud.

"Lucy, stand up," Sally said. "You're all right, he didn't get a chance to do anything. Stand up and help me get him into the cell," Sally said.

Lucy, who had closed her eyes to what she thought was inevitable, heard Sally's voice just behind her. With a gasp of surprised joy, she stood up and turned around.

"Sally! How did you—"

"No time to explain now," Sally said. She pointed to one of Keno's legs. "Grab hold."

With one on each leg, the two women dragged Keno across the floor and into the cell. Then, using the same hairpin, Sally removed the cloth she had used to jam up the lock plate. Closing the cell door, she locked it, then handed the key to Lucy.

"Hang on to that. We'll take the key with us," Sally said. "There is no sense in making it easy for them to get him out."

"They probably have another key," Lucy suggested.

"You're right," Sally said. She jerked open the middle drawer of the desk, then smiled and picked up a key. "Here it is. Let's go."

"Where are we going?"

"The same way we came," Sally answered. "I'm sure Smoke has been following us. He can't be too far behind. We'll catch up with him, then we'll be safe."

Lucy started toward the front door.

"No, not that way, we might be seen leaving. We'll go out the back."

When the two went outside, Lucy turned up her nose. "Oh, what is that awful smell?" she asked.

Looking around, Sally saw an outhouse just across the alley. She chuckled. "Give me the keys."

Taking the keys from Lucy, Sally opened the door to the outhouse, then dropped them down into the hole. When she turned back, she saw a huge smile spread across Lucy's face.

"That's the first time I've seen you smile since we left," Sally said. "It's good to see it."

Lucy's smile turned into a chuckle. "There hasn't really been anything to smile about until now, but I have to admit"—she pointed toward the outhouse— "dropping the keys down there is funny."

"Come on, our horses are in a stable back here," Sally said.

"How do you know?"

"I was looking through the back window when I saw them put away."

"You've just put your finger on the biggest difference between us, Sally," Lucy said. "Here I was, crying and feeling sorry for myself, while all along you were figuring ways for us to escape. I saw you pick the piece of material out from the lock. You put that in there, didn't you? That was how you were able to get out of the cell once he locked you in."

"Yes," Sally said. She peeked into the stable. "Here they are. Can you saddle your own horse?"

Lucy chuckled. "I know I haven't made a very good impression so far," she said. "But I'm not totally hopeless. Yes, I can saddle my own horse."

"Then let's do it and get out of here," Sally suggested as she spread the blanket across the back of her mount.

The two women worked quickly and quietly, their efforts illuminated only by the moon that splashed a pool of silver light in through the large stable window.

When both horses were saddled, Sally held her finger across her lips to suggest quiet. Then she led her horse out into the alley. Lucy followed until they reached the end of the alley. Then they mounted their horses and rode off into the dark.

"What the hell are you doing in the jail cell?" Van Arndt asked in a loud and angry voice when he and the others returned to the jail.

"I came back to check on the women," Keno said. "Somehow, they had gotten out of the cell and as soon as I stepped in through the door, one of them hit me from behind."

"Are you telling me a couple of women managed to escape from my jail?" Craig asked.

"Yeah."

"That's impossible. In all the time I have been here, not one person has ever gotten out of that cell, not one," Craig said. "And now, you are telling me that a couple of women escaped?"

"Well, it ain't my fault," Keno said. "If you want to blame someone, blame your deputy there. Like as not, he didn't even lock the cell door shut."

"You know better than that, Keno," Laney said. "You saw me lock the door." Laney looked over at Van Arndt. "And you even tried to open it yourself."

"That's right, I did try to open it," Van Arndt said. "It was locked."

"Well, it don't matter none whether he locked the door or not," Keno said. "The thing is, the women got out, and now they are gone."

"What I want to know is, what were you doing back here in the first place?" Van Arndt asked.

"I told you, I come back here so I could check up on them," Keno said.

"Nobody asked you to check on them," Van Arndt said.

"Yeah? Well, it's a good thing I did check on them, ain't it?" Keno asked. "Because it turns out they was gettin' away."

"What do you mean, they *was* getting away? They did get away, you dumb son of a bitch, and you did nothing to stop them," Van Arndt said.

"You got no right to talk to me like that, Van Arndt," Keno said. "And anyhow, how could I stop them when they hit me from behind as soon as I come into the room?"

"If you ask me," Boswell said, "ole Keno just come back here so he could get hisself a poke. I wouldn't be surprised if he wasn't the one that opened the cell door to let them out in the first place."

"Is that what happened, Keno?" Van Arndt asked.

"Get me out of here," Keno said.

"I ought to leave you in there till you rot," Van Arndt said.

"Huh-uh," Craig said. "I don't want the son of a bitch lyin' around in my jail. Get him out, Deputy."

The deputy started toward the key, but seeing the hook empty he turned back to Keno. "Where's the key?"

"They took it with them," Keno said.

"No problem," Craig said, "There's another one in the middle desk drawer." Craig started toward his desk.

"No, there ain't," Keno said.

"What do you mean?"

"They took that key, too. They took both of the keys with them."

"Really? Well, boy, looks to me like you are in a lot of trouble here," Van Arndt said. "Without a key, I don't know how we are going to get you out."

"You'd better figure out a way if you want me to tell you where they went," Keno said.

"To hell with you. I'll find them without you," Van Arndt said.

"Van Arndt, don't you leave me in here!" Keno said.

Craig sighed. "I can get him out," he said.

"How?"

"Fred Loomis is the locksmith who put the lock in. He always keeps a master key so he can make a spare just for such things as this."

"All right," Van Arndt said. "Go get him."

"Jerry, go down to Fred Loomis's house. He's probably in bed by now but wake him up. Tell him there is an emergency down at the jail. Then I want you to round up Miller, Coleman, Billings, Deekus, and Agnew. Tell them I want them in a special posse."

The deputy frowned. "Marshal, I know it ain't my place to say nothin', you bein' the marshal and me just bein' a deputy and all, but there ain't a one of them boys you just named that is worth the gunpowder it would take to blow 'em to Kingdom Come. Are you sure they're the ones you want for your posse?"

"You're right, Jerry," Craig said.

The deputy smiled.

"It ain't your place to say nothin'," Craig added. "Now you go get Loomis, then round up them men like I told you to."

Laney nodded. "All right, Marshal, if you say so."

As the deputy left, Craig stepped up closer to the jail cell to look at Keno. "What the hell happened to your face, boy?"

"Nothin'," Keno said, lifting his hand self-consciously to his face.

"Jensen's wife stuck a hot stove lid into the face," Van Arndt said, laughing. "Yes, sir, she burned him good."

"Son of a bitch. Does it hurt?" Craig asked.

"Hell yes, it hurts," Keno replied irritably. "You got any more questions?"

Craig laughed. "You sure you want to go chasing off after her? I mean, it looks to me like ever'time you an' that woman tangle, you come up on the short end of the stick."

"I'm sure," Keno said.

Chapter Twenty-one

It was about fifteen minutes after Jerry Laney left before the locksmith showed up.

"Loomis, thanks for coming," Marshal Craig said.

"What took you so damn long?" Keno asked from inside the cell. "I want out of here now, do you hear me? Get me out of here now."

"I take it this fella isn't supposed to be in there?" Loomis asked.

"Hell, no, I ain't supposed to be in here," Keno replied irritably.

"Well, hold your horses," Loomis said. "I'll get you out as quick as I can."

"It's already too late for quick," Keno said. "You should'a been here half an hour ago!"

"You're a little feisty, ain't you, sonny?" Loomis asked. Then, seeing Keno's red puffy face, he squinted. "What the hell happened to your face?"

Van Arndt and the others laughed at the locksmith's question.

"Did I say something funny?" the locksmith asked, puzzled by the laughter.

"I've heard enough about my face," Keno said. "It ain't none of your business what happened to my face. Just get to work and do whatever you have to do to get me out of here."

"Marshal, I had to make a new key," Loomis said. "I guess you know that's going to cost the city a quarter."

"A quarter? I thought it only cost fifteen cents to make a key."

"That's in the daytime during normal business hours," Loomis said. "Your deputy got me out of bed, so it's goin' to cost you extra."

"Send the city a bill," Craig replied.

Loomis snorted. "Yeah, I thought you might say something like that," he said. "All right, let me see what I can do here."

Loomis walked over to the cell, inserted the key, and tried to turn it. It wouldn't turn.

"What's wrong?" Keno said. "Son of a bitch, you are a locksmith. Can't you even make a key that works?"

"Hold your horses, sonny, hold your horses," Loomis said. Removing the key, he filed on one of the tangs for a moment, then reinserted it, and when it still didn't work, withdrew it and filed on it again. It took him a full five minutes before the key worked. As soon as it did, Keno pushed the door open so quickly that the locksmith had to jump to one side to get out of the way.

As the locksmith was leaving, two men came in.

"Miller, Coleman, I'm glad you could come," Craig said.

"The deputy said you wanted us to join a posse?" Miller said.

"That's right."

Miller laughed. "All I can say is, it must be one hell of a posse if you want me and Coleman."

"Not just you and Coleman," Craig said. "I want Billings, Deekus, and Agnew, too."

The smile left Miller's face. "What the hell is up, Marshal?" he asked. "Me and Coleman ain't exactly the posse kind. And them other boys you just named are even less so. What makes you think we would be interested?"

"You came down here, didn't you?"

"Curiosity got us down here, Marshal," Coleman said. "But that ain't enough to get us to join no posse."

"What if I told you there is fifty dollars for each man who is willing to ride with me?" Craig said.

"Fifty dollars? Just for riding in a posse? Are you serious?" Miller asked.

"I'm very serious."

"Ha, who do we have to kill for fifty dollars?" Coleman asked, laughing out loud.

"Smoke Jensen," Van Arndt said.

Coleman quit laughing. "That ain't funny," he said.

"I didn't intend it as a joke."

"Smoke Jensen ain't someone to mess with," Miller said.

"There will be ten of us," Craig said.

"Ten of us?"

"Like you said, Smoke Jensen ain't someone you want to mess with," Craig said. "But I figure if there is ten of us, we can handle it all right."

"That fifty dollars," Miller said. "It'll be for all of us, right? I mean, you ain't sayin' you are goin' to give fifty dollars just to the one that does the actual killin', are you?"

"It's for all of you, no matter who does the killin'," Craig said.

"As long as we kill the son of a bitch," Van Arndt added.

Miller and Coleman looked over at Van Arndt.

"Who's this pasty-faced feller?" Coleman asked.

"He's the one who is going to pay the fifty dollars once we kill Smoke Jensen," Craig said. "Do you have a problem with that?"

"No, I ain't got a problem with it," Coleman answered. "If the others go along with it, I'm willin' to go, too."

"Van Arndt, wait a minute, if we kill Smoke Jensen, how are we ever goin' to get the money?" Keno asked.

"What money?" Billings asked. He, Deekus, and Agnew came in at that moment.

"Fifty dollars apiece if you ride with my special posse," Craig said.

"That ain't—" Keno started to say, but Van Arndt held up his hand to stop him.

"Harlan, why don't you take your posse outside and tell 'em what's goin' on?" Van Arndt suggested.

"Good idea," Craig replied. "How about you boys

step outside with me, and I'll tell you everything you need to know."

Van Arndt waited until Craig and the posse were outside. Then he looked over at Keno.

"You are going to need to learn how to keep your mouth shut," Van Arndt said. "As far as those men are concerned, fifty dollars is all the money there is. Unless you want to start sharing."

"Sharing what?" Keno asked. "How are we going to get the ransom if we kill Smoke Jensen?"

"You said you know Jensen's ranch," Van Arndt said. "How well do you know it?"

"I've rode all over it," Keno said. "Hell, I know it like the back of my hand."

"If Jensen and his wife are both dead, along with them two that ride with him all the time, there ain't goin' to be anybody left to look after the ranch. Do you think you could show us the best way to cut out about five thousand head and get them off the ranch before anyone notices?"

For a moment, Keno's expression was blank. Then it showed surprise, followed by a big smile spread across his face.

"Hell, yes, I know exactly how to do it," he said. "We can ford them across Elk Creek, then take them up the other side of Red Butte. But what would we do with them once we had them? C.D. Montgomery and Red Cliff are the only cattle buyers around."

"They are paying twenty-five dollars a head up in Wyoming at the railhead in Harney, " Van Arndt said. "We're going to drive the herd up there."

"Twenty-five dollars a head for five thousand

head?" Boswell said. "That's—" He paused to try and figure it out.

"One hundred twenty-five thousand dollars," Van Arndt said. He looked at Keno. "A hell of a lot more money, and more certain, than collecting a ransom from Jensen, don't you think?"

"Yeah," Keno said, nodding. "Yeah, it is."

"What about them other boys, the ones the marshal is talkin' to now?" Jeeter asked. "What do they get out of all this?"

"You heard my brother," Van Arndt replied. "They're gettin' fifty dollars apiece for ridin' in the posse."

"They goin' to be satisfied with that?" Boswell asked.

"Yeah, 'cause they ain't goin' to know about anything else unless one of you starts runnin' off at the mouth," Van Arndt said. He looked directly at Keno.

"I ain't goin' to say nothin'," Keno said, holding his hands up palms out, as if distancing himself from even the idea of such a transgression.

"Where do you reckon Jensen is right now?" Boswell asked.

"It doesn't matter where he is now. He has to come through Ptarmigan Pass to get here—and that's where we'll be waitin' for him."

After Deputy Laney rounded up the posse, he returned to the jail. He was just outside the window when he overheard Van Arndt telling the others of his plan to kill Jensen and the others. Not wanting any part of that, he went back to the stable, saddled his horse, and rode out of town at a gallop.

Seeing the two women in front of him, he circled around a butte and waited for them. When they approached the end of the butte, Laney rode out in front of them.

"Sally!" Lucy shouted in panic at Laney's sudden appearance. Her horse, started by Lucy's reaction, reared up and Lucy fell from the saddle.

Laney jumped down quickly and went to her.

"Get away from her!" Sally ordered and, looking up, Laney saw that Sally was holding a pistol and it was pointed at him.

Laney chuckled. "That would be Keno's gun, wouldn't it?"

"Yes."

"Well, you can put it down, Mrs. Jensen, I'm on your side."

"You know who I am?"

"I do now, yes. That's why I'm here. And like I said, I'm on your side."

"Why should I believe that?"

Laney shook his head. "I don't reckon you have any reason to believe it," he said. He grabbed the reins of Lucy's horse and held them until she was able to remount. "Especially given the way I acted back there," he added. "But once I found out you were telling the truth, and once I found out what their plans were, I figured I couldn't just stand by and watch it happen."

"You don't have to worry about it now," Sally said. "There won't be any ransom paid."

Laney shook his head. "That's not the plan," he said. "And to be honest, I don't think it ever was the plan."

"What are you talking about? Of course it was the plan."

"No," Laney said. "The plan is to hold you two as bait. Then, when your husband comes after you, they are going to kill him and anyone who was with him. They also plan to kill you, Mrs. Jensen. After that, they are going to cut away about five thousand head of cattle from your herd and, before anyone realizes what is going on, they'll drive them up to Wyoming and sell them."

"Ha," Lucy said. "Do you expect us to believe that?"

"I do believe it," Sally said.

"What?"

Sally lowered her gun. "It's brilliant," she said. "It is incredibly evil, but it is brilliant."

"I assume you are heading back to join up with your husband now?" Laney asked.

"Yes."

"If you would accept my help, I would be honored to ride with you until you join up with him."

"I would be glad to have you accompany us, Deputy," she said.

Chapter Twenty-two

Cal saw them first, three riders coming out of the dark.

"Riders coming," he said, snaking his rifle from the saddle holster.

"No, wait! It's Sally!" Smoke said, holding up his hand.

"How do you know? You can't see from here," Cal said.

"It's Sally, and I assume Lucy," Smoke said again. "But I don't know who the third rider is."

One of the approaching riders broke from the other two and started galloping toward them. Smoke mounted his horse and started toward the approaching rider.

Pearlie watched the two riders come together, then dismount and embrace and kiss. He laughed and pointed.

"If that's not Sally, it should be," Pearlie said with a little laugh.

"I think you are right," Cal answered, and they urged their horses into a gallop to catch up.

Lucy and the other rider arrived at about the same

time Pearlie and Cal did, and Pearlie helped Lucy down from the horse. Wrapping his arms around her, he pulled Lucy to him and for a long moment, Pearlie and Lucy, like Smoke and Sally, enjoyed a kiss.

Cal and Laney remained mounted, looking on.

"Uh, don't none of you all worry none about me," Cal said. "I'm just fine. Really."

Sally laughed. "Poor Cal. Feeling left out, are you?"

"Well, yeah, seems like ever'one has someone huggin' 'em but me," Cal said.

"Well, let's see what we can do about that," Sally said. Reaching up toward him, she pulled him out of the saddle.

"Whoa, what are you doin'?" Cal asked, fighting to stay afoot.

"I'm giving you a hug," Sally said, putting her arms around his neck and pulling her to him.

The others laughed.

"Who is this?" Smoke asked, nodding toward Laney, who as yet had said nothing.

"This is the deputy marshal from Salcedo," Sally said.

"The name is Laney. Jerry Laney," the deputy said.

"Have you come with another ransom demand?"

"No," Laney said. "It never was about ransom."

Laney explained to Smoke what he had overheard about using Sally as bait so they could kill them all.

"There will be at least ten of them," Laney said.

"Ten?"

"Yes, sir."

"I appreciate the information, Deputy. And I appreciate you helping Sally and Lucy escape."

Laney smiled. "I wish I could take credit for that," he said. "But somehow, your wife managed to do that all by herself."

"You should have seen her, Mr. Jensen," Lucy said. "She poked some cloth into the jail cell door, then managed to get it open. Your wife is wonderful."

"You'll get no argument from me on that," Smoke said. "Sally, why don't you take Lucy on home?" Smoke said. "We'll take care of Van Arndt."

"I'm not leaving," Sally said. "Smoke, I watched that son of a bitch kill Carlos and Maria, right in front of my eyes. I intend to be there when he pays the price."

"All right, I know you better than to try and argue you out of something once your mind is made up. Pearlie, it looks like you are going to have to take Lucy home."

"Smoke, I—" Pearlie started to protest, but Laney interrupted him.

"If you trust me to do it, I'll take her home," Laney said. "I couldn't stand by and let you folks be murdered, but this ain't my fight, so I don't intend to take part in it."

"You don't have to take part in it," Smoke said. "Like I said, I appreciate you bringing us word. Lucy, why don't you go along with the deputy?"

"I'm not going anywhere," Lucy said. "I'm staying right here with the rest of you."

"No, I don't think so, Lucy," Pearlie said. "Smoke is right. You need to get out of here."

"No," Lucy said.

"Miss, if it's because you don't trust me, I can understand that," Laney said. "But I swear to you, I mean only to help."

"It isn't that," Lucy said.

"Then what is it?" Pearlie asked.

"Pearlie, would you want to be married to someone who is such a coward that she would run out on her friends?"

"What?" Pearlie asked. "What did you say?"

"They are my friends, aren't they? Sally, Smoke, and Cal? Would you really want me to run out on them?"

"No," Pearlie said. "I'm not talking about that part. I'm talking about the married part."

Lucy smiled. "Well, would you want to marry such a person?"

"Are you saying—Lucy—are you saying you would marry me?" Pearlie asked.

"Well, I don't know. I haven't been asked yet," Lucy replied.

"Yes, yes," Pearlie said. "Uh—that is, I mean—well, I hadn't planned on asking you in front of everybody like this but—will you marry me?"

"I'll marry you on one condition," Lucy said.

"What is that?"

"That you don't make me run out on my friends. After all, I have a personal bone to pick with him."

Pearlie looked at Smoke.

"What should I do, Smoke?"

Smoke laughed. "Don't ask me," he said. "You saw

how much success I had in telling Sally she couldn't stay."

"Yeah, I saw that," Pearlie said. He looked back at Lucy. "All right, you can stay," he said. "But you do exactly as I tell you to do, do you hear me? Exactly what I tell you to do."

"Yes, dear," Lucy said.

Smoke looked up at Laney. "Well, Deputy, it looks like we won't be needing you after all. I expect you'd better be getting on now, while the getting is good."

Laney nodded. "I expect you are right," he said. "I wish you folks good luck."

"Thanks."

Behind Smoke, the horizon showed a thin line of gray. In half an hour, it would be light enough to see. During the night, they had heard the sounds of several horses and men, so they knew that Van Arndt and his men had arrived and were setting up an ambush. Now, by the gray light of early morning, they could see that Van Arndt, Craig, Keno, and at least seven more men were in position in the rocks on each side of the pass. They would have been ideally situated to spring an ambush when Smoke came through had Laney not warned Smoke of the possibility.

But Smoke and the others were ready for Van Arndt. They were just inside the pass, in covered positions ready to commence the operation when the time was right. Sally, who was also armed, was right beside Smoke. Looking to his left, he saw that

Lucy, who was not armed, was with Pearlie, but well down behind the rock so as to be out of any line of fire. Cal was just beyond Pearlie.

Smoke heard Van Arndt's voice floating up from below.

"Coleman, Miller, you boys get over there," Van Arndt called out. "When they come through the pass, wait until I give the word. Then, start blasting away. I want Jensen and everyone with him killed."

"He might have them two women with him," someone called back. "What do we do about them?"

"Didn't you hear what I said? I don't care who he has with them, I want 'em all killed," Van Arndt said.

"Craig, you didn't say nothin' 'bout killin' no women. That don't seem right to me."

"Would an extra fifty dollars make it seem right to you?" Van Arndt asked.

"An extra fifty? Yeah, hell, yeah. For an extra fifty dollars I'd kill my own sister."

"Hell, your sister don't count none, Coleman, she's a whore," someone else said.

"Don't make no never mind, whore or not, she's still my sister, and I'd still kill her for fifty dollars," Coleman said.

The others laughed.

"You people keep quiet," Van Arndt shouted. "And keep your eyes peeled."

Smoke saw Van Arndt come down to stand just at the edge of the little rocky ridge that marked the end of the pass. He stood there for a moment, staring in the direction from which he believed Smoke and the others would come.

Quietly, Smoke jacked a round into the chamber of his rifle, then drew a bead on Van Arndt's chest. He could drop him from this distance, and Van Arndt would never know what hit him.

Smoke lowered his rifle.

"Why didn't you shoot?" Sally asked.

"It's not a very sporting way to kill a man," Smoke replied.

"If you won't do it, I will," Sally said. "How sporting is it for a man to shoot a nine-year-old girl in the head from one foot away? Remember, I saw that son of a bitch do that very thing."

Smoked nodded, and sighed. "You're right," he said. He raised his rifle again, but when he looked back, the target of opportunity was gone. Van Arndt had stepped back behind the saddle of rocks.

"I'm sorry," Smoke said. "But I promise you, he will not get out of here alive."

Sally reached over and gave Smoke's arm an affectionate squeeze. "Bless Maria's little heart," Sally said. "I've been too furious with Van Arndt to even grieve properly. But I will grieve when all this is over. I have promised myself that."

Nearby, Cal tried to change positions and when he did, he dislodged a rock and lost his footing. As a result, he began to slide down the side of the little hill, managing to stop himself before he actually fell to the floor below.

Cal stopped his fall, but he was now in full sight, and he started scrambling, trying to climb back up to the relative safety of the rocks.

"What the hell was that?" a voice asked, drifting

up from the area where Van Arndt had set up his ambush.

"Up there!" someone shouted. "There's someone trying to crawl up the side of the hill."

"That's Cal!" Keno's voice shouted. "He's one of Jensen's men. Shoot him! Shoot the son of a bitch!"

Several of Van Arndt's men opened fire then and the bullets started snapping by, hitting rocks and singing as they ricocheted through the narrow confines of the pass. Many of them kicked up dirt and sand all around Cal, but he managed to get back behind the rocks before any of them hit him.

Although the position Smoke and the others had chosen had been well selected to engage Van Arndt's men if they had entered the pass, it was not particularly well situated for what was happening now. Smoke's position had been detected, and whereas Van Arndt's men had a broad plain upon which they could maneuver, Smoke and the others had no such opportunity. As a result, the advantage fell quickly to Van Arndt.

Had either Van Arndt or Craig the slightest experience with military tactics, they would have realized the superiority of their position and stayed put, all the while maintaining a steady volume of fire designed to keep Smoke at a disadvantage. But tactics was not a strong point of either brother, and growing anxious, they started trying to improve their position.

"Miller, move up on the left!" Van Arndt ordered. "Billings, you go up the right side! The rest of you boys, cover them! Keep firing!"

Miller was first one to move out and, firing a

couple of shots from his pistol, he darted from one rock to another, thus moving closer. Billings moved up on the right side.

"Ha! It was easy!" Miller shouted. "Coleman, Deekus, Agnew, come on up!"

When the other three committed themselves, Smoke shouted to Pearlie and Cal.

"Now!" he said.

Smoke, Sally, Pearlie, and Cal opened fire and, with the first broadside, Coleman, Deekus, and Agnew went down.

"Damn," Pearlie said. "I wonder which one of them we shot twice."

Cal laughed.

Smoke began shooting at the rock where he saw Miller take cover. He knew he couldn't hit him from where he was, but he could get close enough to make Miller very uncomfortable.

"Ahh!" Miller shouted. "Craig, get us out of here!"

"Stay where you are!" Craig called up to him.

For the next few minutes, all was quiet. Then, somehow, Billings managed to improve his position so he could take a shot. His bullet came so close to Smoke that it kicked sand into his face. Smoke moved around to return fire, but it wasn't necessary because Cal brought Billings down with one shot.

"Harlan," Van Arndt said. "How well do you know this pass?"

"I've come through it a lot of times," Craig said.

Van Arndt pointed. "You think we could get above them if we went up that way?"

Craig smiled, and nodded. "Yeah," he said. "Yeah, we could. But we'll need to keep someone down here to keep them busy."

"I'll stay," Boswell said.

"Good enough," Van Arndt said. He looked at the others. "Let's go."

Boswell watched the four of them leave. Then he started shooting up toward Jensen.

"Hey, Miller!" Boswell called. "Miller, you still alive?"

"Yeah," Miller called back down.

"Then start shootin'!" Boswell shouted. "I ain't doin' this alone."

Boswell punctuated his shout with another shot from his rifle, and Miller started shooting as well.

For the next few minutes, the shooting continued. Then Smoke saw someone raise up to improve his position and when he did, Smoke snapped off a quick shot. He saw a little spray of blood fly out from the top of his target's head; then the man fell forward.

"That one is Boswell," Sally said.

At that moment, Miller stood up and raised his hands. "Don't shoot, don't shoot no more!" he shouted. "I give up!"

Pearlie raised his rifle.

"No," Lucy said, putting her hand on Pearlie's shoulder. "He wasn't one of them."

"Don't shoot, don't shoot!" Miller shouted again.

"Get out of here then," Pearlie yelled. "Go on, get!"

Miller turned to run.

"Leave your rifle and drop your gunbelt!" Smoke called.

Miller did as ordered, then ran down the hill from where he had taken position, and on out through the end of the pass.

"Smoke, where are the others, do you see them?" Cal called.

At that moment, Van Arndt, Craig, Jeeter, and Keno stood up on a rock above and behind them. The four men were less than one hundred feet away, and had put themselves in perfect position to shoot Smoke and the others in the back. No doubt they would have done so, had Sally not seen the barest flicker of a shadow and turned, just as the four were raising their rifles.

"Smoke, behind us!" Sally shouted.

Smoke, Pearlie, and Cal spun around, even as the four men above them began shooting.

For the next ten seconds, the narrow pass echoed and reechoed with the sound of gunfire as guns blazed and bullets flew. Craig and Jeeter were the first two to go down; then two bullets hit Van Arndt in his forehead, fired from the pistols of Smoke and Sally. For just a moment, the blood was bright red on the white skin; then Van Arndt fell forward and slid the rest of the way down.

Amazingly, Keno had not been hit, and he suddenly dropped his gun and threw up his hands.

"No!" he shouted. "No, don't shoot, don't shoot!"

Smoke, Sally, Pearlie, and Cal held their fire.

"Keno, I hope you know this isn't buying you

anything," Smoke said. "We're taking you back to hang."

"I didn't kill nobody. It was Van Arndt that done it," Keno said.

"I don't care whether you killed anyone or not, you're going to hang," Smoke said. "Come on down here."

"I'm comin', I'm comin'," Keno said, still holding his hands in the air. He started climbing down, then had to turn around and lean forward to grab onto a rock in order to be able to come down from a high ledge.

"Is anyone left down there?" Pearlie asked.

"I don't think so," Cal replied as he and Pearlie both looked back down the trail to make certain everyone was accounted for.

As it happened, Lucy was the only one who saw the gun. When Keno reached down to improve his hold, the pistol Van Arndt had dropped was right there in front of him. Keno grabbed the pistol, then spun around.

"No!" Lucy shouted, and she jumped in front of Pearlie just as Keno fired. The bullet struck her in the chest.

"No!" Pearlie screamed, the guttural shout a cross between an anguished cry and a roar of rage.

Pearlie's first shot hit Keno in the arm, causing him to drop his gun. Then Pearlie shot Keno in the other arm, then in both knees. Keno went down, screaming in agony.

Pearlie shot off each of his ears, then pointed the pistol at Keno's face and fired, putting a hole right between Keno's eyes. Pearlie pulled the trigger three more times, but the hammer fell on empty cartridges.

It didn't matter.

Keno was dead.

Pearlie spun around then, and dropped to the ground beside Lucy. With each breath Lucy drew, blood frothed at her mouth. The bullet had hit her in the lungs and she was dying right before Pearlie's eyes.

"Lucy, Lucy, why did you jump out like that?" Pearlie asked.

"He would have killed you," Lucy said. "I couldn't let him kill you."

"Lucy, oh, my God, Lucy," Pearlie said. Sitting on the ground beside her, he cradled her head in his lap.

"I only wish that we could have been married," Lucy said.

"You can be," Sally said. "Smoke, marry them."

"I don't have a Bible, I don't have a book, I don't—" Smoke started to say.

"For God's sake, Smoke, just do it!" Sally said. "You've been married twice now, you know what to say."

"Lucy?" Smoke said. "Do you want me to do this?"

"Yes, please," Lucy said, taking Pearlie's hand in hers and squeezing it hard. "Please marry us."

"All right," Smoke said. "Pearlie, do you take this woman, Lucy, to be your lawfully wedded wife, to love, hold, and honor, as long—" Smoke paused, and when he spoke again, his voice broke. "As long as you both shall live?"

"I do," Pearlie said.

"Lucy, do you take Pearlie to be your lawfully wedded husband, to love, obey, and honor, as long as you both shall live?"

"I do," Lucy said, the words so weak that they could barely be heard.

"By the power vested in me by the state of Colorado, I pronounce you man and wife."

"We are married," Lucy said. She smiled through her pain. "Pearlie, you are my husband."

"Yes," Pearlie said. "And you are my wife."

"Kiss me, Pearlie. Kiss me quickly."

"Lucy?" Pearlie asked, his voice breaking.

"Kiss her, Pearlie," Sally said. "Kiss her before it is too late."

Pearlie leaned over and kissed her, holding it for a long moment before, suddenly, he stiffened, then raised up. He looked into Lucy's face, which, despite her death agony, wore an expression of rapture. The joy of her marriage was her last conscious thought, because Lucy was dead.

When Pearlie looked up, tears were streaming down his face. Stepping over to him, Sally knelt beside him, then held him as he wept.

One month later

As Pearlie tightened the cinches on his saddle, Sally came out to see him, carrying a cloth bag. "I baked a few things for you," she said.

"Shucks, you didn't have to do that."

"I know I didn't. But I wanted to."

"I appreciate it," Pearlie said, tying the bag to his

saddle horn. He looked back toward the bunkhouse. "I thought Cal would come tell me good-bye."

"Cal's having a hard time with the fact that you are leaving," Sally said. "So am I. So is Smoke."

"Yeah," Pearlie said. He ran his hand through his hair. "Truth is, I'm having a hard time leaving."

Running his hand through his hair messed it up a bit, and Sally licked her fingers, then reached up to smooth it out.

"It's just that, well, with what happened to Lucy and all, I need myself some time alone." Pearlie held his hand up. "This is no knock on you and Smoke and Cal," he said. "Lord, there can't no man anywhere in the world have any better friends. It's just that—" He paused.

"I know what you mean, Pearlie," Sally said. "And I understand your need to get away. I just hope it isn't permanent."

"Pearlie!" Cal called, coming from the bunkhouse then.

Pearlie turned toward his young friend and smiled broadly. "Well, I'm glad you came out to see me. I was beginning to think I might have to leave without saying good-bye."

"I want you to have this," Cal said. He held out his silver hatband. "You can see that I have it all polished up for you. You have to keep it polished, otherwise it gets a little tarnished."

"Cal, I can't take this," Pearlie said, pushing it back.

"I ain't givin' it to you permanent," Cal said.

Sally started to correct Cal's grammar, but she realized that this was a very emotional time for the two young men, so she said nothing.

"I figure if you've got my silver hatband, you'll come back for sure," Cal said.

Pearlie looked at the hatband for a moment, nodded, then slipped it onto his hat. Without another word, he swung into the saddle and rode off.

Smoke came out of the house then, and stood with Sally and Cal as they watched Pearlie pass under the entry gate.

"You didn't try and talk him into staying," Sally said.

"No," Smoke said. He put his arm around Sally and pulled her to him. "I've been there, Sally. Pearlie has to make up his own mind as to whether or not he's coming back."

"He's coming back," Cal said resolutely.

"How can you be so sure?" Smoke asked.

"I gave him my silver hatband," Cal said. "Pearlie ain't no thief. He'll bring it back."

Smoke chuckled. "You know, you might just be right," he said.

"Damn, what was I thinkin'?" Cal said.

"What do you mean?"

"I'm goin' to the dance tonight. Without that hatband, there ain't goin' to be girl one look at me. Most especially without Pearlie there to act up and get 'em all to comin' around us."

"Cal, I've never told you this before, because I didn't want it to go to your head," Sally said. "But I think you are one of the best-looking young men I've ever known. You just keep that in mind at the dance. Why, I'll just bet the girls won't be able to stay away from you."

"What? Wow, Miz Sally, are you serious?"

"I'm very serious," Sally said.

A broad smile spread across Cal's face. "Well, I'll be," he said. "Comin' from you, that's somethin' special, seein' as you're about the prettiest woman there is."

Cal looked at his hat and turned it a few times in his hand before he put it back on. "Shoot, I don't need no silver hatband," he said, turning and walking back toward the bunkhouse with a decided swagger. "No, sir, I don't need me no silver hatband a'tall."

Smoke chuckled at Cal walked away.

"You laid it on a little thick, didn't you?"

"He needed a little cheering up," Sally said.

"Don't we all?" Smoke replied.

The stood there for a moment longer, looking at Pearlie as he and his horse receded in the distance.

"Do you think he'll be all right, Smoke?"

"Yeah," Smoke said. His voice was gruff. "He'll be fine."

Turn the page for an exciting preview of

THE FIRST MOUNTAIN MAN:
PREACHER'S PURSUIT

by William W. Johnstone and J. A. Johnstone

Coming next month from Pinnacle Books

Chapter One

Preacher pressed his back against the gully's rock wall and tightened his hands on the flintlock rifle he carried slantwise across his chest. He listened intently, ignoring the thudding of his heart and trying instead to pick up the stealthy sounds of the man creeping up the gully after him.

His side stung a little where a rifle ball had ripped his buckskin shirt and burned across his flesh. He put that pain out of his head, too. 'Tweren't nothin', he told himself. He'd been hurt lots worse plenty of times.

A tall man in his thirties, dark-haired and bearded, lean-bodied but still powerfully built, Preacher knew these mountains as well as most men knew their own faces . . . or the bodies of their wives. The two varmints who'd tried to ambush him had made a bad mistake in doing so.

One of them had already paid the ultimate price. He lay dead or dying on one of the slopes higher up, his guts torn open by a shot from Preacher's rifle.

His companion was still alive, though. He was the one trying to sneak up on Preacher now. Normally, Preacher would have just waited for the man to come along and then blown a hole through him, but that was hard to do without any powder.

A lucky shot aimed at Preacher had clipped the rawhide thong by which the powder horn was slung over his shoulder. It had skittered over the edge of a long drop, gone before he could even try to grab it. He had already emptied his rifle and both pistols while trading lead with the two would-be killers, so he couldn't reload.

But that didn't mean the man called Preacher was helpless. Far from it.

He'd been toiling up a long, steep slope to check on some traps. His horse and dog were down at the base of the slope, left behind because there was no real reason for them to have to make the tiring climb. He was halfway to the top when he heard the shrill neigh from Horse and the half-snarl, half-bark from Dog and recognized them as warning signals. Somebody was close by who shouldn't be.

The first shot had rung out as Preacher started to turn. The heavy lead ball struck a small rock near his feet and blew it to smithereens. He saw the puff of powder smoke from a clump of fir trees, and was bringing his rifle to his shoulder to return fire when another rifle cracked from above him and he felt the fiery lance slice across his side.

They had him between 'em, drat the luck.

He let loose with a round aimed at the fir trees anyway, then turned and dashed along the face of the slope, figuring to work his way around a rocky shoulder that jutted out ahead of him. More shots came after him, but his long legs carried him too fast for the lead to find him.

He reached the shoulder, ducked around it. Behind him, a couple of men yelled at each other. White men, Preacher noted. They were speaking English, peppered with a lot of cussin'.

"I got him, I tell you!"

"The hell you did! Did you see the way that bastard was runnin'? No son of a bitch who was wounded could move that damned fast!"

He could tell from the sound of their voices that they were angling toward him from above and below. He set the rifle down and drew the pistols from behind his belt. Both were double-shotted, with powder charges heavy enough that the recoil from them might break the wrist of a normal man.

Preacher was anything but normal.

He heard rocks clatter close by, kicked loose by the man who was closing in from above. Preacher swung around the rugged knob and saw the man trying to skid to a stop about fifteen feet away and bring his rifle to bear. Preacher squeezed the trigger of his right-hand pistol before the muzzle of the rifle could line up on him.

One of the balls missed, but the other one plunked itself in the man's belly. He screamed as he doubled over and pitched forward, rolling a couple of times before he came to a stop. He kept writhing and wailing.

"You son of a bitch!"

The cry came from the other man, who fired a pistol at Preacher even though he was still a good forty feet away. The ball missed, but it came close enough that Preacher heard the hum of its passage through the air. He darted around the rocky shoulder, stuck the empty pistol behind his belt, grabbed up his rifle, and started running again.

He had gotten a good look at the man he'd shot, and knew that he had never seen the son of a buck before. The fella was squat and bearded, with a big felt hat that had fallen off when he collapsed. Preacher hadn't taken the time to study the other fella's face, but he had a feeling he had never seen that one either.

Now, why would two men he had never met before want to kill him? He had a decent mess of plews back at his camp, but nothing worth killing—or dying— over.

Preacher didn't spend a lot of time pondering the question. It was enough to know that they'd tried to ventilate him, which, according to his way of thinking, meant it was perfectly all right for him to blow their lights out.

He kind of wanted to talk to that second man, though, and maybe find out what was going on here. That meant he had to take the rapscallion alive.

For that reason alone, Preacher hurried along the side of the mountain, looking for a spot where he could turn the tables on his pursuer and get the drop on the man. Otherwise, he never would have run.

Fleeing from trouble stuck in his craw. He had always been one to face up to it head-on. That was the way he had lived his life ever since he came West some twenty years earlier.

Of course, he hadn't come straight to these mountains. There'd been a little matter of fighting the British first at New Orleans under ol' Andy Jackson . . .

Preacher put those thoughts out of his mind, too. Bein' chased across a mountain by some son of a gun who wanted to kill him was no time for reminiscing.

Preacher threw on the brakes as he leaped over a rocky hump and found himself teetering on the brink of a hundred-foot drop. Footsteps pounded behind him. He still had one loaded pistol, so he whirled around and brought the gun up. He and the man chasing him fired at the same time.

That was when the ball clipped Preacher's powder horn loose, just as neat as you please, and over the edge it went without even bouncing once. The two balls from his pistol powdered rock at the man's feet and made him skip backward with a yelp of alarm.

Left now with empty weapons and no way to reload, Preacher turned and stepped off the edge of the cliff, vanishing into empty air. The fella chasing him let out a startled yell.

Preacher hadn't done away with himself, though. He had spotted a narrow ledge about a dozen feet below the rim with some hardy bushes growing on it. He landed with a lithe agility and grabbed hold of some branches to steady himself and keep from plunging the rest of the way to the bottom.

Once he had his balance, he began working his way quickly along the ledge. The cliff face jutted out above him, cutting him off from the other man's view. More importantly, the varmint couldn't get a shot at him from up there.

But the man could hear the pebbles that Preacher kicked off the ledge clattering all the way down the drop-off, so he could track his quarry by the sound of Preacher's passage. Likewise, Preacher heard the fella scurrying along up above.

The ledge angled down, and eventually Preacher found himself at the bottom where a narrow creek twisted its way along the base of the cliff. He followed it and came to the gully. During snowmelt season, a stream probably ran through it, but it was dry now, so Preacher followed it, deliberately making enough of a racket so that the man behind him would be able to tell where he had gone.

So that was where he found himself now, wounded slightly, a little winded, and with empty guns.

But he still had a hunting knife with a long, heavy, razor-sharp blade, and there was a Crow tomahawk tucked behind his belt as well. He wasn't defenseless, not by a long shot.

He hadn't moved for several minutes. The fella chasing him had to be wondering by now if Preacher had given him the slip. Preacher heard him drawing closer, hurrying along now and muttering frustrated obscenities to himself.

"Sumbitch couldn't've got away. Maybe Jonah

was right. Maybe he *was* wounded. I know he came along here, damn his hide."

The words came clearly to Preacher's ears, along with the panting breaths that the man took. He was right around the bend in the gully where Preacher waited . . .

The man stepped around the bend and yelled in alarm as Preacher lunged at him, swinging the empty rifle. He jerked his own rifle up, not trying to fire the weapon, just making a desperate effort to fend off Preacher's rifle.

The flintlocks came together with a loud clash of wood and metal, knocking the rifle out of the man's hands, and the blow Preacher aimed at his head bounced off his shoulder instead.

That still had to hurt. The man yelled again and lowered his head, driving forward with powerful thrusts of his legs while Preacher was slightly off balance. The man was almost as tall as Preacher and weighed more, and when his head slammed into Preacher's chest, Preacher was knocked backward.

The collision sent both men sprawling to the ground. When Preacher slammed into the earth, it jolted the rifle out of his hands.

No great loss, he thought. The rifle was empty, and it wasn't very good for fighting at close quarters anyway. A long-barreled flintlock only made a good club when you had room to swing it.

He snatched his tomahawk from behind his belt and swung it instead. The other man rolled out of the way, his desperation giving him the speed to barely avoid the tomahawk's slashing head.

He kicked out at Preacher as he went by. The heel of his boot caught Preacher on the elbow, making Preacher's entire right arm go numb. The tomahawk slipped out of his fingers, but he caught it with his left hand before it hit the ground.

The man grabbed Preacher's arm and twisted it. Preacher aimed a knee at the man's groin and sank it deep. The man screamed in Preacher's face, but didn't let go.

They rolled over and over, grappling with each other. The man's hat came off. Long, fair hair flopped over his face. A mustache of the same shade drooped over his mouth. Preacher was more certain than ever now that he had never seen this varmint before.

That was mighty curious, too. Usually when folks tried to kill him, they had a good reason, or what they *thought* was a good reason anyway.

The man drove his face at the side of Preacher's head. His mouth was open, and Preacher knew what was coming next. The son of a bitch wanted to bite his ear off!

Preacher jerked his head to the side, avoiding the snapping teeth. He whipped it back the other way so that their skulls banged together. Preacher would match the hardness of his noggin against anybody else's, but he had to admit that he saw stars dancing around behind his eyes. Both men groaned and seemed a little addlepated.

The feeling was coming back into Preacher's right arm and hand. He reached for his knife and closed his fingers around the leather-wrapped handle. He pulled the weapon free of his belt and slashed at the man's legs with it.

The blade cut through buckskin and flesh. The man howled, let go of Preacher's other arm, and drove the ball of his hand hard against Preacher's jaw. Preacher's head was forced back until it felt like his neckbone would crack.

Whoever this fella was, he could fight! He was almost as adept at rough-and-tumble as Preacher.

But there was only one Preacher, and he had come by his reputation as the toughest he-coon in the mountains honestlike. Preacher kneed the man again, in the belly this time instead of the balls. He walloped him across the face with the brass ball that was at the end of the knife's grip. The man's struggles were growing weaker now.

Sensing maybe that he was losing the fight, the blond man made a last-ditch effort. He heaved himself up off the ground, arching his back so that Preacher was thrown off to the side. Then he rolled over and scrambled frantically for the rifle he had dropped when the fight began.

He was closer to the weapon, and got there before Preacher could stop him. Grabbing the rifle, he lunged to his feet and swung around, earing the hammer back to full cock. Preacher scrambled up, too, and saw the barrel swinging relentlessly toward him.

The survival instinct took over then. Preacher still gripped the tomahawk in his left hand, but he was almost as deadly with his left hand as he was with his right. His arm swept up and back and then flashed forward.

The 'hawk spun across the space between the two men with blinding speed and landed with a meaty *thunk!* just as the man pulled the trigger. The flint-lock roared, but its owner was already going over backward, his skull split open by the tomahawk that had landed with terrific force in the middle of his forehead. He fell on his back and lay there twitching as blood and brains oozed out around the blade.

"Well, *hell*!" Preacher said with heartfelt disgust. The man wouldn't be answering any questions now.

And Preacher still had no earthly idea why the two varmints wanted him dead.

Chapter Two

The settlement had no name. It wasn't even much of a settlement, at least so far. And it would be just fine with Preacher if it stayed that way.

First had come the trading post established by a pair of cousins, Corliss and Jerome Hart, who had been brought here to this beautiful valley in the shadow of the Rocky Mountains by Preacher. They'd had some mishaps and adventures along the way, but things had finally settled down once they got here. Corliss and his wife Deborah had even unofficially adopted the boy Jake, who had run away from his brute of a father in St. Louis and come along on the wagon train journey that had ended here.

Another wagon train had followed close behind, bringing with it a handful of settlers—and customers for the trading post, which was doing a brisk business even before the building that housed it was completed.

Word of the trading post and tiny settlement had spread among the fur trappers and traders who made their living from the beaver and other animals in the mountains. There had been other trading posts out here far beyond the normal reach of civilization—one in almost the same spot as the Hart cousins' venture, in fact, some twenty years earlier, not long after Meriwether Lewis and William Clark returned from their epic journey to explore the Louisiana Purchase.

None of those posts had lasted for more than a few years, though. Savage Indians, brutal weather, disease . . . something had always happened to either wipe out the businesses or send their owners fleeing back to civilization.

Corliss and Jerome Hart swore that their trading post would be different. They would stick it out, they said, come hell or high water. The fact that Preacher had befriended them during their journey West gave their claims some credence. Everybody west of the Mississippi and north of the Rio Grande knew Preacher, knew the sort of man he was.

So the trappers came to the post, and so did the traders. Some of them had Indian wives, and they built a handful of cabins near the post, sturdy log cabins that reminded them of the homes they had left behind back East.

Of course, not all the men *wanted* to be reminded of such things. Some of them had come West to get away from unpleasantness back East. But the little no-name settlement grew anyway. A few of the trappers even went back to St. Louis and brought out their *real* wives, the ones they had married in a church or a judge's chambers instead of the ones they just shared buffalo robes with in lodges made of hides.

There had been a minister with that first wagon train, and as time went by more missionaries showed up. Not black-robed Jesuits like the ones who had been some of the first white men to penetrate the vast Canadian wilderness and on across the border into the northern reaches of the United States. No, these missionaries were Baptists, and they brought their wives and even their children with them. Within a year, nigh on to a hundred people lived within rifle shot of the Harts' trading post.

It made Preacher's skin crawl to think about it. Having so many people around in St. Louis was bad enough, but he could handle it because he made the trip down the Missouri River only once or twice a year. But he visited the trading post more often than that, and whenever he did, he felt cramped, like he didn't have any elbow room, and it seemed like there were too many folks breathing the mountain air. They might use it up, he worried, although that seemed unlikely when he looked at the vast blue arch of the sky above the mountains.

He could see the trading post and the settlement far below him as he rode through South Pass. The big, sure-footed horse he had named Horse— Preacher was nothing if not a practical man—picked its way down the trail with ease. The shaggy, wolflike cur Preacher had dubbed Dog bounded ahead.

Preacher was leading three horses: his own pack-horse, which carried his supplies and the load of pelts he had taken since his last visit to the trading post, and the two that belonged to the pair of dead bushwhackers. He had found the animals tied to a tree not far from the spot where the men had ambushed him, but there had been nothing in their belongings to tell him who they were or why they had tried to kill him.

The would-be killers were lashed facedown over their saddles. Preacher had thought seriously about leaving their carcasses for the wolves. He had even considered burying them. But in the end, he had decided to bring them with him since he was less than a day's ride from the trading post and the dry, cool, high country air helped keep dead varmints from rottin' too fast.

He wanted to see if anybody at the settlement recognized them.

It took him almost an hour to make his way down from the pass to the broad, grassy park where the trading post was located. Folks had seen him coming. Dogs barked and kids ran out to meet him. Most of the youngsters were 'breeds, the children of trappers and their Indian mates, but some belonged to families that had come out here from St. Louis and other places in the East, looking for a place to call their own.

A stocky, round-faced boy of eleven or twelve grinned at him and called, "Hey, Preacher! What you got there?"

"Couple o' skunks in human form, Jake," Preacher answered the boy as he reined to a stop. "Ever seen either one of 'em before?"

Some folks would've tried to keep the boy away and not expose him to the sight of the dead bodies, but Preacher figured anybody who was going to live in these mountains had to be tough enough to handle such things. Death was a fact of life, and it didn't do any good to coddle young'uns and try to hide that fact from them.

Jake wasn't bothered by it. He'd been through hard times already despite his young age. He grasped the hair on one of the dangling heads and lifted it so he could see the man's face. After a moment, Jake let go and the head flopped down again.

"Nope," Jake said. "He's a plumb stranger to me, Preacher. Lemme look at the other one."

Jake studied the face of the second corpse with the same result. Other kids crowded around him while he was holding the man's head up, and Preacher asked the same question of them, only to have all of them shake their heads in the negative. It was beginning to appear that the two bushwhackers hadn't visited the settlement before coming after Preacher.

He hadn't asked any of the grown-ups yet, though, so he hitched Horse into motion again and rode toward the big log building that was the center of the community.

Corliss and Jerome Hart's trading post was solidly built, with thick walls that had been notched out here and there to create plenty of rifle slots. In addition, a stockade fence made of vertical logs with sharpened tops had been erected around the place, with watchtowers at the corners and a parapet that ran inside it where defenders could stand and fire. The cousins had run into enough Indian trouble on the way out here that they had built the post with fighting off attacks in mind.

So far, the Indians in the area had left them alone. But a man who was prepared for trouble, whether it came or not, usually lived a lot longer on the frontier.

The double gates in the stockade fence stood open right now. Preacher glanced up and saw that all of the watchtowers were manned. If the sentries saw any sign of hostiles approaching, they would sound the alarm and the gates would be closed and barred before the Indians could get there. Everyone in the settlement knew to listen, and if they heard the bell mounted on top of the trading post tolling, they knew it meant to get inside the wall as quickly as they could. All the settlers would gather there in case of trouble.

Today, though, peace reigned in the valley, and folks strolled in and out through the gates, visiting the trading post for supplies or just some conversation, then heading back to the log cabins that dotted the grassy park. With a procession of youngsters trailing him, Preacher rode through the gates as well, and brought Horse to a stop before the trading post just as Corliss Hart stepped out onto the shaded porch.

Corliss smiled and lifted a hand in greeting. He was a muscular man in his thirties with a friendly face and a shock of dark hair.

"Howdy, Preacher," he called. "Didn't expect to see you back here quite this soon."

"I was lucky and already got a good load o' plews," Preacher drawled. He shifted Horse to the side so that Corliss could see the other two saddle mounts and their grisly burden. "Got a load o' something else, too."

Corliss's smile disappeared and his eyes widened. "Good Lord!" he said. "Who's that?"

"You tell me," Preacher said. "They tried to kill me this mornin'."

"Well, that was a foolish mistake," Corliss muttered as he came down the steps from the porch and moved forward to get a closer look at the bodies. Grimacing a little in distaste, he did what Jake had done, lifted the heads by the hair and studied the faces of the dead men.

He was shaking his head when he turned away from the horses. "I'm sorry, Preacher, but I never saw them before. They look like pretty unsavory sorts, though."

"They ain't any sort anymore 'cept dead."

Corliss looked at the youngsters crowding around and said, "You children run along. You don't need to see this." He added to his adopted son in particular, "Jake, go inside and give Deborah a hand."

"Aw, Corliss," the boy complained. "I seen dead folks before, you know."

"You've seen too much in your life. Run along."

Grumbling and dragging his feet, Jake went inside. The other kids went back to whatever they had been doing. Dead bodies started to lose their novelty pretty quickly. They didn't *do* anything.

As Preacher swung down from the saddle, Corliss asked, "Is that blood on your shirt? You're hurt, Preacher!"

The rangy mountain man shook his head. "Naw, not to speak off. Just got a little hide scraped off where a rifle ball come too close for comfort. I already slapped a poultice on it. It'll be fine."

"Deborah could take a look at it if you'd like."

The idea of Corliss's pretty, dark-haired wife poking around at his bare torso made Preacher a mite uncomfortable, so he shook his head. "No, thanks. It's all right."

"Suit yourself. Anyway, you probably know as much about treating bullet wounds as anybody else in this part of the country."

"I've patched up a fair number of 'em," Preacher admitted. "On me and on other folks, too."

A short, slender, sandy-haired man wearing a thick canvas apron over his clothes bustled out onto the porch. "Preacher!" he said. "What's this about dead men?"

"They tell no tales," Preacher said. He inclined his head toward the corpses. "Wish they would, though. I'd kinda like to know why they wanted to kill me."

Corliss's cousin Jerome came down the steps. Unlike the easygoing Corliss, who sometimes seemed to be on the verge of dozing off even when he was wide awake, Jerome Hart was nervous most of the time, whether there was really anything to be nervous *about* or not.

During the journey out here, there had been a rivalry between Corliss and Jerome for Deborah's affections, a rivalry in which Corliss had emerged victorious. For a while, it had looked as if the resulting bitterness would divide the cousins permanently. But they had made their peace and as far as Preacher knew, there had been no more problems between them.

"I've never seen them before," Corliss said, referring to the two dead bushwhackers. "Take a look, Jerome, and see if you recognize them."

Jerome frowned and hesitated. "I, uh, I'm sure that if you don't know them, Corliss, then I wouldn't—"

"Oh, for goodness' sake," Corliss snapped. "They're dead, they can't hurt you." He lifted the corpses' heads, one after the other.

Jerome paled and swallowed hard as he looked at them. "I'm sorry, Preacher," he said. "I don't know them. I don't think they've ever been here."

"That's what I figured when Jake didn't recognize 'em. That younker keeps his eyes open."

"Jake?" Jerome repeated. "You let Jake look at these . . . these cadavers?"

Preacher nodded. "And the other kids from the settlement, too."

Jerome looked horrified, but he didn't say anything. Preacher knew that the ways of the frontier were different than anything Jerome was accustomed to. Jerome was trying to get used to them, but it might take him a while.

News of what Preacher had brought in was already spreading through the settlement. People began to show up to have a look at the bodies. Anything different, even something like this, was a welcome break from the hardships of everyday life. Deborah Hart, her gently rounded belly starting to display that she was expecting, came outside and took her turn checking to see if she recognized the bushwhackers. It came as no surprise to Preacher that she didn't. Neither did Pete Carey, the stocky jack-of-all-trades who helped the Hart cousins run the trading post.

"Well, Preacher," Corliss said after a while, "you seem to have drawn a blank. What are you going to do now?"

Preacher spat. "Only one thing to do. Reckon I'll need to borrow a shovel."

"You're going to bury them?"

"I killed 'em. I'll plant 'em."

Jerome said, "Surely we can give you a hand with that at the very least. And Reverend Porter can say a prayer for their souls . . . although I'm not sure they deserve it if they tried to murder you, my friend."

"That's for somebody else to sort out, not me," Preacher said. "Once they're in the ground, I figure on sellin' that load o' pelts to you fellas, and then I might buy me a jug o' whiskey."

Corliss frowned. "But they tried to kill you, and you don't know why! Doesn't that bother you?"

"I'm a mite puzzled," Preacher admitted, "but I'll let you in on a little secret . . . this ain't the first time somebody's tried to kill me. And I got a real strong feelin' it won't be the last . . ."

Chapter Three

By nightfall, the two men were buried, Reverend Thomas Porter had said the proper words over the graves, and Preacher had gotten a good meal cooked on a stove in the trading post rather than over a campfire. Now, he sat in a barrel chair in a corner, his long, buckskin-clad legs stretched out in front of him as he took an occasional nip from the earthenware jug he held. Several other trappers of his acquaintance sat with him, swapping windies. Preacher was mostly silent, though, a frown on his face as he pondered what had happened.

Despite the nonchalant answer he had given Corliss Hart, the attempt on his life *did* bother him. Life on the frontier was fraught with enough dangers already. Even though the two strangers had been unsuccessful in their efforts to kill him, the very fact that they had tried told Preacher that somebody else could show up out of the blue and do likewise.

"What do you think, Preacher?" a red-bearded trapper named Bouchard asked.

The direct question shook Preacher out of his brooding. "What do I think about what?"

"Jock thinks there'll be real towns out here someday."

"Aye," another trapper said. "Jus' like Glasgow or Edinburgh, wi' factories and shops and row after row o' houses."

Preacher shuddered at the thought. "Lord, I hope not. If things ever start to get like that, just take me out and shoot me, 'cause I don't wanna see it."

"Maybe that's why those fellows ambushed you," Bouchard suggested with a grin. "They were just trying to spare you from having to witness the ravages of civilization, *mon ami.*"

Preacher downed a snort of hooch. "Yeah, I reckon," he said caustically.

The Scottish trapper, Jock, leaned forward and said, "Ye dinna kin why those scuts came after ye, Preacher?"

Preacher shook his head. "I don't have any idea. Maybe I had trouble with a friend o' theirs in the past, and they were tryin' to settle the score."

He didn't have to explain what he meant. The other men knew that whenever somebody had trouble with Preacher, that somebody usually ended up dead, or at least hurt mighty bad.

Corliss Hart came over and said, "Why don't you stay here at the trading post tonight, Preacher?"

A frown creased Preacher's forehead. "Sleep with a roof over my head? I ain't in the habit o' doin' that very often. Hell, it ain't even been a year since I was last in St. Louis."

Jock said, "Next thing ye kin, he'll be wantin' ye t' take a bath, Preacher!" The Scotsman slapped his thigh and laughed uproariously at the very idea. The other trappers joined in the laughter.

"No, I'm serious," Corliss said. "Surely it would be safer staying here than camping somewhere in the area. Maybe those two men were the only ones who are after you, but you can't be sure of that."

"Fella can't be sure of much of anything in this life," Preacher said. "He gets up in the mornin' not knowin' if he'll see the sun go down that evenin'. But worryin' about that too much will drive him plumb out of his head if he ain't careful."

"Well, the offer stands, if you're so inclined. Deborah and Jerome and I would be glad to have you as our guest."

Preacher took another drink from the jug and wiped the back of his other hand across his mouth. "I'm obliged, Corliss. I truly am. But I reckon I'd have a hard time goin' to sleep without the stars up yonder lookin' down at me." He pulled in his legs and stood up, moving with the easy grace of a big cat. "Fact is, I'm a mite tired, so I think I'll go on and find a place to lay my head."

He said his good nights and walked out of the trading post, dangling the jug from his left hand. The thumb of his right hand was hooked behind his belt, not far from the butt of one of his pistols. The weapon was in easy reach if he needed it, and it was loaded and charged again. He had taken the powder horns and shot pouches off the two men he had killed that morning. They wouldn't be needing 'em again.

Torches burned at the watchtowers and at intervals along the walls, casting their glow over the area outside the stockade. The gates were still open, but a couple of armed guards stood just outside them keeping watch. Preacher paused on the porch to look out at the night. Dog lay on the porch a few feet away. He raised his head and pricked his ears forward as Preacher stood there.

The valley was peaceful. Lights burned in the windows of some of the cabins in the settlement, and silvery moonglow washed over the grass. At moments such as this, it was hard to believe so many dangers lurked in the darkness.

But hostile Indians could be watching the settlement at this very moment. So could lawless white men, for that matter. Bandits weren't common on the frontier, but they weren't unheard of either. Storms could be brewing . . . natural or man-made. A fella never knew.

Preacher gave a little shake of his head. It wasn't like him to mope around like this. He had left his belongings on the porch, wrapped up in his bedroll. He picked them up now, growled, "Come on, Dog," and stepped down from the porch. The big cur rose and padded after him.

He had already put Horse away in the paddock adjacent to the stockade after dickering with Jerome over the load of pelts. They had come to an agreement without much trouble. Preacher knew he could have gotten more for the furs in St. Louis . . .

but that would have meant going to St. Louis. The Harts paid him enough to take care of his simple needs.

He planned to walk out into the trees that came right up to the edge of the settlement in places and find a good spot to spend the night. As he left the stockade, he nodded to the guards and said, "Might as well close 'em up for the night, boys. I don't think anybody else is leavin'."

"All right, Preacher," one of the men said. They knew his reputation. If he offered an opinion about anything, nine times out of ten it could be taken as gospel. The guard went on. "I'm sort of surprised that you're not staying inside the walls tonight."

"Why's that?"

The man shuffled his feet a little uncomfortably. "Well, I mean, since those fellas tried to kill you and all . . . not that I think you'd worry about that even for a second, Preacher . . . !"

The mountain man chuckled. "Forget it, son. I ain't offended. But I ain't worried neither."

To tell the truth, if there was somebody else out there in the night looking to kill him, he almost hoped they'd go ahead and do their damnedest. That beat waiting around. He'd take his chances against almost anybody, especially with Dog around to warn him and pitch in if need be.

And if somebody *did* come after him, maybe this time he'd be able to grab them and make them tell him what in blazes was going on. He had learned a few tricks from the Blackfoot about the best ways to make a fella talk . . .

* * *

Despite the fact that Preacher was halfway hoping his enemies would come after him again, the night passed quietly and peacefully. He slept lightly as always, resting but ready to come fully awake at an instant's notice. His soogans protected him against the nighttime chill, which was year-round at these elevations.

The next morning, he returned to the trading post to pick up Horse, and as he led the stallion out of the paddock, Jake came up to him and asked, "Are you gonna take me with you this time, Preacher?" The youngster asked him that same question almost every time he paid a visit to the trading post. "I could be a big help to you."

"Well, I dunno, Jake. You're a mighty big help to your ma and pa, I expect."

"Corliss and Deborah ain't really my ma and pa. But I reckon you'd know that."

Preacher nodded. "'Deed I do. But they been takin' care of you like you're their own young'un, and I reckon you sort of owe them for that. And with Deborah bein' in a family way, they're gonna need even more help around here."

"Yeah, but Preacher . . ." An anguished expression appeared on the boy's round face. "They say there's gonna be a *teacher* on the next wagon train headin' this way. There's gonna be a *school* here. You just can't leave me to face that!"

Preacher sympathized; he truly did. He had never had much education himself before he left the family farm and headed West when he was about Jake's age. He had learned to read, some on his own, some with the help of other mountain men who'd had some book learning. He could cipher some, too. A fella had to be able to do that if he wasn't going to be taken advantage of by the fur traders.

But the thought of sitting in a building and letting some soft-handed gent try to pound facts into his head while *life* was going on outside . . . well, that was just horrifying.

There was nothing he could do, though, except slowly shake his head. "I'm sorry, Jake," he said. "Maybe one o' these days, but not yet."

"Damn it, I was afraid that was what you were gonna say! Am I gonna have to run off again?"

Preacher knew how badly that would upset Corliss, Deborah, and Jerome, who looked on the youngster as a member of the family. He gave Jake a hard stare and said, "If you do, I'll have to find you and tan your hide good, boy. That what you want?"

Jake swallowed. He knew that there was nowhere he could go in the mountains where Preacher couldn't find him. "All right," he said, not bothering to hide the reluctance in his voice. "I guess I can give it a try, Preacher. But only if you promise me that one o' these days I'll be your partner."

Preacher hesitated. He wasn't the sort of man who gave his word lightly. At the same time, he couldn't really see himself taking some green kid under his wing and trying to teach the sprout how to take care of himself. Jake had him over a damn barrel, he thought.

"All right," he finally said. "But I decide when you're ready to go with me. Deal?"

Jake held up a pudgy hand. "Deal."

Preacher shook with the boy and then handed him the packhorse's reins. "Here, hold these while I mount up." He swung up onto Horse's back and took the reins from Jake. He had already said his good-byes to the Harts and to Pete Carey and Bouchard and Jock as well. He lifted a hand in farewell as he said, "Be seein' you," and nudged Horse into a trot that carried them through the open gates of the stockade.

He looked back once and saw Jake standing there just outside the walls, watching him ride away.

Preacher left the settlement behind him and worked his way up toward the pass. He was going back to the same area where he had been when the attempt on his life was made. He had traps there that still needed tending to, and he sure wasn't going to let what happened scare him off.

When he reached the pass, he paused to look down into the valley at the settlement. Even though he didn't like the idea of civilization encroaching on the mountains, he had to admit to himself that he grown fond of some of those folks down there. Corliss was a bit of a wastrel at times, Deborah could be a mite bossy, and Jerome was just downright annoying more often than not. But they were good people and had demonstrated that on more than one occasion. Jake was . . . well, Jake was Jake. For good or bad, there was no other kid quite like him.